It Started With a Kiss

by Clare Lydon

custard books

First Edition June 2022
Published by Custard Books
Copyright © 2022 Clare Lydon
ISBN: 978-1-912019-12-0

Cover Design: Rachel Lawston
Editor: Cheyenne Blue
Typesetting: Adrian McLaughlin

Find out more: www.clarelydon.co.uk
Follow me on Twitter: @clarelydon
Follow me on Instagram: @clarefic

This is a work of fiction. All characters and happenings
in this publication are fictitious and any resemblance
to real persons (living or dead), locales or events
is purely coincidental.

Also by Clare Lydon

Other Novels
A Taste Of Love
Before You Say I Do
Change Of Heart
Christmas In Mistletoe
Nothing To Lose: A Lesbian Romance
Once Upon A Princess
One Golden Summer
The Long Weekend
Twice In A Lifetime
You're My Kind

London Romance Series
London Calling (Book One)
This London Love (Book Two)
A Girl Called London (Book Three)
The London Of Us (Book Four)
London, Actually (Book Five)
Made In London (Book Six)
Hot London Nights (Book Seven)
Big London Dreams (Book Eight)

All I Want Series
All I Want For Christmas (Book One)
All I Want For Valentine's (Book Two)
All I Want For Spring (Book Three)
All I Want For Summer (Book Four)
All I Want For Autumn (Book Five)
All I Want Forever (Book Six)

Acknowledgements

I hope you enjoyed *It Started With A Kiss*. The idea for this novel arrived when I went to a cheese and wine tasting at Albury Vineyard in Surrey. The cheese was tangy, the wine delicious, and on top of that, the whole setting *screamed* romance. Even though it was a mud-squelching, freezing cold November day, I could still imagine sun-drenched vines and heat. Afterwards, I quizzed the owners about their process, and that only convinced me further. I had the setting, I had the middle-of-the-night bougie lightings, now I just needed a story to bind it all together. Enter, Skye and Gemma, stir in family secrets along with simmering sexual tension, and hey presto! *It Started With A Kiss* was born. If you fancy going along to one of the many fantastic events at Albury Vineyard, I highly recommend it: www.alburyvineyard.com

Thanks as always to Angela and Sophie for their first read and encouraging comments. Also, to my fantastic advanced reading team for their eagle eyes that picked up all the last-minute issues. I couldn't do this without you, so you get all the plaudits!

Lashings of praise to my wonderful team of talented professionals who make sure my books look and read the best they can. Rachel Lawston for the slinky cover. Cheyenne

Blue for her legendary editing. Adrian McLaughlin for his typesetting prowess and general loveliness. Also, to my wife for just being the best.

Finally, thanks to you for buying this book and supporting me on my writing journey. This one took a little longer to mould because of life issues, but I'm glad it's finally out in the world for you to read. Thanks for your continued support in my writing journey. I truly, madly, deeply appreciate it.

If you fancy getting in touch, you can do so using one of the methods below:

Website: www.clarelydon.co.uk
Email: mail@clarelydon.co.uk
Instagram: @clarefic
Facebook: www.facebook.co.uk/clarelydon
Twitter: @clarelydon

For Tom Lydon. 1933–2022.
A dedication on a book about wine. How appropriate.
Cheers, Dad.

Chapter One

"Morning, Skye!"

Annie. The receptionist at the Seasalter Hotel was the first person Skye saw when she entered the lobby. Today, she was the acid test. How far had the news spread? Did Annie know?

Skye tried a smile, but it was half-baked. A little like the banana bread she'd attempted a few months back.

"Morning!"

She'd contemplated calling in sick, but decided that was simply putting off the inevitable. She'd have to face people eventually. Instead, she took a deep breath and decided to get it over with.

"You look knackered." Annie tamped down her curly hair, which was well ruffled by her usual seafront walk to work.

She gave Skye a sympathetic smile.

She knew.

"I didn't sleep well." Not a surprise given yesterday's news. Skye had found out just as she was dropping off to sleep, thanks to a text from her friend Justin that had lit up her phone.

Whatever you do, DON'T look at your Facebook right now, he'd messaged just before midnight.

So of course, Skye had to look.

"I saw it this morning, gotta be rough." Annie shook her head and pursed her lips. "I would offer to go out with you later to rip her to shreds over a glass of wine, but I've got a spin class." Annie had priorities. Also, some dried toothpaste on the corner of her mouth. She leaned in, her cheeks sun-kissed from her recent bargain weekend to Valencia. "Just know, I'm on your side. Everyone is. What she did was *not okay*."

That was one way to put it.

"Thanks." Skye's bum cheeks clenched. Her shoulders stiffened. Was this going to happen with everyone she met this morning? Maybe she should have stayed in bed.

She gestured to Annie's toothpaste, and her colleague grabbed her compact from her desk drawer and gave an embarrassed smile. Skye left Annie wiping her mouth, and slipped along the sleek hallway of the Seasalter Hotel, St Austin's most upmarket place to stay. She breathed in the smell of fresh polish on the parquet floor, mingling with the fresh flowers on the hallway tables. At the end she turned right into the main office. She was the first one in, like always.

Skye sank into her padded black office chair and spun around. She stopped mid-spin, and stared out her window, at the golden sands beyond, lapped by the crisp waves of the Atlantic that stretched as far as she could see. This view could normally be counted on to make her smile, but not today.

Not after the fallout of the past year. Not after last night's announcement.

She spun around to her screen and turned on her laptop.

She had 12 new emails overnight. One from the hotel owner, Mr Cooper, detailing a new wedding for the hotel diary. Eighty guests, platinum wedding package, hotel DJ to be included. And then at the bottom, a line in bold:

50% discount to be applied for head chef, Amanda Cross.

Skye's stomach fell to the floor like an anchor. She narrowed her gaze. Hell to the fucking no. Not on her watch.

She couldn't stay here today. She checked the rotas. Amanda was due in at 3pm, and she couldn't risk coming face to face with her entitled, smug face. Yes, Skye's office view might be stunning, and yes, she'd loved her job until her personal life exploded all over it. But she was the hotel manager, so she could make the rules.

There was a line, and Skye had just drawn hers.

There was no way in hell she was playing any part in booking or organising a wedding for her cheating ex-wife, Amanda.

* * *

Skye contemplated going direct to Beer on the Beach after she got the news, but doing so would mean Amanda had won. She'd done enough of that over the past year since they split. Instead, Skye delayed it, went to the gym and took it out on a punch bag, then jumped on a bike and cycled until her legs shouted at her.

Now it was 6pm, which was a respectable time for dinner and a glass of red. She licked a smudge of ketchup from her index finger as she finished her cheeseburger and chips, then took a sip of her shiraz. Behind the bar, Justin buffed up a champagne glass, but never took his eyes from her.

"What are you going to do about the wedding? Refuse to do it?" He put the glass on the shelf behind him, patted his sandy hair in the mirror, then turned back, a hand on his hip.

"Better yet, you could do it, but drop a vat of chili flakes in the prawn cocktails, then piss in the chicken fricassee."

"I'm not that obvious." Skye hadn't decided what she would do. But as the day wore on, she was coming to the conclusion she needed a new job. However, that brought her back to the same argument she'd been having with herself for the past year. She wasn't the one who'd cheated and broken up a marriage, so why should she be the one to find a new job?

"Maybe you should be. If Marion did that to me, I'm not sure my revenge would be a dish served cold."

Skye pushed away her plate and Justin cleared it from the bar. She stretched out her arms and glanced around the space. Two groups of friends sat by the large windows overlooking the ocean, but other than that, the bar was empty. Give it a couple of months and that would all change. However, it was still only the final week of February, so the tourists hadn't arrived.

Outside, a brunette in a black trench coat paused at the glass front door and peered in. After a few seconds hesitation, she walked in. Her shiny black heels caught Skye's attention, mainly because she was always impressed by women who just casually walked in heels like it was no big deal. It always had been for her. The woman took off her coat and hung it on the hook under the bar, along with her expensive-looking handbag. She hopped onto the bar stool two down from Skye, then gave her a hesitant smile.

She looked like the type who baked banana bread with ease. Someone who not only liked yoga, but probably had a favourite type. Perhaps hatha. Or the hot one. Or was hatha the hot one?

Justin approached her, and the woman wriggled on her

stool, then dialled up her smile. She ordered a bottle, "give me something local, ale or beer, your choice", then pulled down the cuffs of her sharp black shirt, creases still intact, that told Skye it was fresh out of the packet. What had brought her into this bar tonight? The woman's floral perfume wafted along the bar and settled in Skye's nose.

Justin delivered the woman's beer, then sauntered back to Skye.

"When did my life get so complicated?" Skye swung her attention back to her friend. "Was it when she told me she really wanted a goatskin rug for the lounge, and I told her no?"

Justin raised an eyebrow. "A goatskin rug? That's a thing?"

"A smelly thing," the new woman added, then took a swig of her beer.

Skye had expected the woman to ask for a glass, but no. She was drinking it straight from the bottle.

The woman held up a well-manicured hand. "Sorry for butting in, but I couldn't help overhearing. My cousin got a goatskin rug, and it was the singular most anti-social thing he ever did."

Skye threw up both hands. "You see, I knew I was right to stand my ground." She smiled at the woman. "Thank you."

"You're welcome." The woman leaned towards her. "I promise, I won't interrupt anymore."

"Please do," Skye replied. "We're all friends here."

"Careful, I take people at their word." The woman shifted her drink and herself to the adjacent bar stool, then held out a hand. "I'm Gemma."

Skye shook it, thrilled to have someone else to focus on tonight. Especially someone with such smooth, strong hands.

"Skye," she replied. "And this is Justin, barman extraordinaire."

She took in the woman's high cheekbones, and her deep green eyes. Something about her pinged Skye's gaydar, but then, Skye's gaydar was legendary for being faulty. Tonight, it was probably all sorts of wrong, because she was hardly in the best place herself, was she?

If she had to describe herself in a dating profile – she'd set up a profile after her friend Lauren bullied her into it, but it was still totally blank – it would say something like 'divorced, morose, prone to spiralling'. She needed to work on her wording.

Gemma did not look like she spiralled ever. If Skye had to guess, she'd say yoga lady was having a drink to unwind before heading home to have dinner with her wife or husband. She'd probably have sushi delivered on a motorbike, because there was no way she was cooking. Maybe she lived in one of the larger towns in the area. Perhaps Newquay. Maybe she'd come to Cornwall in search of a simpler, more idyllic life, just as Skye had. It hadn't turned out that way.

Justin gave Gemma a salute. "I'm here to serve the beer and sort out your life problems. Consider me not only a bar owner, but also a life coach."

"All the best bar staff are." Gemma grabbed a beer mat from the stack on the bar, then put her bottle on it. She turned to Skye.

"Stop me if I'm completely out of line, but who wanted the goatskin rug?"

Skye stared at this stranger asking personal questions. Did she really want to open up to someone she didn't know at all?

Then again, she'd just been talking to Justin about it. Maybe a stranger would be the perfect person. Someone who didn't know Skye, Amanda, or anyone connected to either of them. Someone who'd never set foot inside the Seasalter Hotel.

"My ex-wife, Amanda. Who cheated on me with her sous chef, broke up our marriage, and is just about to get married again." When she said it out loud, it sounded just as bad as it was.

Justin rested an elbow on the bar in front of them. "And now said ex-wife has booked the hotel that Skye works at for her wedding and reception, and Skye's boss is demanding Skye organise it."

Gemma let out a low, slow whistle.

Skye had never been able to do that. Impressed didn't cover it.

"Holy wedding catastrophe!" Gemma shook her head. "There was me thinking small seaside towns looked relaxing to live in."

"Lies, all lies." Justin rolled his eyes.

Gemma raised a single eyebrow. "Seeing as we're all friends, let me buy you a drink to let you know that not all women are bad. Also, to tell you, you were so right on the goatskin rug. You had a lucky escape. The rug would have ruined your life. It sounds like your ex already did a good job of that herself."

Chapter Two

It was 9pm. She'd missed her train. Gemma got out her phone and looked up when the last one left. She winced. 10.50pm, and it would get her in around 5am. Not ideal, but she could sleep on the train. She'd done it before, and she couldn't leave now. She was invested. Also, a little tipsy. Okay, a lot tipsy. One drink had turned into four, and all on an empty stomach.

Not, however, as tipsy as Skye, the dimpled, blonde, hot mess next to her. Which, as Gemma's sister would tell you, was exactly her type. Particularly cute hot messes. Gemma couldn't help feel for Skye. No matter what heartache had befallen Gemma, her ex had never dumped her and then forced her to plan her next wedding. That was next-level evil. It almost made Juliette appear human.

Almost.

Having got up to speed with the full back story, Gemma and Justin had spent the past hour trying to convince Skye to hand in her notice and get a new job. Gemma understood Skye's argument, though. That she didn't want to be run out of town by her ex. That she'd built a life here, with friends and a job she liked. The only downside was it involved dealing with her ex-wife all the time.

"I really think you should consider it. You work in

hospitality. You live by the coast. It's not like there aren't other jobs out there, is it?" Gemma asked.

Skye didn't look convinced. "I know that. But it still comes back to me having to change my life through no fault of my own."

"But you're cutting off your nose to spite your face." Justin gave her a stern look, then walked down the bar to serve somebody else.

Gemma sympathised. She understood more than most the trouble ex-girlfriends could cause by simply breathing. She reached out and put a hand on Skye's arm.

Skye jolted, then stared.

Had she overstepped? Gemma gave her a hesitant smile, then removed it. She was the tactile type and it had got her into trouble before. Clearly, a couple of hours was too soon to touch Skye.

"I know how you're feeling." She paused. Gemma didn't normally come out so soon after meeting someone, but this situation was anything but the norm. Sitting at a bar talking about how terrible women were took her back to her early twenties, when she used to do it most weeks with her friends. Now she was nearly 40, those days were gone. She hardly ever went out. She had a vineyard to run. Customers to charm. Frost to thaw. But this trip down memory lane was fun in a weird, nostalgic way.

"I was with someone not so long ago who turned out to be not who I expected, too. She wanted something I couldn't give, and she only saw the world from her perspective."

Surprise registered on Skye's face, followed by the glimmer of a smile.

It was always nice to meet someone who understood exactly where you were coming from. Somebody who knew that when women dated other women, the whole idea of a sisterhood went out the window. Nobody could break your heart like a woman.

"I just don't get it. Weirdly, I am mostly over it, despite what this looks like." Skye waved a hand in front of her face. "It's just, these past 24 hours have been a head fuck. I knew they were together, but now they're engaged." Skye threw up her arms. "We were together for five years. She asked me to marry her after two, and things were great then, truly." Skye's eyes misted over for a moment. Then she shook herself. "We had a big wedding – at the same hotel would you believe? – and when I said my vows, I meant them. For better, for worse. In sickness and in health. I don't recall there being a vow that said, 'until the next young thing comes along, and I get a better offer'." She slumped forward and rested her forehead on her forearm.

Gemma put a hand on Skye's back.

This time, Skye didn't flinch. She simply raised her head and gave Gemma a crooked smile. One that showed off her dimple to full effect.

Gemma was a sucker for a dimple. Especially one attached to a face like Skye's. Maybe in another life, where Skye wasn't still hung up on her ex, where they lived within a hundred miles of each other, this might have been the start of something. But Gemma knew this was a time-limited, soon-to-end evening. She was determined to wring the last drops out of it.

"Why are women so terrible, though?" Skye mumbled as she sat up again. "Is it me, do you think? You're a professional queer, right?"

"A paid-up member of the union."

"So in your opinion, am I giving off signs that say, 'welcome, please use me and abuse me'?"

Gemma shook her head. "You are not."

"Yet when I look back at my marriage, and at the two other long-term relationships I was in before that, they were all disasters. All three of them left me for other people. The fact is, women don't stick around. There's never been a happy ending for me. Why don't I deserve that?"

"You do deserve that," Gemma replied, trying to keep Skye upbeat. "You've got so much going for you. You're young, good-looking, intelligent, and you've got a great job."

Skye nodded along with every point Gemma made.

"Plus, you've made a new friend who thinks this Amanda woman is clearly mad to have left you."

Skye gave her a shy grin. "Thank you. I'm glad we met tonight. You've really cheered me up." She slugged back her wine and sighed. "I just feel like I've missed out on certain things, you know? I've never laid on a blanket with someone under the stars. I've never danced naked in the rain. I've never had sex on a beach."

"That last one is way overrated. Far too sandy. Or painful if you're in Brighton: all those pebbles."

Skye flipped her head to stare at the ceiling, then back to Gemma. "You see! You've done these things. You've at least experienced life and love." Skye stared at Gemma. "You've been in love?"

Gemma's stomach rolled. She gave Skye a slow nod. "Yes, I've been in love."

She was lying.

"I've also had my heart trampled on." Gemma had no great desire to do that again.

"I bet you've sat on a blanket with someone under the stars, too."

Gemma knew she should stay silent on that one.

Skye ordered more wine, and drank half the glass in one go. "Do you think life is passing me by? Because sometimes, I do. I go to work, and it's like Groundhog Day. The same thing, over and over. Customers complain. Toilets get blocked. Amanda serves delicious meals, everyone thinks she's a bloody genius, but only I know that it took her six months to give me an orgasm. She's the most clumsy, selfish lover I've ever had." Skye clamped a hand over her mouth and her eyes went wide.

"But I thought she was the love of your life?" Gemma frowned.

"She was my wife. She was a great chef. I thought the rest would come in time. And we were happy enough. Until we weren't."

Gemma stared at Skye, confusion dancing in her eyes. Was she upset at losing her wife? Or simply upset at how it happened? Maybe a bit of both. "I know it doesn't seem like it now, but it sounds like you're better off without her. Better she cheated sooner rather than later. Now you have a chance to find someone who can give you the happy ending you deserve. Someone you can lie with under the stars."

"On a blanket." Skye waved a finger at Gemma. "There has to be a blanket."

Gemma sipped her beer and glanced at the clock. 9.45. She should get going soon. She didn't want to miss this train.

"Nobody's ever found my G-Spot either."

Gemma spat out a little beer. She hadn't been expecting that one.

"You know what else?" Skye snagged her gaze and brought her hand up to Gemma's face.

Gemma should have moved away, but she got stuck in Skye's orbit. Her eyebrows were immaculate, and her eyelashes some of the longest Gemma had ever seen.

She had a train to catch. Her brain told her to leave.

Instead, she moved her head closer to Skye. "What?"

Skye pressed her fingertip into Gemma's right cheek. "I've never met a stranger in a bar, told her she was one of the most beautiful women I've ever seen, and then kissed her." She paused. "You, by the way, are one of the most beautiful women I've ever met."

Gemma's libido lifted its head off the pillow. Okay, she hadn't expected that. But why not? She was in a bar miles from home, with a cute woman she'd never see again.

A gorgeous, sad, dimpled woman who could use some cheering up. Maybe kissing Skye might be just the tonic Gemma needed, too.

Before she could talk herself out of it, she leaned forward and laid a kiss on Skye's full, pink lips. A delicate whisper of a kiss.

Just to make something go right for Skye today. Nothing else.

Only, Skye's soft lips made her linger. When Gemma took hers away, she wasn't ready.

It turned out, neither was Skye.

The hustle and bustle of the bar faded into the background

as Skye shuffled her stool forward, stared into Gemma's eyes and leaned in. This time, she took Gemma's face in both of her warm hands, held her gaze with her intense azure stare, and pressed her lips to Gemma's with such tender confidence, Gemma wobbled on her bar stool. Desire and surprise held her in place.

Until they didn't.

Skye slipped her tongue into Gemma's mouth, and Gemma slipped left.

Her stool tipped slightly.

Her heart lunged in her chest.

Gemma flung out a hand to hold on to Skye's waist, but only grabbed a piece of her T-shirt.

She let out a startled cry as her lips pulled away from Skye.

Skye's eyes went wide.

It all happened as if in slow motion, as Gemma's bar stool tipped onto two legs, then past the point of no return. In desperation, she tried to grip onto whatever she could. That was Skye. As she fell sideways, her hand took Skye and both bar stools with her, and all four landed with a thump on the wooden floor.

Gemma's shoulder took the impact, as well as her pride.

She lay on the ground, noticing an errant Smartie under the bar, before she raised her gaze to meet Skye's.

She wanted to laugh, and she also wanted to cry. She mouthed the word 'sorry' to Skye, and then Justin's face appeared between them, concern stamped across his features.

"What the hell just happened? I turn away for a moment, then I look up and see the two of you falling to the floor."

Skye reacted first. She untangled her legs from the stool and pushed it away. She sat up, then stood, before offering Gemma a hand.

Gemma took it, then winced as she cupped her shoulder.

"Nothing broken? Are you going to sue me for faulty bar stools?" Justin picked the stools up and checked the legs, then patted the seats as he put them back.

"More likely, it was faulty operators," Skye replied, a sly grin threatening her face.

From feeling tipsy, Gemma was now way more sober. She rolled her shoulder. "I might nip to the loo."

"I'll come with you."

They walked together, Gemma rubbing her arm and the side of her face, the clack of her heels strong on the wooden floor.

Skye pushed open the door and held it for Gemma.

She smiled as she walked past, breathing Skye in.

When they got to the sinks, Gemma checked her face in the mirror. Still intact. No blood. She took a deep breath, washed her hands, dried them with white paper towels, then walked over to the metal bin and threw the used towels away. Then she walked to the far wall, and pressed her back against the cooling white tiles. She glanced at the three cubicle doors reflected in the sink mirrors. All empty.

Skye washed her hands, then turned to her.

The electricity that had been in the bar hadn't left. If anything, now they were alone, someone had turned up the dial.

Gemma swallowed hard as Skye approached her, then stopped.

"Sorry about spoiling your happy ending."

Skye smiled. "It's not over yet. Besides, I liked the beginning. Every ending needs a strong beginning too, right?"

Gemma nodded.

Skye stepped closer.

"The middle was wobbly, but I think we can work on the ending. Especially now we're on solid ground."

Desire fizzed through her. Gemma's bones melted. Skye closed the gap between them, then her expert lips fixed Gemma to the spot, to this red-hot moment of pleasure she couldn't turn away from.

They'd only just met, but already, Skye's lips were the only place Gemma wanted to be. She pulled her close, a hand lingering on Skye's shapely bum. Like this was what she did every day.

It wasn't.

Gemma's heart boomed. She'd expected to be on a cold train platform right now. She hadn't factored in being roasted by Skye's pitch-perfect lips. Being caressed by Skye's firm fingers. Where the hell had she come from? And why the hell couldn't Gemma take her with her?

Skye kissed like the world might end tomorrow. Like Gemma's lips were gold, and Skye was going to protect them at all costs. She hadn't expected that either. Amanda's cast-off was Gemma's gain. Whatever else she took from tonight, she'd leave with the knowledge she was eminently kissable. That women like Skye existed. That kisses like these were not just the stuff of folklore.

When they broke apart, Skye blinked, then stared. Her chest heaved.

Gemma lifted her index finger and traced a line through

Skye's dimple, and onto her lips. She did it without thinking. Like it was the most natural thing in the world.

In return, Skye kissed Gemma's fingertip.

Wicked sensation skittered across her skin.

It was one of the most erotic things to ever happen to Gemma. She'd love to take it further. See where else Skye's lips could leave their mark on her.

But she had to leave. She had a train to catch. Yet at this moment, she didn't want to move. She wanted to build a life in this bar, with Skye at her side. Available to kiss her whenever she needed it. Skye's golden lips on tap. But real life didn't work like that.

A customer entered the loo.

Just like that, their bubble popped.

Gemma flinched.

Skye stepped back, and blinked as if she was trying to process what just happened.

The woman hesitantly smiled at them, then closed her cubicle door.

Without a word, Skye took Gemma's hand and pulled her back into the bar, and back to their bar stools. Back to where it all started.

Only, it wasn't the same as when they left. The music was louder, the air was thicker. Next to her, a man asked for a large glass of house white. How dare he intrude on their short time together. Only, this moment wasn't just theirs, was it? It belonged to the bar. To tonight. To Cornwall. Gemma couldn't pack it into her bag and whisk it back to Surrey no matter how much that appealed. She dropped her gaze to Skye's lips once more. She wanted to throw herself on them.

"I'm not sure what just happened." Skye's blue eyes shimmered under the lights.

Gemma wasn't, either. She traced the tip of her tongue along the back of her top teeth, and shook her head. She couldn't find the words, so what was the point of trying? Instead, her eyes dropped to Skye's denim-clad thighs, her scuffed Nikes. Yep, she was just Gemma's type, damn her.

Skye gulped. "I never asked, but do you live local?"

Disappointment sat heavy in Gemma's gut as she shook her head.

"I don't. I live in Surrey. I came down today to visit a vineyard."

Skye glanced at her bottle. "But you're drinking beer."

Gemma shrugged. "I've been tasting wine all day long. I fancied something a little different. Something to refresh my palate. Something I wouldn't normally have at home." Gemma could equally have been talking about the beer or Skye.

"Did you find it?" Skye matched the words with an intense stare.

"I think I did." Gemma balled her fist so she didn't raise her fingers to Skye's face again. It was just one kiss. She could keep herself under control. She'd done it before, and she could do it again. She glanced at her watch. She *really* should go. But all she truly wanted to do was kiss Skye again.

Damn it.

"But now, with really bad timing, I have to catch a train. It's the last one of the night, and if I don't get it, I'll be sleeping on the beach. While that sounds romantic during the summer, in February, I fear I might freeze to death."

Skye frowned. "The trains back to Surrey are going to be a nightmare now."

"You're not wrong, but I can sleep on the train." Gemma winced. "I had a seat booked on the earlier train, but I didn't want to leave. I was enjoying chatting to you." The anonymity had been freeing. In St Austin, she was a stranger. It was the opposite of her neck of the woods, where everybody knew every facet of her life. "It's fine. I'm a big girl. I'll get home."

"Why don't you come back to mine?" Skye licked her lips. "I have a sofabed. You could at least get a bit of sleep, and then get the early train in the morning."

Gemma ground her teeth together. It was tempting. Only, she knew very well she wouldn't be on a sofabed. She'd be in Skye's bed. Naked as the day she was born.

Her skin flared hot. All of which made the offer doubly tempting.

However, she had to get back for work in the morning. She had meetings to attend, events to organise. She couldn't spend the night with a random stranger in Cornwall.

"That's very kind, but I think it's best if I get my train. Plus, I think we both know I wouldn't get much sleep."

Skye stared, her rich blue eyes flecked with honey and gold. Skye had almost illegal lips and eyes. Gemma wasn't going to allow herself to ponder what the rest of her might be like.

"I promise I'll let you sleep."

Gemma's stomach lurched, but she shook her head. "Thank you, but no." She reached out and took Skye's fingers in hers. A shiver of delight danced up her spine. What was she saying no to? Something special, she had no doubt. Even if it was just for one night. But maybe cutting her losses now was the best thing all around. She hoped she'd helped Skye in some way.

Plus, they'd always have *that* kiss.

"I think we should leave it here. A small slice of heaven in a seaside bar. The perfect kiss. A happy ending for us both." She ran her thumb over the top of Skye's knuckles.

Skye let out a shallow breath and her eyelids fluttered briefly shut. When she opened them again, she gave Gemma a slow nod.

"I think we nailed the happy ending." She gave her a crooked smile.

Gemma took a deep breath, then gathered herself, her hand still warm from Skye's touch. When she glanced up, Skye stared at her own hand, too. Gemma shrugged on her coat and grabbed her handbag from its hook. When she'd hung it earlier, it had seemed like a different lifetime. In a few hours, her world had changed. This wasn't how she expected her night to end. With feelings of want, and of regret.

But she couldn't go back to Skye's place.

It wasn't what Gemma did. Her life was ordered.

"It was really lovely meeting you."

Skye held her gaze. "Let me walk you out."

Gemma sucked on her top lip. Her blood roared, her heart thumped. How to end it? She should just say, "be seeing you." But when she snagged Skye's stare a final time, it drew her back in. Just one more kiss. What could it hurt? They both deserved it.

Gemma stepped forward and pressed her lips to Skye's for a final time. They were even better than she remembered. When she slipped her tongue into Gemma's mouth, the world swayed, and electricity sparked inside.

She felt the tremble of Skye's body, the pull of her touch.

Seconds later, with supreme regret, Gemma wrenched herself away.

"Good luck with everything. And promise me you won't organise her wedding."

Skye smiled. "I promise." She paused. "One final question. Do you like yoga?"

"Jeez, no," Gemma replied. "You have to be far too bendy and balanced. My sister Martha loves it. I, on the other hand, fall over and off things all the time. As I think we just saw." She grinned. "Why do you ask?"

Skye shook her head. "No reason."

Gemma squeezed Skye's fingers, let go, then turned and walked towards the door. Past the two blokes playing pool on the left. Past the couple sharing a plate of chicken wings. Past the woman pouring two glasses of white wine.

She put her fingers on the door handle, and only then did she turn. She lifted her gaze and connected instantly with Skye.

The intensity, even from so far away, rooted Gemma to the spot. She wanted to run back into Skye's arms. To go back to hers and pretend her real life didn't exist. Just for one day.

But she'd made her decision. She was going home.

Skye gave her a small wave.

Gemma returned it.

Then, before she changed her mind, she wrenched open the door and walked away.

Chapter Three

"We're going to need about 15 tables. We think there's going to be a fair bit of interest, but 150 guests should be the max we get judging by past years. Can your space fit that okay?"

Brandon Tyler loosened his navy tie as he spoke. He was an insurance salesperson by trade, whose first love was cricket. Skye had once sung a terrible karaoke version of "Don't Go Breaking My Heart" with him at the Dog & Duck. Neither of them had been able to hit the high notes.

A little like Skye today. Brandon's lips were moving, but she couldn't quite pin down what they were saying. She ran them through her brain again. 150 guests. 15 tables.

But then a different image landed at the front of her brain. Gemma's hot lips on hers. Pleasure endorphins whizzed around her body. Her cheeks warmed. The hairs on the back of her neck prickled.

Skye drew in a breath. She had to focus. But today was not going well. She'd spent the first part of the morning staring at the sea from her office window. Now she was talking to a client about a cricket awards dinner, but her mind was still in the bar last night. Back on that bar stool. Plus, her lips were definitely still on Gemma's. To top it all, she had the mother of all hangovers. Both physical and emotional.

"Are you okay? You seem a little spaced out today." At least she wasn't in danger of losing this job. Brandon knew her. They'd sung together. He'd cut her some slack.

She shook her head. "Just got a bit of a headache. But yes, 15 round tables are no problem. Did you want buffet or served?"

"Served," he replied. "I want it to be upmarket. Three courses, coffee, wine, champagne for the toast. I want people to feel like they're getting their money's worth."

Skye nodded. "Got it. 150 people on a Thursday night. I'll check the calendar, but I'm pretty sure it'll be fine. I'll do some sums and send you an email this afternoon?"

"Sounds perfect, thanks Skye. The best deal you can do, please."

"Of course."

Skye saw him out to reception, smiled at Annie who was on the phone, then glanced down the corridor and stopped in her tracks.

Amanda. In full chef whites. Just the sight incensed her.

Skye really didn't need to see her this morning. Not after last night. Not when the jury was still out on whether or not Skye was going to vomit. However, even though Skye's feet had paused, Amanda's had not. Wasn't that just typical? Amanda didn't stop for anyone. She bulldozed her way through life, and didn't care who she might hurt in the process. So long as she got what she wanted.

Amanda came to a stop a few feet away, and gave Skye a half-smile.

"I was just coming to see you."

She was? At least this way, Skye had seen her coming. She should be grateful for small mercies. Skye said nothing, just tried to keep her face in neutral. It took all her powers.

"I wanted to tell you about something before it became public knowledge, but I think I might be a bit late. I came by yesterday, but Annie told me you'd left for the day. Very unlike you. Were you sick?" She peered closer. "You do look a little grey around the gills."

How very Amanda. Come to share her good news, and also to pick holes in Skye's appearance. Whenever Skye felt bad about their break-up, she should always remember the reality.

"I'm fine." Skye bristled. "And yes, you're a little late with your news."

Amanda's face twisted. "I really did mean to tell you first."

"You don't owe me anything."

"I feel like I do. Also, I didn't plan to have the wedding here, but it just makes sense financially. I hope you understand."

Skye's head began to pound a little more. In the past year since their break-up, she'd never come out of a meeting with her ex feeling better than when it started. Today was going to be no exception.

"You do what you need to. Don't start worrying about me and change the habit of a lifetime."

Skye closed her eyes. She hadn't meant to snap, but it was what Amanda did to her. Turned her into someone she wasn't. Made her brittle, snide. She didn't like who she was with Amanda. On the contrary, she'd very much liked who she became with Gemma. Perhaps it really was time to cut Amanda out of her life. Skye had the feeling her ex enjoyed meetings like these.

"Don't be like that, Blue."

Skye's face twitched. She'd never liked Amanda's nickname for her. "Blue Skye, no clouds at all, just like you!" She liked it even less today.

"You're getting married to your new wife in the exact same spot you married me a handful of years ago. How do you expect me to be? But like you said, it makes financial sense." She shrugged. She wanted this meeting over as soon as humanly possible. "Is there anything else?"

Amanda stared at Skye, trying to read her. She'd always been bad at it. She opened her mouth, and then closed it.

Probably her wisest move yet.

"No, I just wanted to come and check you were okay."

Skye pushed down her automatic response. She wasn't going to be drawn into anything else today. Amanda's goading days were over.

"I'm fine."

Amanda nodded, then went to walk away.

"And Amanda?"

Her ex turned.

"Whatever you do, don't include me on the guest list."

Skye walked into her office, sank into her chair and tipped her head to the ceiling.

Her mind flashed a snapshot of that kiss with Gemma, and her body relaxed in an instant.

She needed a break. Most of all, she needed another kiss from Gemma, but she didn't even know her last name. All she knew: great kisser, wears heels like a boss, likes wine and beer.

Skye tapped in 'Gemma, Surrey' into Google. A hairdresser, an events manager, a professor at Surrey university who specialises in mixed research methods. Plus, Emma & Gemma, a wedding band duo. The last one made Skye smile. None of them were Gemma.

Her Gemma.

She spun around to face the sea. She had to face facts. She was never going to see her again. Gemma had been 'her Gemma' for a few short hours.

But something inside Skye told her they weren't done. That if she went to Surrey, they'd meet again.

She had no facts to back up her conviction. It was illogical, it was stupid, but it already made far more sense than her marriage to Amanda ever had.

Chapter Four

Gemma parked in the cheese shop car park, and eyeballed the sky. Fat raindrops bounced off the bonnet and the windscreen with glee, which only made her yearn for summer that little bit more. January had been mild, and she and Martha had high hopes of a good year weather-wise. But February had soon put paid to those fanciful ideas. If it would just stop being so damn cold and rainy, she might find cause for optimism. However, the forecast for the next few days was rain, with a possible chance of hail and snow. At this rate, their harvest was going to be one of the worst they'd had since she and her sister took over the vineyard. It might be time to do a sun dance. She could rope Leo in, her nephew loved that sort of stuff. His younger brother Travis, on the other hand, might prove harder to convince.

She reached around to grab her Martha's Vineyard-branded umbrella, but her hand hit empty air. She twisted in her seat and scanned the back seat. It wasn't there. She gritted her teeth and glanced outside. The rain was so hard, the car park was now a pop-up swimming pool with drains that simply couldn't cope with the deluge. At least she'd worn leather boots and not heels today. She had nobody to impress. Not another vineyard owner, not a customer, and certainly not a random stranger who might kiss her until she went limp.

That thought brought Tuesday night crashing back into her brain with flashing lights all around it. The warmth of the bar. The press of Skye's fingers on her cheek. The way her lips had caressed Gemma's. She smiled at the memory. It had only been two days, yet it felt like another lifetime. A different world to this one, where she was picking up supplies for the weekend cheese and wine sessions after their marketing manager called in sick.

When Gemma had arrived home on Wednesday morning, she'd stood and stared at her lips in her hallway mirror. It really wasn't like her to go kissing total strangers in bars. Gemma was purposeful in most things she did. She never slept around, never had a crazy story to tell anybody. Now that she did, she wanted to keep it close to her chest. It was a secret only she knew, a memory she intended to treasure. If she told anybody else, the excitement might seep out and fade away.

Instead of sharing, she'd spent her time replaying the evening in her mind. How she'd kissed Skye to cheer her up, but that reason had quickly been cast aside once their kiss had taken flight. Despite falling off her stool. She chuckled at the insane memory. What must they have looked like? Never in her life had Gemma had a kiss so great, it knocked her off her stool. Literally. She'd had the chance to leave. Instead, she'd flirted. Snogged Skye in the toilet like she was 21 again. Should she have taken Skye up on her offer to stay over? That question had blazed in her heart ever since.

Part of her wished she'd been brave enough, and had one night of full blown, caution-to-the-wind sex. She'd never had a one-night stand before. When it came to sex, her sister, Martha, was far braver than her. She'd had one-night stands and regaled Gemma with high tales. Meanwhile, Gemma had a handful of meaningful relationships, but none that had ever progressed to anything more serious.

Both she and her sister were still single, aged 40 and 43. Martha thought it was because their job scared suitors off. The fact they owned a vineyard left people overawed. Gemma could understand it when it came to men. But the women she'd met had never appeared overawed. They were just the wrong women. Gemma had a knack for choosing them. She had no idea if Skye would be any different. What she knew for sure was that none of her past relationships had started off with the kissing equivalent of dynamite.

A bang on her car window shook Gemma from her thoughts.

A man stood huddled under an umbrella. He mouthed something to her through her window. Gemma couldn't hear him, but his hand signals told her he was asking if she wanted to come under his large, blue golf umbrella. Ordinarily, getting under an umbrella with Harvey Drinkwater – local landlord and brother of her most recent terrible idea for a girlfriend – wouldn't thrill her. Not that Harvey wasn't lovely. He was. Much nicer than his sister, in fact. But she knew he'd try to apologise for Juliette's behaviour, and Gemma didn't want to hear it. Normally, she'd have shaken her head and waved him on. Today, though, Harvey's umbrella would stop her getting drowned.

Instead, she nodded, grabbed her handbag, and jumped out. Yes, it was just as wet as it looked.

"Lovely day for it!" Harvey shouted over the thud of water on nylon and concrete.

Gemma gave him a wire-tight smile. "You're going to the cheese shop, right?"

He nodded, then held out an arm.

She threaded hers through his, and together they sploshed across the car park. Once inside, Harvey stashed the umbrella in the ceramic umbrella stand, then shook himself in the manner of a dog. Rain skittered off his bright-blue waterproof jacket.

The intoxicating, powerful smell of the shop hit her nose at speed as always. Creamy, ripe, cheesy deliciousness.

"Two of my favourite people all at once!" Shop owner Davina came out from behind the wide counter laden with artisan cheese. She gave both Gemma and Harvey a hug. She had the energy of a puppy, and the complexion of gorgonzola. She tilted her head at Gemma. "How are you, dear? After *everything*?"

Gemma wished the whole community would stop mourning her failed relationship. It wasn't like she and Juliette had been married. They'd been together for six ill-advised months. Nothing more.

"I'm fine," she said, brushing off Davina's comment like the rain.

Davina gave her a sad smile in return, before turning to Harvey. "Glad to see you're both still friends, anyway. No point one bad apple spoiling the barrel, is there?"

Harvey ignored the slight to his sister, and gave Davina a polite smile.

"I'm here to pick up the cheese for Saturday's tastings," Gemma said. "We've got a full house for both sessions, so the usual portions please." Dalton Cheeses was noted for their

Surrey Blue, along with their crystal-rich cheddar. They also stocked a brilliantly gooey brie and a local goat cheese. All four were the stars of Martha's Vineyard's cheese and wine tastings, along with some honey, walnuts and their signature quince paste. The vineyard's wine was exceptional, but so were the cheeses they paired with them. Gemma didn't like to brag, but their tastings were best in class.

"They're all ready for you, let me just go and get them." Davina peered out the window. "I hope the weather clears up for you soon, too. Maxwell and I were out last night doing a sun dance for all the vineyards."

"Thanks Davina, you're a star." The local businesses worked together and looked out for each other in any way they could. At least, most of them did.

Gemma waited for Davina to disappear before she turned to Harvey. As expected, he gave her a sympathetic smile. She almost wished she had a photo of Skye snogging her to thrust in his face. Anything to stop her being 'poor old Gemma' to all the locals. Successful in business (weather-permitting); unlucky in love.

She'd full-on kissed a complete stranger in public! She was someone to be reckoned with.

"How have you been?" He had the same hazel eyes as his no-good sister, the same shaped mouth, the same shock of jet-black hair.

Gemma tried not to focus on that.

"Good." She gave him an emphatic nod. "Been down to Cornwall, and we've got some tastings this weekend, all full. Business is good."

He held her gaze. "I wanted to say, I'm sorry about not

restocking your wines at the pub. It was Juliette's doing, and you know what she's like."

Flighty. Impulsive. Deceitful. Yes, Gemma was aware.

"I'm hoping we can put them back on soon. It's just, when you broke up, she didn't want any chance of you coming in."

"She broke up with me." Plus, as there was nobody else involved and no valid reason, Gemma hadn't understood why she'd stopped serving their wines. Pure spite? That, Gemma could well believe. "And you've had our wines in your pub for years."

He put his hand on her arm. "I know and I'm sorry. It's temporary. I've tried talking to her, but she's not ready to listen just yet. But she will. She knows it's ridiculous and petty. She'll back down eventually."

"We support local business around here. We always have. I send customers your way, you stock my wine. You know how it works." Gemma bristled. She thought she'd dealt with her feelings on this, and she had when she didn't have to think about it. But it was still a sore point. She'd wanted to blame Harvey, but she knew what a brat Juliette could be. Her brother preferred a quiet life.

Harvey nodded. "I do, and I'll get it sorted. I still don't fully understand why you broke up? I asked Juliette, but she was vague."

Gemma made a strangled sound. "She was vague with me, too. Something about our values not being aligned. Anyway, it's over. Probably for the best." Definitely for the best, but she didn't want to be cruel. Juliette wasn't Harvey's fault. Juliette was 100 per cent her own worst enemy.

"I miss you at the pub. So does Gravy."

Gravy was the pub terrier. "I miss Gravy, too. I will come back at some point, but not just yet. Things need to heal. There are always casualties of war."

Harvey nodded, then studied his wet trainers. "How's Martha?"

"Fine. You can still come and see us, even if Juliette has banned us from the pub." She gave him a wry grin. "I am joking." She put a hand on his arm. "But we all know if I did drop in, she'd set Gravy on me."

"And she'd lick you to death."

They both smiled at that.

Davina appeared from the back of the shop, carrying two boxes of cheese. She gave one to Gemma, and one to Harvey. "I put a little extra for you both to enjoy at your leisure, too. Don't want to give the customers all the good stuff, do we?"

* * *

Harvey escorted her back to her Jeep. Gemma put the cheeses onto the back seat and got behind the wheel. She slammed her door, and took a breath. It was still raining cats and dogs.

Harvey drove off ahead of her, waving as he went.

She waved back.

There were days when she didn't give a single thought to Juliette and what she'd done. Then there were days when Gemma fixated on her, and had to sit on her hands to stop herself from driving to the next village, walking into The Haunted Hare and giving her a piece of her mind.

At least now, whenever she had the red-mist thoughts, she had something else to nudge them out of her head. Kissing

Skye by the seaside, a place where Gemma could be whatever she wanted to be. A debonair, sophisticated out-of-towner who waltzed around coastal towns, snogged locals, and then vanished into thin air. Only, she hadn't particularly wanted to vanish when it came to Skye. She'd simply wanted more, but that wasn't possible. So now she was going to hang that kiss on her memory mantlepiece. Buff it up regularly, keep it dust free. It was worth it. She could live off the energy of that kiss for a while yet. Then, she simply had to find someone else who kissed just like Skye. It was a tall order.

She was just about to start the car when her phone buzzed in her pocket. She pulled it out. It was a text from her marketing manager, Andi – she of the cheese-collection-no-show – telling Gemma she couldn't do the tasting sessions on Saturday due to a medical emergency.

Gemma closed her eyes and let out a sigh. It wasn't like Andi to bail on them – she was normally Mrs Reliable. But Gemma knew what it meant. That she and Martha would have to take a session each. Another job to add to her ever-growing list. She messaged back telling Andi she hoped everything was okay and to keep her updated. If this was going to impact any more of her time, they needed to know so they could arrange cover.

She plugged her phone into the car's entertainment system so any messages would be flashed up on-screen and read out. She liked it when it did that. It made Gemma feel like she was living in the future. Unlike running a biodynamic vineyard, at the mercy of the weather and pests, which often felt like anything but. She set her wipers to blitz mode and put the radio on. The DJ blathered about lost love. She rolled her eyes, pulled out of the car park and onto the country lane that led back towards Frinton, where their vineyard lived. She had to drive past The Haunted Hare too, but she wasn't going to stop. Not today, or any day soon.

A jaunty Taylor Swift number came on. Gemma turned it up and sang along. Taylor was a woman on her wavelength. She knew her worth, didn't settle for second best, but also seemed perpetually unlucky in love. Gemma often thought she'd love to invite her over for a glass of wine and some cheese. Taylor understood her world like no other.

Her mum, though, had other plans. A message flashed up from her, interrupting Taylor's wise words. A measured female voice narrated it to Gemma.

'Hey darling, hope you're good! We've had a great day today, won big on the gee-gees! Your dad and I are running low on the fizzy vino collapso, so if you could ship another couple of cases, that would be great. The cheap Cava does the job normally, but we like to impress our friends with the good stuff. Thanks honey. Kisses!'

Gemma gripped the wheel that bit tighter. Between her parents and Juliette, she wasn't sure who annoyed her more. Of late, Juliette. But for the grand title, it had to be her mum and dad. Thank goodness for her sister, artists like Taylor, and strangers like Skye, who all gave her hope there was a better world out there.

The sign for Martha's Vineyard came into view and Gemma slowed, then flicked on her indicator.

She was up for a world with more glamour, more melody, more kissing.

More up for it than perhaps she was even willing to admit.

Chapter Five

Skye sat on the sea wall, facing the ocean. Ahead of her, three surfers rode the waves as if they were a part of them. Just like always, Skye was impressed. One of them was Justin: she recognised his bright yellow wet suit. It was the reason he'd moved here from London, so he could pursue his passion to surf. She admired that. This week, after Amanda's news on Monday and that kiss on Tuesday, Skye had started to wonder whether she should do the same. Not surfing, but following her passion. Now, all she had to do was find out what that was.

Skye hadn't moved to Cornwall because she wanted to surf, or get out of Reading. She'd moved because of Amanda. Skye's favourite band had played a night in Bath, and she'd gone over for the gig, where she'd met Amanda. Six months later, she'd moved to Cornwall and taken a job at the hotel where Amanda worked. The stars had aligned and Skye believed in fate. It turned out, fate didn't believe in her.

But what was keeping her here now? Nothing but her own stubbornness. She hadn't wanted to be driven out of her home, but when she really thought about it, was this her home? It was definitely Amanda's. She had family here. Skye's family were back in Reading. Was it time to start building her life nearer to where she was from? Was Cornwall sending her a message?

She stared out to sea. She'd miss this, though. She'd got used to living by the waves. The smell of the sea, the gentle chime of metal against boat masts, the cry of seagulls. A coastal chorus just for her. Living by the sea was something she'd always wanted to do, and moving here had fulfilled that dream. It had also given her a wife. Had she jumped into life and marriage too quickly? Her parents certainly thought so. They'd come to the wedding, but Skye knew they hadn't been onboard with Amanda. It turned out, they had better instincts than she did.

But moving away from St Austin was a major life decision. An admission she'd been wrong. A levelling of the ground of her life, a flattening of the foundations so she could start over. She sucked in a long breath. Starting over wasn't a bad thing, but it was daunting. However, moving back home had the added advantage of a support network already in place. Her parents. Her brother. Lauren. She'd have people she could call, dinners she could share, friends to moan about the mess she'd made of her life. Maybe there might even be a woman in her fresh start.

Skye's mind immediately jumped to Gemma, as it had done for the past couple of days. To their hot bodies pressed together. She flushed at the memory. Despite fate giving Skye the massive middle finger when it came to a happy marriage, Skye still had faith in it. After two days replaying that night with Gemma, she'd come to the conclusion that Gemma had been sent to her for a reason. Her fleeting nature had a reason behind it.

Gemma was a signpost, someone sent to show Skye there was another way to live. That there were hot women out there who were willing to kiss her. However, if Skye wanted to find another Gemma, she might have to leave St Austin. Leave Cornwall. Start all over again. Gemma had been sent to show her it was a little early to put herself on the shelf. Skye was not done. There was life to yet be lived.

Justin was out there, catching another wave and living his best life. It's exactly what Skye needed to do. Catch another wave of her own. She rose and began to walk along the sea wall.

Her phone rang. Lauren. One of the people Skye would hopefully be hanging out with more if she decided to change her life for good.

"Hello stranger." Guilt rose in Skye as she said the words. She and Lauren had been friends since school. She'd come to her wedding, but over the past year, Skye had been too wrapped up in her own gloom to keep long-distance friendships ticking over. She needed to remedy that.

"Hello to you, too!" Lauren's voice was comfortingly familiar. "Can you talk? Is this a good time?"

Skye stared out to sea, and combed through her recent thoughts. "It's the absolute perfect time. More perfect than you could ever imagine."

"Okay, I've no idea why, but I just wanted to ask a quick question. Are you coming for Seb's birthday bash this weekend? And don't just say no like you normally do."

She blinked. Seb's birthday. It was this weekend. Damn it, she was a really shit sister. He'd left a few voicemails over the past few days, but she hadn't got around to listening to them.

"I hadn't thought about it." That was the truth, but it wasn't very palatable. Wind buffeted her from one side as she walked. Shivering, she made a beeline for a straggly wooden shelter to give her some protection.

"Are you standing in a wind tunnel?"

"Just on the seafront, you know what it's like around here."

"You're not at work?"

Skye kicked a stone as she sat on the rickety wooden bench inside the shelter, crushing her knees together. Even her woollen work trousers couldn't cope with this wind. "Just having a break to clear my head." She did some brief maths in her head. "Is it Seb's 40th?" But she knew the answer. He'd always been two years older than her. That had never changed.

"Nothing gets past you does it, Sherlock." Skye could almost feel Lauren's eye roll down the phone. "Which is why he's having a party. I'm going, your parents are going. It would be nice if his sister turned up as well."

Skye had the weekend off. Was this phone call a sign, too? Perhaps it was. Lauren hadn't called her for a few months, but perhaps she knew things had shifted and Skye needed a prod.

"I know he'd like to see you. I'd like to see you, too. We've all been worried about how you're doing since Amanda. You've kind of fallen off the face of the earth."

She dropped her head and studied her feet. It was the truth. She'd been a shit friend and sister.

"I know, and I'm sorry. But I promise I'm coming this weekend."

"For once, I believe you. Are you going to stay with me?"

"If I'm still invited."

"Lucky for you, I'm the forgiving sort." Lauren paused. "Another question. Can you make it here by eleven on Saturday morning?"

Skye nodded. "I can. I'll get the train Friday night. Why?"

"I've got a spare ticket for a cheese and wine thing Saturday lunchtime if you want to be my plus one? Mum bought it for my birthday, but she can't make it now. We could make a day of it?"

"Making a day of it sounds brilliant. Let me look up train times and I'll message you when I get in?"

"Sounds great. I'll pick you up from the station even though you don't deserve it. You might want to let Seb know, too. He looked a bit sad he hadn't heard from you when I saw him last."

"I will," Skye promised. "And Lauren?"

"Yeah?"

"Thanks for calling and for sticking by me, even when I've been a shit friend."

"You can buy me wine to make up for it," her friend replied. "I gotta run, I'm on my lunch break. See you Friday, can't wait!"

Chapter Six

Gemma walked into the vineyard tasting room, then gave a satisfied nod. The weekend team had set the space up perfectly for the midday tasting, with every place set with three branded champagne flutes, along with cutlery and a place mat for the cheese course to follow. Water jugs and glasses had also been placed on the thick wooden tables that formed a U-shape looking out onto the canopied terrace, and the wines, their origins and prices were well showcased on the vineyard literature in every place setting. They were ready to roll. All she had to do was guide it.

She glanced out at the vines beyond, climbing the fields in neat, ordered rows. Sometimes, if she stared hard enough, she could still see her granddad in his trilby hat, crouched and pruning them back. He'd always chat to the vines, just as Martha still did. He said there was nowhere on earth more idyllic. When the sun shone, Gemma agreed. Today though, on February 28th, the buds had yet to burst and the sky was the colour of indecision. May and June were Gemma's favourite months of the year, when the weather warmed up and the sun came out. There was still some way to go until that happened.

In the meantime, what had shown up this morning was a brand-new spot on Gemma's chin. But her clients today would never know, because Gemma had slipped on her professional persona. Along with her Charlotte Tilbury Flawless Finish Micro-Powder to hide said spot. As her grandma used to say, it didn't matter how you felt: "Hunters always get things done."

She didn't need to be quite so formal for a tasting as for a meeting, so this morning she'd put on her favourite long-sleeved bright yellow shift dress to cheer herself up. Wearing it was an act of self-care. It transformed Gemma into a ray of sunshine.

Her sister Martha poked her tongue at her from beyond the wall of glass that separated the tasting room from the vineyard's shop and bar. They'd designed it like that when they'd refurbished the venue a few years ago, so that customers doing tastings could see others buying and enjoying their wine. The wall also retracted for larger events. Martha walked to the doorway and popped her head inside. She held her pruning gloves in her hand, and her wellies glistened with morning dew.

"Do you need a hand before I run Travis to his game?"

Her sister was doing the later tasting so she could ferry her younger son to his weekend football match.

Gemma shook her head. "It's under control. Polly and Brianna are doing the cheese boards, Leo and Jack are serving. You go and enjoy the football." She gave her sister a grin. Martha couldn't stand most sports, but being a widow and a single-parent, she had to pretend. She'd been spared it with her eldest son, Leo, who'd never shown any interest in kicking a ball of any shape around a muddy field. Leo was interested in wine and how to make it. Martha had lucked out with him.

"I like the look today." Martha waved her hand up and

down, appraising Gemma. "With your black scarf and boots, you look like a stylish bumble bee."

"It was exactly what I was going for."

Martha pointed to the notice board. "By the way, I put the ad up for the marketing manager position on a few job sites, and also on the notice board. People come in here all the time and they might fit the bill, so I figured why not."

Their marketing manager's health was not looking good, so they'd decided to advertise for a temporary replacement while she hopefully got sorted. Gemma already had enough on her plate running the day-to-day operations without everything else, too.

"Makes sense."

"Good luck today, sell lots of wine. And if you could hire a temporary marketing manager so we don't have to present again, that would be great."

Gemma rolled her eyes. "No problem."

"Have you got a full house?"

Gemma nodded. "Yep. The full 25. Let's hope they're a fun bunch, otherwise it might be a very long 90 minutes."

Martha's son, Leo, sauntered up behind her. At 15, his hair sported a regulation flop. "You still here? Travis will be going mad." He glanced at the clock on the wall. "You know he likes to get there early to get a *feel* for the grass." Leo rolled his eyes, putting the word 'feel' in air quotes.

Martha poked her son in the ribs. "Leave your brother alone. He finds football soothing." She kissed his cheek, and Leo didn't rub it off. He was used to it.

"Love you," Martha told him, then turned to Gemma. "Love you, too."

She gave them both a wink, then walked out the main door, keys swinging off her right index finger.

Gemma watched her go, then shook her head. Martha had so much love, it spilled out of her and she had to share it around.

Meanwhile, Gemma kept all of hers locked up inside.

* * *

"Okay, if you could take your places and get settled, that'd be great!" Gemma scanned the room. They were missing two people. She checked her watch. One minute to midday. It didn't matter how many times she did a tasting – and she'd done many in her decade at the vineyard – there was always one party that ran late. She always gave them five minutes grace, and it was rare people overran that. Wine-lovers on the whole were a punctual bunch.

The woman sat nearest the patio doors on the other side of the room raised her hand, as if she was a student. It always amused Gemma that people fell back into such roles even with wine in front of them. The woman was dressed head to toe in beige. Gemma would lay bets that every wall in her house was painted magnolia.

"Yes?" She gave the woman an encouraging smile.

"Will there be a chance to buy the wines we've tasted?"

"Of course!" Gemma pointed through the glass to the shop. "When we're done, feel free to linger and taste in our bar, and buy from our shop which you can see right beside us." Just as she finished speaking, two women with red bobble hats walked in the main door to the bar. These must be her two stragglers. Gemma rubbed her hands together and grinned at the group. "We're just waiting for two more, and then we'll get going."

She walked behind the small table in front of the patio doors and took the first bottle from the ice bucket. Gemma focused on untwisting the wire from the cork, as she heard the last two walk in. She glanced up and smiled.

But when she saw them properly, something inside her stalled. Gemma flinched, then shook her head. Her brain buzzed in her skull, and her palms began to sweat. She was back in that toilet, the cool press of its wall hard against her back. She stared hard at the bottle as she took the wire off and put it on the table.

She kept her head down.

She must be seeing things.

One of the newcomers looked *incredibly* like Skye. Same height, hair, face. But it must be a doppelganger. Skye lived in Cornwall, miles away from here. This was Gemma's brain playing tricks on her. After all, she'd hadn't slept well, and this had been a weird week.

That must be it.

When she looked up again, the woman would not be Skye. Rather, she'd simply be someone who looked incredibly like her. Someone else Gemma was attracted to. At least it would make this tasting more interesting. Customers who were easy on the eye never hurt, did they?

Gemma's fingers gripped the cork, twisted and eased it out. She expected the resultant pop to reset her vision. That when she looked up, the person sat next to the woman in the bubble-gum-pink top would be someone else altogether. However, when Gemma dared to move her gaze, she connected with

Skye's piercing blue eyes. That's when her stomach fell through the floor. Gemma gripped the bottle of blanc de blancs as tight as she ever had. Her heart thumped in her chest.

In response, Skye frowned. There was her tell-tale dimple, too. The one Gemma had traced with her finger. Just to the right of the lips Gemma had kissed for days. The lips she thought she'd never see ever again. What on earth were those lips – and the person attached to them – doing in her tasting room on a Saturday lunchtime? Very far away from where Gemma had left them four days ago?

Gemma had questions. *Soooooo many questions.* Like, had Skye sought her out? And who was the woman beside her? Friend? Sister? The latest person Skye had snogged in a bar? That final option made her vision sway. But she couldn't ask. What's more, she had 24 other people waiting for her to tell them about wine and how it was made.

For now, she had to avoid looking Skye's way – or at least pretend she didn't know her at all – and slip into professional mode. Be the wine-maker extraordinaire. She'd done this talk with a colossal hangover, with a broken ankle, the morning after the girlfriend before Juliette had dumped her. She could do it today.

She put the open wine back in the ice bucket, then smiled at the woman in beige. Then at the man directly ahead wearing a thick black jumper and white-collared shirt. Then, automatically, she turned her head to the left too, and her gaze rested on Skye.

It really was her. Gemma needed to have a proper, full-on look one more time to confirm it.

Once she did, she knew. It was definitely Skye, in all her

glory. With her cool Nikes, her striped shirt, her artfully frayed jeans.

She couldn't seem to stop staring at Gemma either, probably in disbelief.

The feeling was mutual.

"Welcome to the last pair." Gemma decided to style it out like it was nothing. She addressed the group. "My name is Gemma Hunter, and I'm the co-owner of Martha's Vineyard. I run it alongside my sister, Martha. She looks after the vines, I look after the business. And no, the vineyard is not hers, despite what the name suggests. Martha's Vineyard was started back in 1974 by my grandparents, Victor and Martha Hunter. If you know a little about geography, you may know Martha's Vineyard is an island off the coast of Boston in the USA. Back in the 1970s, my grandparents weren't aware of Martha's Vineyard in the US – or so they told us. This vineyard was named in honour of my grandmother. If my sister tries to tell you otherwise, it's all lies."

Gemma waited for the gentle laughter to die down. That story was always a great ice-breaker, and Gemma had managed it even with Skye right in front of her. She hadn't imploded, or launched herself into Skye's lap to kiss her again. These were good signs.

She could absolutely do this.

"Can I have a show of hands who knows something about wine? Don't worry, I'm not going to whip a wine quiz out and challenge you."

Gemma waited. This question was an ease-in. A gentle audience participation, and one that showed her who might be prepared to talk, who knew something, and who liked the sound of their own voice. The woman in beige raised her hand, as did a couple in the left-hand far corner. Also, out of the corner of her eye, the woman beside Skye raised her hand.

Then Skye promptly grabbed it and pulled it down.

The brunette gave Skye a stern look and put it back up.

Gemma's heart, which had switched to jog mode, now went into overdrive.

It turned out, the woman in beige had visited three vineyards in the US and two in Australia, so she knew a little about wine. The couple in the corner had done an evening class on the topic at their local college. Gemma encouraged them to speak up and tell the group what they knew. The couple both blushed bright red, so she didn't expect much. However, she'd definitely engage them in conversation later.

Then Gemma turned to Skye's companion, studiously avoiding any eye contact with Skye. Which wasn't easy.

"There seemed to be some difference of opinion whether or not you know anything about wine?"

Pink lady shook her head. "It's not me, it's her." She nodded towards Skye.

Of course it was. Why hadn't Martha taken this tasting session, and Gemma the later one? It was all Travis's fault. It might be harsh to blame her 11-year-old nephew, but it was fair.

Gemma looked Skye dead in the eye.

Skye grimaced, then folded her arms across her chest.

Had Gemma's face coloured red? Hopefully she had enough makeup on to cover it up. Thank goodness for foundation, powder, bronzer. For Charlotte Tilbury and her magical powers.

"My shy and retiring friend here is a hotel manager in

Cornwall, and she deals with wine people all the time," Skye's friend continued, oblivious. She'd said friend, not *girlfriend*. "She knows her wines."

Skye had not applied makeup this morning, and her cheeks were currently the colour of a ripe plum. She glanced up at Gemma, but didn't hold her gaze for long. "I know some things, but I'm always happy to learn more," she mumbled.

That made two of them. Gemma took the opening to find out more. "What brings you here from Cornwall? I assume not purely this wine and cheese tasting, although it is the best in the area."

Skye stared at her.

Gemma could almost see the internal dialogue going on in her head.

Her friend jumped in. "It's her brother's 40th birthday party this weekend. This is an added bonus. Because who doesn't like wine?"

"Who indeed?" chimed in beige lady.

Okay, so she was fairly sure Skye wasn't stalking her. Her brother lived nearby and it was his 40th. A perfectly logical explanation.

Gemma held up the bottle of blanc de blancs she'd just uncorked. "First off, I'll be giving you a background on all our wines, how we grow them, what our expected harvest is, that sort of thing. We'll also be tasting all the wines, but I would encourage you to ask questions. I've worked here for ten years, plus I grew up here, so I know a thing or two about wine-making. All your burning questions, do let me know."

Gemma walked around the group, starting with beige lady, filling the glass on the left a third-way full with their blanc de blancs fizz. Martha's Vineyard specialised in organic sparkling wine, and its three main sellers were a Classic Cuvee blanc de blancs, a blanc de noirs and a sparkling rosé, alongside a signature still rosé. They also made sloe gin, vermouth, and port, but their mainstays were sparkling.

"Many people are surprised when they come for a cheese tasting with sparkling wine, but I'd encourage you to try different wines with cheeses, and you might be pleasantly surprised." She reached the pair before Skye, filled their glasses and took a deep breath. Then she poured for Skye and her friend.

"In life, people tend to stick to what they know. Only red wine and port with cheese, that's what they say, right?" Gemma stared at Skye. Delicious friction crept up her spine.

Skye gave her a slow nod.

"But you can enjoy something different, like a riesling, a sauvignon blanc, a bottle of our sparkling, or even an ice wine. They're all great with cheese, as you're about to find out." Skye's long lashes framed her rich blue eyes. "Don't always do the expected in life, whether it's wine or whatever. My motto is, live a little, because you never know where stepping outside your comfort zone might take you."

Chapter Seven

Gemma had disappeared somewhere, which allowed Skye to take in the impressive vineyard without fear she was about to inadvertently collide with her full-on gaze. She'd spent the past hour and a half trying to avoid it, and it had been exhausting. Lauren kept giving her strange looks as if asking what the hell was wrong with her. Luckily, they'd had the wine-and-cheese tasting to keep them occupied, and Gemma had her hands full dealing with the rest of her customers.

Skye focused on the food and drink, even though her body was on high alert. The signature fizz had been worth it, as had the cheddar infused with salt crystals. Skye made a note to buy some fizz before she left.

She pushed back her chair just as Gemma reappeared in the doorway. She looked absolutely stunning in her sunshine dress, subtly different from the suited executive Skye had kissed earlier this week. However, both Gemmas shared an air of professionalism, a casual confidence and love of what they did. Skye had always found casual confidence attractive in a woman. It was what had drawn her to Amanda.

Okay, bad example.

Gemma was different from Amanda. Plus, Gemma's

confidence was matched with her fabulous cheekbones you could cut bread with, along with her memorable lips.

Their gazes collided and Gemma stopped in her tracks.

Her gaze skittered across the floor and landed at Skye's feet. Gemma licked her lips, then raised her stare.

Was she thinking about running away too? Skye understood the urge. This was the woman she'd blurted out far too much to, after all. The woman who knew that nobody had yet found her G-Spot.

Skye's insides curled at the memory. She pressed it down, as she and Lauren walked to the doorway.

"If you'd like to buy any wine, or have another glass, feel free to move into the bar." Gemma addressed Lauren. "We need to set this room up again for a final tasting at 2.30."

"Another glass sounds like a top idea," Lauren said.

She had no idea what she was saying.

Skye forced a smile and addressed Gemma. "Are you doing the next session as well?"

Gemma shook her head. "No, my sister is. We're sharing the load as our normal presenter is off sick."

"You did an amazing job."

Gemma blushed, and gave them a tight smile.

Skye was instantly transported back to the bar. Her heartbeat thumped in her ears, but nobody else seemed to have noticed.

"That's very kind." Gemma's gaze didn't move. "Whereabouts is your brother having his party?"

"Reading," Lauren replied.

Skye glared at the side of her friend's head. She was being as loud as her top today.

Lauren walked over to the shop and its tall, wooden racks

of wine. She picked up a bottle of fizz, then stared at the notice board beside it.

Skye focused on her friend, willing her to come back. But she wasn't going to, was she?

She had to face Gemma alone, but she was going to put it off for as long as she could. Her gaze took in the table in the middle of the shop, laden with wine gift boxes, jars of locally grown honey, and artisan chocolate. But eventually, Skye turned her head and brought her eyes level with Gemma's.

A million first lines and then a million nothings skidded through her mind. She'd had no trouble chatting with Gemma on Tuesday. No trouble kissing her forever. But Tuesday had been a break from reality. A very short holiday. Now her feet were planted firmly in the here and now, it was a very different prospect. Plus, were they going to acknowledge anything? Skye had no idea.

"I couldn't quite believe it when you walked in." Gemma's eyes flicked up to Skye's.

Hers were still an incredible shade of green.

"That makes two of us." Skye stared at Gemma's lips. She rolled her eyes internally. She was so obvious.

"Skye, come look at this!"

Lauren's raised volume made Skye wince. She glanced over to where Lauren was pointing at the noticeboard.

"They're looking for a temporary marketing manager. This could be perfect for you! You said you wanted a change and that you were considering moving back this way."

Gemma's eyes widened. "You are?"

"Maybe." Skye joined Lauren at the notice board, and Gemma followed.

"See!" Lauren stabbed the job ad. "It could be perfect." She glanced at Gemma. "I assume you'd be hiring. Would you consider Skye?"

"Lauren!" Skye's tone held a note of warning, but Lauren didn't spot it. Skye's defensive walls shook.

"I'd have to speak with my sister. We're interviewing candidates next week." Gemma looked as freaked as Skye felt.

She put up a hand. "Right now, I live in Cornwall, and I have a job, so this conversation is not one that's going anywhere. So let's buy some wine and leave." Skye walked over to the rack, picked up two bottles of the blanc de blancs, and gave Gemma an apologetic smile.

Gemma shook her head. "If you want to apply, please do send me a CV. I'm always happy to hear from potential candidates. Plus, it might be nice to have some fresh blood, somebody from outside the area who could bring some different knowledge to the team." She sighed. "Also, we're just revving up into our busy season, so I really need to find someone capable quickly." She shook her head. "Sorry, enough of my problems. You don't live here. You live in Cornwall." Gemma's gaze dropped to Skye's lips. "Lovely place, Cornwall."

Skye swayed on her feet. The sun came out in her heart.

"You see!" Lauren cooed. Then she leaned toward Gemma. "Leave it with me, I'll work on her."

Gemma gave Skye a tight smile. She went over to the cash desk, grabbed something, then returned. She held out a card to Skye. "It's got my email address on it, and my phone number, so feel free to call me with any questions if you do decide it might be something you're interested in."

Was she talking about the job or her? Skye couldn't quite

work it out. As she took the card from Gemma, their fingers brushed and she stilled. A shock of desire travelled up her arm and radiated down her whole body. When Skye looked up, she could see Gemma had felt it too. They both froze in each other's gaze. Skye tried to regulate her breathing once more. It wasn't easy.

Skye stared at the card. She had Gemma's details in her hand. But there was no way she could work for her. No way she could see her every day and not kiss her again and again. The job was a non-starter. However, now Skye knew how to contact her. If she moved back to Reading, she'd be close. If she moved in with Lauren, who lived in a small village just a ten-minute drive from the vineyard, Gemma would be just around the corner. She might end up living near to a woman who kissed her like nobody else *ever* had.

It already sounded appealing. Suddenly, her potential move took on a completely different slant.

* * *

Skye was still processing meeting Gemma again when they arrived at her brother's Victorian terrace for his party later that day. Three red balloons were stuck to the black front door, along with a banner that proclaimed *40 & Still Gorgeous!* She pushed it open and was hit by the sounds of 60s Motown and loud laughter from the lounge to their right. When she glanced up, Seb came down the stairs. He wore a black Ramones T-shirt and tight jeans, hair slicked into a quiff as always.

"There's my baby sister, the one who never comes to see me!"

She deserved that. But Seb's words came with a smile and

a hug. When he let her go, Skye handed him a bottle of the blanc de blancs they'd bought today.

He gave her a wide grin. "I love Martha's Vineyard wine! Did you go there today?"

Skye nodded, a vision of Gemma radiant in her mind. "We did."

"And they had a job going which Skye would be perfect for!"

Lauren was not giving up on this, was she?

"Are you thinking of moving back?"

Skye gave Seb a non-committal shrug. "Maybe. It's early days. But I need to find a place to live and a job before anything can happen."

"I might have the answer to your prayers." Seb smiled at her again. "I've met someone, and I've handed my notice in at work."

Skye shook her head to make sure she'd heard right. Seb had worked at Reading Council in the housing department for the past 20 years. He was part of the furniture. She'd assumed he'd stay there until he could draw his pension, and consider it a life well lived.

"You've met someone? Who are they?" Her brother had always been open to persuasion.

"They're a woman called Imogen and she lives in Sydney. I'm moving to Australia!" He raised both arms in the air and gave her a triumphant smile.

Australia? Even saying the word winded her. Skye glanced at Lauren. "Did you know about this?"

Lauren winced, her shoulders lifting in guilt. "He mentioned it a couple of weeks ago, but he wanted to tell you himself."

Seb had told Lauren, but he hadn't told her. That fact made her brain tilt, and her teeth ache. But she had no right to feel hurt. She was the one who'd not picked up any of his messages forever. The one who'd opted out of her family. She'd heard about people buying sports cars when they hit 40, or blowing all their money on booze and drugs. But moving halfway across the world? That was a new one. "Are you sure, because that's an awful long way if you're not." That was a midlife crisis with no recall button.

Seb shrugged. "I've been stuck in the same job for years, and I've just accepted it. But now, I've met a woman online, and I'm taking a chance. I want to be with her and she wants to be with me."

Skye pictured her brother arriving in Sydney, being greeted by a surfer chick and living happily ever after. Just like Gemma had told her she deserved. She pushed that thought from her mind.

"Have you seen photos?" Because the surfer chick could just as easily be a bloke living in a basement. Worse still, a scammer from a far-off land. Although, Australia was a far-off land. She didn't want her brother to lose everything he'd worked for. A sense of doom slipped through her. "Have you actually spoken to her live on a video call?"

"Many times." Seb grabbed her shoulders. "Baby sister, I'm taking a chance. Maybe you should, too. Why are you still down in Cornwall when your bitch of an ex-wife is getting remarried? I'm leaving in ten weeks, and I was going to rent out my house. But if you want to rent it, I'll give you a reduced rate as long as you take Winston, too."

Winston was Seb's much-beloved cat. "You're leaving

Winston? This woman must really mean something to you." Her brother doted on his 12-year-old tabby. She couldn't believe he was leaving him.

He dropped his hands to his sides, then gave her a sad nod. "I think me and Imogen could really be something, but obviously, Winston was a sticking point. I'm going to miss him like crazy, but if you're here, it would soften the blow. Mum and dad said they'd have him, but you know Fizz wouldn't be keen." Fizz was their parents' ancient German Shepherd who liked to be the centre of attention.

"Think about it, you don't have to give me an answer right away." He squeezed her shoulder and kissed her cheek, then held up the bottle of fizz. "I'm going to put this in the fridge and we can open it at midnight, when I officially turn the big four-zero."

Seb walked off, and Lauren gave her a tentative shrug. "It's not just me who thinks you need a change of scene. I know change is hard, but you can build a new life. It can be different to the one you lived before, too. You can live with me, live here, do whatever. Even if you don't go for the vineyard job, there are others out there. You need to remember who you are and where your heart is, Skye." Lauren paused. "Do you remember that?"

Skye hadn't before Tuesday. But then Gemma had given it a jumpstart. Now, the stars appeared to be aligning, didn't they?

As if backing up that thought, Skye's dad appeared at her elbow and gave her a hug. "My lovely daughter in the flesh. I heard a rumour, but I had to come and see it with my own eyes."

Her family was acting like she'd been away for years. It had only been five months. Maybe seven.

"Sebastian tells me you might be moving back! That is good news." Her dad never shortened her brother's name under any circumstances.

"Has he told you he's moving to Sydney?" She bet that went down like a bowl of cold sick. Seb had always been her parents' favourite.

"He's going to see what he thinks. Taking a chance. We're all for it. You only live once, or YOLO!"

YOLO? Since when did her dad say YOLO?

"Especially if you make the move back home. One in, one out. Plus, if you move back, it means Winston doesn't have to move. Winston would be very happy about that. Even though he's currently hiding in the spare room upstairs, being aloof. What do you say?"

It seemed like her friends and family thought the move was a done deal. Was it for Skye, too? She had a house lined up, and a possible job. The only snag? She might not be able to keep her hands off the boss. Was the boss even available? Didn't vineyard owners normally have someone waiting for them at home? Skye couldn't factor the job or Gemma into this decision. It had to be about her and her alone. She glanced at her dad's expectant face.

"I'll think about it," Skye said.

He gave her a squeeze. "You do that. But I know if nothing else, you won't say no to Winston."

Chapter Eight

Gemma packed up her easel and stretched her arms into the drowsy evening sunshine. The soil was soft from the morning rain, but in the afternoon the weather had finally edged into spring, and not a moment too soon. They'd done the hard yards in January and February, pruning the vines, and getting the admin in order for the year. It was March tomorrow, and a few weeks until bud burst. After that, the vineyard tipped into overdrive and the real fun began.

She stroked one of the vines, as Martha always told her to do. Gemma had been suspicious of adopting biodynamic principles for their vineyard at first, blaming her sister for making everything more difficult than necessary. However, surveying the wildflowers just springing to life, and the insects buzzing all around, Gemma was glad they had.

Taking the step from organic to biodynamic meant they respected the land and the seasons, and they worked to the natural order of the moon and its cycles. Yes, adhering to the principles had its moments, especially once the buds burst and their main objective was keeping them alive with no help from chemicals. They were one of only ten UK vineyards who had gone the biodynamic route, which told its own story.

It wasn't something her grandparents or parents had done,

but Martha had wanted to signify a new dawn. A fresh start after their parents left them in the lurch, with an ultimatum: they were leaving, and the sisters could run the vineyard, or sell it. They'd opted for the former, even though Gemma had reservations after it caused so much heartache in her childhood.

However, her sister had seen the bigger picture. That the problems were more to do with their parents than the vineyard. She wanted to honour their grandparents' legacy and turn its fortunes around. Gemma was grateful she had. She loved running the place, even though dealing with payroll, accounts and suppliers meant it was difficult to carve out more time for art, her true passion. Once they hired a marketing manager, maybe she'd be able to snatch back more hours like these.

A barking interrupted her thoughts. Gemma looked down to see Steve, her sister's tan-and-white Jack Russell dashing towards her. Her sister followed, marching as always in her walking boots, her fair hair in a loose ponytail, her favourite Gap sweatshirt pulled down over her dark jeans. Only her face, still made up, told the story she'd presented a tasting today. Steve jumped up when he got to Gemma, and she leaned down to pet him.

Steve growled in return, which was his way of telling her he loved her.

"I was just stroking the vines and now, here you are. I feel like I magicked you with my hippy vibes."

Martha gave a throaty laugh. "Definitely, you woo-woo goddess. But look at all the nature in full bloom!" She gestured to a bee that flew by. "I was just taking Steve for a run and came to let you know the afternoon tasting is done, our staff are flogging extras to them like mad and the bee-keeping session was a great success. Plus, the Hunter Rosé is being delivered in a month. Excitement! Craig just stopped by to let me know." She raised both shoulders, along with the sides of her mouth in glee.

The bulk of their sales were sparkling wine, but that took two years to ferment. However, for a bit of variety, they also bottled a signature rosé every year, which took six months from harvest to bottle. It sold out in a matter of weeks as soon as it was released every May. Wine critics and consumers alike loved it, and they were currently looking at planting more fields with vines, which would eventually feed the rosé demand further. But that was in the future. Today was all about this year's wine.

"By the way, you need to say thank you to Steve." Martha crouched down and held up Steve's front paw.

Gemma leaned down and gave him a high five. "Has he been chasing partridges and foxes away again?"

"He did indeed, saving our vines and our livelihoods." Martha bent down to pet him. "They should make a cartoon of Super Steve, shouldn't they, buddy?"

In response, Steve licked her face. Martha often said Steve was far more appreciative of her than her children. They never licked her face, no matter how hard she encouraged it.

"Patrick's spraying the organic fertiliser next week, and the rosé is nearly done, I feel a new energy in the air today, don't you? I love this time of year. It feels like anything is possible."

Anything was possible, as Gemma had found out earlier when Skye turned up at her tasting. "I love your optimism. You know May is my favourite month, and it's still to come." And who knew what the future might bring?

Gemma shook her head. She couldn't think about if she'd

hear from Skye again. Theirs had been a one-off kiss. A moment in time. One forever framed in gold. But it was in the past.

"What time did you book the pub for later?" She began walking back towards the house.

"Eight o'clock." Martha tapped her thigh, and Steve did a twist in the air at her command.

* * *

Flying in the face of the traditional country pub, The Blind Badger focused on super-charged pies to bring in its customers – and bring them in they did – along with a side-line in competitive darts. Where some pubs had karaoke, The Blind Badger chose arrows as its entertainment of choice. Which is why on this particular Saturday night, while Gemma and Martha tucked into their pies and wine, there was a barrage of shouts coming from the other side of the pub as punters attempted to discover their inner darts champion. Playing darts at this pub had given Gemma a whole new appreciation for the players on TV. The dartboard was tiny in real life, and you had to stand *so* far away from it. Getting a double was like trying to skewer an ant. Nevertheless, she and Martha had finished their pies, and were next up to play.

Perhaps Gemma would bring Skye here for a pie and some darts. She rolled her eyes. Skye was not her girlfriend. They barely knew each other. But it was her smile Gemma kept thinking of. That dimple. She blinked, then brought herself back to the here and now.

"Did I tell you Mum called?"

Martha rolled her eyes. "You didn't. Was it to tell you how much she loves us both?"

Gemma's laugh was brittle. Their parents had never once told them that in their whole lives, which is why Martha told her sons every day.

"Close. More that she loves our wine, she's run out and could we send some more."

Martha snorted. "Dad sent me a message asking for some, too. Do they think we don't talk to each other?"

"Who knows what goes on in the minds of those two?"

After everything, Gemma was just surprised her parents were still together. They were the opposite of her grandparents: volatile, unstable, and unpredictable. Plus, they should never have had kids. Her dad's drinking and affairs had meant a childhood built on shaky foundations, one that had driven Gemma away as soon as she could leave. But even though her mum had threatened to leave many times, their bond was unbreakable. Their parents now lived the life they wanted in Benidorm, and left her and Martha to it.

"Life is far simpler if I don't speculate about that." Martha sipped her glass of pinot noir. It was from the vineyard 20 minutes down the road. She rolled it around her mouth, swallowed, then gave Gemma an appreciative nod. "This is good. Fabulous flavour. Have you tasted it?"

"I have, and I agree." Often, people thought Gemma wouldn't want healthy competition from other local vineyards, but it was the opposite. She and Martha wanted the perception and the quality of British wine to shine. They wanted it on every menu in every pub and restaurant around the UK. There was always a Spanish or French option. Why not a British one, too?

"We should talk to the producers about working together. Are you doing an Easter wine box?" Martha left the marketing and sales to Gemma, while she concentrated on the vines and the harvest. The split of duties played into the sisters' skill-sets perfectly.

"I am, when I get the time."

Behind the bar, Rick aimed a low whistle their way. Gemma gave him a thumbs-up, then the pair took their wine and put it on a high wooden table next to a large frosted window by the dart board. Martha picked up the three arrows with their bright-green flights, and started to throw. Gemma always found the thud of the dart as it hit the board soothing. To their right, two men drank pints and ate fish pie. The smell tickled Gemma's nose.

"Did I tell you I ran into Harvey? He asked after you."

Martha handed Gemma the darts, then stuffed her hands in the pockets of her jeans. "You did not." She paused. "I've started to see a new side to Harvey of late. He's lovely. Unlike his sister. Is she still not stocking our wines?"

Gemma shook her head. "They're still on the menu, but she's telling people they're out of stock. Which is ridiculous when the vineyard is literally a couple of miles down the road."

"I hate to think what she would have done if you'd been a terrible girlfriend."

"So do I." Gemma took a sip of wine, then threw the darts. Three 20s. She'd never be able to replicate that when it counted.

Just thinking about Juliette again made her stomach tight. She was trying to train herself to be more sanguine, because there was nothing she could do about it.

Martha took another turn, then Gemma, then they decided to play for real from 501.

Martha's first three darts scored 30. She stamped her foot with displeasure.

Gemma steadied her foot behind the white oche, squinted her left eye, then threw her first arrow. Treble 20. She'd skewered the ant.

She punched the air. "Have some of that!"

Every time they played darts, they reverted to being 12.

Her sister narrowed her eyes. "Don't get too cocky, there's a long way to go."

Gemma's next two darts scored five and one. When she turned and clocked her sister's smirk, she punched her in the arm.

Martha's face paled, and she rubbed her arm in mock-shock.

"Have you seen her at all since you broke up?" Martha threw another three darts. She chalked 70 off her score. Respectable.

Gemma shook her head. Thud. Thud. Thud. 43.

"She's kept a low profile, which I should be thankful for. But I'm still mad at her for dumping me because I couldn't be around more at weekends. Just because Harvey let her duck out of any weekend work in the pub, she thought I could as well."

"Wasn't it also because you couldn't tell her you loved her?"

"That was nothing to do with my usual reticence of saying the words. That was because I *didn't* love her."

Martha studied her sister's face, before throwing again. She scored 88. When she walked back from collecting her darts, she strutted like a peacock. She was the one with a dartboard in her house, and it showed.

Gemma rolled her eyes, threw 22, then stamped her foot.

When they both then threw 55 and 21 respectively, Gemma let out a howl of frustration.

Martha put an arm around her shoulder and kissed her cheek. "This is meant to be relaxing, remember?" She gave her a wink.

Gemma resisted the urge to stamp on her sister's shiny Doc Martens.

"How was your group today? You didn't say. Mine included a ten-strong hen party and they were very keen on slugging the fizz, rather than simply tasting it. However, they did then drink more and buy a case, so I'm not complaining."

"We love hen weekends because they love fizz, remember?" Heat flushed through Gemma as she recalled her group. Or more specifically, one customer in particular.

Had Skye wanted to kiss her right away, too? Gemma had wondered if Skye might leg it. But she'd hung around. They'd chatted. Skye had taken her card. She didn't expect to hear from her about the job, but just knowing Skye had her details made Gemma a little dizzy. Their Hollywood kiss had planted a seed of hope in her she couldn't ignore.

Martha threw another high score, then another, while Gemma's mind tripped over memories of Skye. She'd given up now, anyway. Martha had hit her stride.

"Have you been practising with Leo?"

"Might have." Martha's grin could only be described as cheesy.

"In answer to your question, my group was great. Engaged. Lovely, in fact." Gemma's cheeks ran hot.

Martha narrowed her eyes. "Why have you gone the colour of a tomato?"

Gemma was glad there was no temperature check in The Blind Badger. She reckoned she'd be off the charts right now. Even though the sisters were close and they shared most things, she wanted to keep this secret. Have a memento of a moment when she was not quite herself in the best possible way. The last time she'd told Martha she liked someone, it had been Juliette. Gemma didn't trust herself or her judgement. Whether she saw Skye again or not, this memory was just for her. She hadn't even known her last name. Still didn't. She was just Skye. Gorgeous, perfect-lipped Skye.

"Because I'm shit at darts and you've been cheating."

Martha's mouth dropped open as she took her score down to the final double to win. "Practising is not cheating. Leo needed a sparring partner, and I'm available. Besides, having a skill like this is always a good surprise. You never know who might be watching."

"Someone who wants to snap you up for the next world darts championship?"

Her sister rolled her eyes, then pressed the tip of her finger to Gemma's chest. "Maybe. Or perhaps the woman of your dreams who's always wanted to learn darts, and you could be her in."

"She's more likely to want you, seeing as you've got 34 left, and I still have 156." Gemma stepped up, threw her darts, and chalked off another 45 from her total.

Then Martha stepped up and got a double 17 with her first dart.

Gemma sucked through her teeth, then gave her sister a begrudging hug.

"I promise," Martha said, holding her at arm's length.

"If any lesbians come after me because I'm irresistible with a dart, I'll send them your way. So long as you do the same for me with men. Deal?"

She couldn't stay mad at her sister for long. "Deal."

Chapter Nine

Skye walked into the massive Waitrose and stopped by the door. What did she need to cook dinner for Lauren tonight? Her friend had asked for Skye's speciality, which was chicken escalope with aubergine parmigiana. It wasn't particularly Skye's speciality, more her dad's that she picked up along the way. However, Lauren requested it whenever they were together, and Skye figured she owed her. Even if she'd been a little too over-familiar with Gemma. Then again, Lauren didn't know Gemma and Skye had met before. Skye was all too aware.

At the front of the shop, a stand of offers winked at Skye. It was nearly Mother's Day, which meant every form of chocolate you could ever want was displayed, along with flowers, posh bath salts that cost the same as a meal for two (with wine and service), and a pyramid of candles that were only a toddler tantrum away from toppling over. Skye contemplated a box of posh truffles for after dinner, but then decided her palate wasn't quite that advanced. When push came to shove, she was far happier with a box of Cadbury's Heroes than the more sickly offerings.

She wandered up the vegetable aisle, scanning the shelves for aubergines. She wasn't sure when the humble aubergine had been turned into an object of comic significance, but it had happened. She grabbed a bag of value onions – nobody needed beautiful onions lounging in string bags, did they? – and spied the aubergines opposite. Her basket banged against her hip as she walked. Skye picked up one, and squeezed it. Too soft. She picked up another so shiny she could see her face in it. She tried to check her hair, then stopped. Focus. Plus, this aubergine, while shiny, was too small.

Skye put it down, and reached for another one. Just at the moment when another hand reached for exactly the same one.

Their hands touched.

Skye glanced up.

Something kicked in her chest.

It was Gemma. And her face was almost as purple as the aubergine.

Skye opened her mouth to speak but nothing came out.

Gemma did the same. Her wispy brown hair was tussled but tamed under an over-sized flat cap. She looked like she might produce an easel and start to paint Skye at any moment.

They gawped for a few seconds, until someone behind Gemma muttered an "excuse me".

They both dropped the aubergine and stepped back. The man grabbed one without a second glance, and hurried on.

Gemma was the first to break. "Could we have been reaching for anything more cringey?"

"A tube of Vagisil?"

"Some haemorrhoid cream?"

"A Katie Hopkins biography with foreword from Jeremy Clarkson?"

They grinned at each other.

Skye let out a breath she'd only been vaguely aware she'd been holding. That's when she noticed Gemma actually did have some paint on her floaty white shirt. Maybe her guess had been more real than she imagined.

"I thought you were only here for the weekend?" Gemma motioned towards Skye's shopping basket. "Have you moved already? You look very at home."

Skye stepped aside for someone else to get an aubergine. They were popular vegetables.

"I'm here until tomorrow, and Lauren has requested my speciality for dinner."

"Aubergine surprise?"

"Close enough." Skye motioned towards Gemma's paint splat. "Are you an artist as well as a wine expert?"

Gemma cast her eyes to the paint stain, then nodded. "It was what I trained in, until I had to step into the family business. I still squeeze it in when I can. I did a few hours this morning, but then I realised I had no food in my fridge. That's the trouble with living on your own and working so much. You need to remember to do the boring life admin, too. Like eat, sleep, that sort of thing."

"It's why Steve Jobs ate the same thing every day and wore the same clothes, too. It saved his brain space."

"I heard that, but I think that would be kinda boring, don't you? I like to change up my food and clothes. It makes me happy." She nodded towards the aubergines. "Just like cooking aubergine surprise."

"What's the surprise in yours?"

"That I've no idea what I'm doing?" Gemma laughed. "Seriously, what are you cooking? Maybe I could copy you."

72

Skye told her.

Gemma raised an eyebrow. "I love that! Let's pick up the ingredients together. You can send me photos of yours and I'll send you mine."

Skye snorted. "You want me to send you photos of my aubergine? There's a joke there somewhere, but I can't quite land it."

Gemma picked up two and put them in her basket.

No squeezing. She was a risk-taker. Skye applauded that. "Is that enough?"

Skye shook her head. "I use five or six." She grabbed the required number.

"Are you feeding an army?"

"I like aubergines."

"I feel like I've talked about aubergines more in the past five minutes than ever before in my whole life." Gemma paused. "What else do we need?"

"Tomatoes, basil, mozzarella, chicken and parmesan. Then you can make it your own with whatever herbs and additions you want to add. Breadcrumbs if you like texture."

They set off down the vegetable aisle, Skye's arm brushing against Gemma's with a pleasing tingle. This meeting already felt a little more relaxed than their first two.

In the bar, Skye had fallen apart, laid out all her woes, and kissed Gemma. The second meeting had been a shock, and all Skye could think was, "this woman knows far too much about me, make it stop!" But this time, they'd just bumped into each other. Like old friends. Plus, it didn't feel weird. If anything, it felt natural. Calm. Not the words that Skye had associated with Gemma so far.

"How was last night's party?" Gemma appraised her. "You don't look too worse for wear."

Skye smiled. "I am cooking a cheese-laden dish, though. But in fairness, Lauren's worse. She's laid up on her couch watching football. Tonight, we're eating food that's terrible for us and watching *Dirty Dancing*."

"Sounds fantastic. Maybe I'll copy your film choice, too."

They stopped at the end of the aisle. Skye picked up a packet of basil, then offered one to Gemma.

She shook her head, reached down and got a plant. "You'd think, being an expert on keeping vines alive, I'd be able to keep a basil plant alive, wouldn't you? But so far, this has not been the case."

"I feel like you're ready. I feel an energy sparking off you. The plant will feel it, too."

Gemma held up the plant. "I'm taking it as a sign. Maybe next time I see you, Beyonce the Basil plant will still be alive."

"She's a survivor, just like her namesake."

"I see what you did there. Anyway, I'll let you go. Good to see you again."

Gemma's gaze raked Skye's face so intensely, she was rooted to the spot.

Then Gemma snapped her fingers. "Mozzarella, right?"

"And parmesan." *And my number*, Skye wanted to say, but she didn't. Instead, she stared at Gemma's face, taking in the fine lines beside her eyes, the uncertainty of her smile. What caused that uncertainty?

At the tasting, she'd wanted to put as much distance between her and Gemma as possible. Now, she wanted to know all about her. She didn't want this to be the end of the road. She wanted... Skye wasn't entirely sure. As long as she was in Gemma's orbit, she'd be happy.

Gemma's phone began to ring. She put the basil plant in her basket, and answered it. "Hey," she said, waving a hand at Skye, telling her she was free to go.

Skye's feet dragged, but she could hardly hang around. She gave Gemma a wave and wandered into the meat aisle. She grabbed some chicken breasts, then refocused. Cheese, wine, dessert, then she could get out of here. But when she inhaled, she could still smell Gemma. Her laugh still rang in Skye's ears.

She stopped abruptly, and the woman following banged into her. It was busy in here today. Sunday shoppers. Skye apologised, and the woman gave her a thunderous stare before moving on. She twisted, walked back to the top of the vegetable aisle, but couldn't see Gemma where she'd left her. Skye exhaled. She'd lost her for today.

She walked to the top of the cheese aisle, then stopped beside a pyramid of kitchen rolls at least ten feet tall. Some merchandiser was pyramid crazy in this store. She got out her phone to check the recipe one more time. When she looked up, a man (also looking at his phone) barrelled straight into her with his trolley. Skye staggered backwards, alarm rattling through her. She put out an arm to steady herself, but only found kitchen rolls. Her slow-mo fall must have looked spectacular to any onlooker. As she fell backwards, she let out a yelp and dropped her basket. However, her landing was soft, among an ocean of Plenty. When she opened her eyes, a small crowd had formed around her.

Including Gemma.

It was she who crouched down beside Skye, her face creased with concern. She smelled of vanilla and spice.

"We really must stop meeting like this." Gemma put a hand on Skye's thigh.

Skye's body lit up, but she tried not to focus on that.

"Are you okay? No broken bones? If you're going to fall into anything, kitchen roll's a good shout."

Skye's cheeks roared red. "It was planned, totally."

Gemma tilted her head. "I feel like we're sort of unfinished business." She held Skye's gaze. "Shall we finish up, pay, and go for a coffee? Do you have time?"

Skye didn't need to think about it. "I have time."

Chapter Ten

They paid, then walked across the car park to the Costa Coffee which stood in the corner like the lonely kid at a party. Skye bought them both a coffee, then offered Gemma a big smile.

Gemma had been bold, just telling Skye they should go for coffee. But sitting across from her felt all sorts of right.

"Here we are again," Skye said. "It feels like someone is trying to tell us something, doesn't it?"

"That Sunday shopping is dangerous?"

"It is. I now understand why I normally watch a movie and order a takeaway."

"A much better option." Gemma paused. "Is that your normal routine?"

"When I'm not working."

"Ah yes, the hotel. With your ex. Are you going to carry on, or will you be tempted to move this way?" Gemma raised a single eyebrow. "Or was turning up at my wine tasting a clue that you're stalking me?"

Skye smiled. "I believe you stalked me this morning."

"I never said my theory was watertight." She took a sip of her coffee. "My question still stands."

"You're very inquisitive for someone who doesn't really know me that well."

Gemma shrugged. "Maybe I'm intrigued. Maybe I want to get to know you a little better." She couldn't quite believe the relentless line of words dropping from her lips, but she was powerless to stop them.

"Honestly, I don't know. It's all been a bit fast. I only found out about Amanda this week. For the record, I still can't believe we only met on Tuesday."

"The feeling's mutual."

"I only came here to have a break, but maybe other things are calling me back. My brother says I can have his house when he moves. There will be jobs here. I have savings. Maybe it's time to make a move." She held up a palm. "But I don't plan on applying for your job, so don't worry."

"I wasn't worried."

Skye blinked. "Okay then. I mean, I'm not sure how it works when the person who might be your future boss knows too much about you."

"I don't know that much."

"Why do I feel like you're humouring me?"

Gemma shook her head. "I'd had a drink that night too."

"Not as much as me."

"Well, no. You did have a few hours head start. And a reason to drink. But you only showed me you're human and not afraid to show your feelings, which isn't a bad trait."

"I'll take your word for it."

"Shall I tell you something about me so you feel things are a bit more even?"

Skye's cheeks coloured crimson. "I believe you know some

quite personal things about me, so the 'making it even' bit might be a bit too embarrassing without booze included."

"I'll go a little more high level. Leave the true revelations for another day." Gemma tapped her fingers on the wooden table. "I once threw up on a train platform on the way to work. Terrible hangover. Tried to vomit into a rolled-up newspaper. Ending up making the world's worst paper cone, and in my haste to get rid of it, then spilt the warm sick all down myself."

Skye made a face. "If you're trying to woo me, your efforts are a little off-base."

Gemma grinned. "Okay, how about this? My last few relationships have all been a bust. I've wasted time and energy on them, but they were ultimately going nowhere. So if anybody knows about the futility of love and relationships, it's me. I'm not going to judge you for your relationship not working out."

"But you didn't marry your mistake."

Gemma shook her head. "True. But if they'd asked, maybe I would have. People do crazy, reckless things when they want something. I've been guilty of wanting love and trying to shoehorn something that's not quite right into a box that it had no business being in. Sometimes, we all want a fairy tale, don't we?" Gemma gestured to Skye with her right hand. "Take us, for instance." She couldn't control her mouth today, that much was clear. "We met, you poured your heart out, and then you kissed me. It was a great kiss." It was still living inside Gemma in glitzy, cinema-sized widescreen, but she wasn't going to admit that.

"Did we kiss?" Skye's face was blank.

Well.

Hot damn.

Did she not remember?

Gemma's facial muscles tightened, as if being turned like a screw. "You don't remember?" A chill sailed through her. This was beyond embarrassing.

It was only then Skye cracked. "I'm kidding." She leaned forward, then licked her lips. "I remember. That kiss was off-the-charts great."

Gemma blinked. "That was cruel. I was about to hide under the table." Then crawl out the door and across the car park, get in her car and sob. "But back to us before you rudely wound me up."

"Sorry."

Skye's dimple winked at Gemma. She took a deep breath and continued.

"We met. We shared. We kissed. But we'd be foolish to read anything else into it. One kiss is not something you can build a relationship on. I don't believe in fairy tales any more than the next person." She was lying, but she wasn't about to fess up everything today.

"It was a pretty great kiss, though. From the fragments I recall." Skye's eyes sparkled as she spoke.

Gemma's stomach flip-flopped. "It was. But do you think we're destined now? Isn't that buying into fairy tale talk?"

Skye shrugged. "I like a fairy tale. Who doesn't? Apart from you, of course. Maybe you just haven't seen the right ones?"

"Maybe."

"I always wanted to be Prince Charming when I was a little girl."

"Me, too." Gemma snagged Skye's gaze, and she heated from the inside out.

"I think you might be lying about the whole fairy tale thing."

Gemma shook her head. "I prefer to focus on my work. It's easier. Sometimes. Or at least, it will be when I fill this marketing manager position. I desperately need the help."

Skye sipped her coffee, then furrowed her brow. "Do you want me to apply?"

"I wasn't saying that."

"I know, but I could." She paused. "I know enough about wine, and I know loads about hospitality and sales. What do you need this new person to do?"

"Shore up our business, make it weather-proof, basically. We need more avenues into restaurants and pubs not in the local area. Plus, getting into supermarkets like the one across the car park would be huge. Getting us into magazines would help, too."

"I've got experience with that. I got our hotel in Cornwall onto the right influencer sites and it put us on the cool hotel map. Plus, I boosted our visibility as a venue for all occasions: conferences, birthdays, wakes, and especially weddings." Skye gulped when she said the final one. "Maybe I did too good a job with the weddings part."

Gemma winced along with her. "Maybe you did."

Skye held up a finger. "And I know people in magazines who I could tap up. I can definitely get your name out wider than it is. I even got the Seasalter into an in-flight magazine as a romantic destination hotel. Bookings went through the roof."

Attractive and capable. It was all music to Gemma's ears.

"Exactly what we need. Plus, help with social media. I mean, it's just me right now, and it's a lot."

"From what I saw yesterday, you're doing a good job. The tasting went well, the shop was great, and the vineyard looks immaculate." Skye tilted her head. "But I could apply. It'd only be temporary, and you'd be helping me out. Plus, I love your biodynamic ethos, and your products taste delicious. I totally buy into it."

Gemma fixated on Skye's lips. Was she still talking about the wine?

"The biodynamic part is great, but it does mean more work for us at the start. But ultimately, it's where the world's going. We're on the right path: a winning and profitable one. I just need to introduce more people to our wine, because I know what we've got is good."

"I could definitely help you with that."

Gemma stared at Skye. "Maybe it could work. But there is a condition."

"What's that?"

"We can't kiss again." Her stomach lurched once more, but this time for very different, sad reasons.

Skye frowned. "We can't? But you just said it was a great kiss. Not a fairy-tale kiss, but great nevertheless."

"Touché. It was a good kiss. Great, even." The impact still flickered in Gemma's soul. "But if we work together, nothing can happen between us. It's a hard rule my sister and I came up with after my dad nearly ran the vineyard into the ground with his affairs. Let's just say, I don't tell that part of the story at the wine tastings. You only get my grandparents, how they met, fell in love and started Martha's Vineyard. I sell the romance, not the fact our parents nearly ruined the business, and we had to rescue it after my dad drank the wine and shagged the staff. Because of that, we've always agreed we'd never sleep with anyone that could impact the business. No exceptions."

Gemma assessed Skye's reaction. Her face didn't flicker as she spoke. Was she sad? Did she care? Maybe she thought Gemma wasn't her fairy-tale ending either.

"I can abide by that rule. Although it's not a rule that works in your favour if you want to meet someone. What happens if the woman of your dreams runs the Sainsbury's wine department?"

Gemma laughed. "Most of the people I deal with are balding, middle-aged men. I don't think a siren is suddenly going to emerge from the buying department."

"All I'm saying is, those kind of rules are fine in the moment, but maybe in time they're not going to work for you. Although maybe if I'd stuck to those rules, I wouldn't be in the mess I am right now." Skye frowned, then sat forward. "Maybe you and your sister have a point." She held up both palms. "No kissing, I can manage that." She stared at Gemma's lips. "Are you offering me a job?"

"Not quite yet. We are interviewing this week. But if I did, and everything else fell into place, would you say yes?"

Skye thought about it for a few seconds. "Definitely maybe. But I need a few weeks to sort out my life before I get here."

"That sounds reasonable."

"Shouldn't we talk money? Start dates? Conditions?"

"I'm desperate. I need someone on-board asap to help with everything. Someone who's up to speed in time for May when the vineyard year truly kicks off, with the launch of our rosé towards the end of the month. Preferably someone who knows what they're doing. Which you do. Tell me what you want. I'm not offering you a job. I'm just enquiring."

"That's not a good negotiating tactic."

"I know. Never tell my sister." Martha would kill her. But when it came to hiring this position, Martha trusted Gemma implicitly. "You've got my card. Send me an email telling me what salary you expect. It would be a three-month contract initially. I'll send you a job spec, you tell me if it's what you fancy doing."

"What if you can't afford me?"

"There's a lot of perks to consider. Wine. Cheese. Delicious honey." She held her chin. "This face every morning."

Stop flirting, Gemma!

"That is a hard sell." A devilish smile sauntered across Skye's face.

"I haven't even got around to mentioning frost alarms."

"Frost alarms?"

"That's for after you've signed."

Skye nodded, then drained her coffee. "I have a question." She brought her gaze up to meet Gemma's.

Damn, she was cute. But Gemma could totally do this. She made the rules. Which meant she must not think of sliding a hand around Skye's neck, pulling her close and kissing her.

Totally out of bounds.

"Shoot."

"What if I accidentally fall on your face one day and our lips get stuck together?"

Gemma let out a hoot of laughter, but not before her mind totally pictured it. She gulped before she answered.

"Like you just fell into that stack of Plenty kitchen towels?"

Skye shrugged. "You see, I have form."

"You unstick yourself, get up and forget it ever happened. Just like you did with the first one." Gemma gave her a knowing look. "I need a marketing manager more than I need a girlfriend. You need a job more than you need a girlfriend. It might just work."

"It might."

"Think about it."

Chapter Eleven

Living in St Austin was set to be the death of her. Which was why it was a good job Skye was moving this week. In the end, it had been an easy decision. Plus, her notice period had been cut to just two weeks after the hotel owner's know-it-all son came back from his travels and retook the manager reins. Maybe he'd succeed this time, but Skye had promised her boss she'd be on the end of a phone to answer any questions. She wanted to leave on good terms to ensure a positive reference, which had been promised after everything she'd done. She could live with Lauren first, move into her brother's place eventually, and she had a job waiting for her.

It was an especially good move because in the past week, Skye had run into Amanda and her fiancée not once, but twice. She was an expert at avoiding them when she was at work, but out in the mean streets of the village, it proved nigh-on impossible. The first time, she'd been with Justin in a tapas restaurant overlooking the water. It was a rare night out for both of them, and she wanted to make the most of their coinciding time off before she left. However, halfway through the meal, Amanda and her intended had arrived.

"As much as I'll miss you, the faster you move out of here,

the better you're going to feel. This is not your life anymore. Or at least, it shouldn't be," Justin had told her.

After she bumped into them again in the local kitchen shop – she needed a new whisk, they needed a kitchen island – she realised it was definitely time to call it quits. Amanda had always dismissed her ideas of home improvement. Yet now, she was all for it.

Lauren had been over the moon when Skye told her.

"The nights out we're going to have! We can recreate our youth."

"But with less pink wine?"

"Slightly."

Plus, true to her word, Gemma had sent her a job description, a package that was more than Skye had anticipated, and a three-month contract to start next week. That had been the final piece of the puzzle, and Skye had already given her notice in. If you'd told her this time last month she'd be moving and starting a new job next week, she'd have said you were crazy.

Being an adult wasn't always easy. Like a sour drink, Skye had settled in St Austin. But now, she was shaking up her life to make it come alive. Skye had scanned the contract Gemma sent through for a kissing clause, but there was none listed. Maybe she was going to be strict and enforce the verbal agreement. She'd seemed resolute when they spoke.

That was fine for Skye. She was freshly divorced and didn't need a new love interest. Plus, having the rule in place gave them boundaries. She liked Gemma, and she could see out three months with no kissing easily. It was a new job, which is what she needed most. A new industry. A fresh start.

For the first time since Amanda had broken up with her, there was a glimmer of hope.

Skye got her suitcase down from the top of her wardrobe and started packing.

* * *

"You never told me your last name was Tuck."

Gemma held Skye's CV in front of her as if she were about to sing from it. Behind her, vineyard trainee Patrick wheeled in crates of sparkling wine on a metal trolley. He sliced open the box with a yellow Stanley knife, and began to stack the bottles on the wooden racks located on the far wall of the vineyard bar.

"Don't I get the job now?"

Gemma peered over the top. "Skye Tuck, though. Your initials are S.Tuck. Stuck."

"Nobody's ever pointed that out to me before." Did Gemma think this was news?

"Is this move an attempt to get unstuck?"

Skye inclined her head. "If this was an actual job interview, I'd tell you I'm moving for a myriad of reasons, but mostly for a new challenge, a fresh start. But you've seen me at my worst."

"Worst is a strong word. You were drunk. Perhaps a little over-shary. But you still had skills."

"I thought we weren't talking about those skills?" But Skye's chest puffed out at the fact Gemma brought it up.

"We're not." Gemma mimed zipping up her lips and throwing away the key.

"So yes, this move is to get unstuck, although I'll always be S.Tuck, won't I? There's no getting away from that."

"Unless you marry someone and double-barrel. Or take their name."

"What's your last name?"

Gemma laughed, and her cheeks turned bright pink.

Skye kept her face straight. No kissing probably meant no overt flirting, too. They could be friends. She was confident of that.

"Whatever, the reason – stepping-stone job, to get away from your terrible ex or to nab someone else's surname – I'm glad you're here. Especially looking at this." She put the CV down. "Hotel management degree and all. I know we discussed it when we spoke on the phone, but your CV is impressive. The only question left to ask is, do you know your Aldi plonk from your Surrey vineyard?"

"The short answer is, yes. I like to think my palate is advanced. I've drunk a fair bit of wine dealing with local Cornish vineyards and beyond. Plus, what I don't know I'm happy to learn. Particularly if that involves drinking your delicious wine."

"Flattery will get you everywhere."

"Duly noted." Skye tapped her finger against the side of her nose. "The main thing is that organising events, cultivating relationships and making sure things run smoothly is my jam. So long as you deal with the wine while I'm getting up to speed, we'll be golden. And if it doesn't work, just let me know."

This was Skye's first time back at the vineyard since the tasting. This morning, the sun glistened and melted over the vines, and without any customers, everything was calmer. The blue skies and lush greens made it look like a holiday brochure. Skye was used to picturesque views from her workspace, and this fitted the bill. It wasn't quite the Atlantic Ocean, but it wasn't a city, either. That was important. She was used to working in open spaces. Maybe this job was more of a bonus than she'd first considered.

"You must be the famed Skye!" A taller woman with fair hair and a winning smile walked into the bar and approached the table. A get-shit-done vibe bounced off her. Whoever she was, Skye loved her energy.

Gemma got up and motioned towards Skye. "She is. This is my sister and co-owner, Martha. What she doesn't know about wine and grapes isn't worth knowing. Don't get her started on soil and manure, unless you want a very long conversation."

Skye stood and shook Martha's hand. "Who doesn't love some good soil chat? Good to meet you." She was well aware of the need to charm Martha as well as Gemma. Feigning an interest in soil was step one. Judging by Martha's wide smile, it seemed to work.

"You, too. You come highly recommended by Gemma, so you must have impressed my sister with your knowledge at the tasting. She's never hired someone so quickly before."

"She keeps telling me she's desperate. I've tried not to take offence."

Martha laughed. "I like you." She glanced at Gemma. "Anyway, I just came to tell you that bud burst is *this close*." She held up her thumb and index finger with barely a gap between them. "This is where the fun starts. I fucking love my job!"

Skye followed Martha's retreating form, then turned back to Gemma. "She's a dynamo."

Gemma nodded. "Martha is one of the only women I know

who never worried about her weight. She never stops moving, so she never has to."

"Generation Z would tell you weight is something you should never worry about. You are exactly the weight you're meant to be."

"They do say that, don't they? They've clearly never had a bra get so tight it cuts off your circulation. That's when I know I should cut down on the toasted teacakes." Gemma glanced down at Skye's CV again. "Your resumé is very impressive, though. I wasn't joking."

"Would you have considered me if we hadn't known each other? I have no direct vineyard experience."

"I like to think so. Skills are transferable, right?"

Was it just Skye thinking of the other skills Gemma had referred to at the start of their meeting? Perhaps. "When I was in Cornwall, I got experience working in a smaller business that demanded I learn a little bit of everything. That's a plus point. Hopefully that will stand me in good stead here. What are the things you want me to focus on first?"

"That's easy. What I told you when we went for coffee. First, get the vineyard name out a bit more. Also, think of ways to use our facilities more." Gemma counted off the points on her fingers as she spoke.

Skye's gaze was instantly drawn to her long fingers and her styled, shiny, short nails. Her insides woke up. She squashed them down and focused on what Gemma was saying.

"Second, have better connections with local businesses. Not just vineyards for wine boxes and subscriptions and all of that, but also with local pubs and restaurants, and further afield. There's a big world out there. We want to identify the businesses

that really want to promote good-quality, home-grown fizz."
Gemma paused to check she still had Skye's attention.

She did.

"Third, as I told you, wines into supermarkets. I know this is tricky. Andi and I have tried half-heartedly before, but I'd love you to give it a real go. Finally, social media. Get ours in order." She gestured out the window. "We've got pretty photos to promote, and wines to be popped that would make great boomerangs. We just need to do it."

"And you want me to reach out to influencers and bloggers to get your stuff noticed?"

"We do." Gemma paused. "That's a lot to do, right?"

Skye smiled. "It is. But I'll tackle it just like I tackle everything. One step at a time."

Gemma sat back and assessed Skye. "You're very chill. Are you like this with every job you start?"

"Only when they involve women I've kissed." It was out before Skye had a chance to think. She gave Gemma a grimace. "Sorry. It'll be out of my system soon. I promise. I know the deal. Raise the profile of the vineyard, no flirting with the boss."

Gemma's gaze dropped to Skye's lips, then quickly pulled back up. "You're a quick learner."

"It's been said." Skye picked up her teaspoon, then put it down again. The clatter on the saucer reverberated around the bar. She was suddenly very aware of her breathing, and that of Gemma.

"We're all good? You can start Monday?"

"Absolutely." Skye raised her gaze and fixed Gemma with her stare. "Just to be crystal clear, definitely no kissing?"

Gemma couldn't help the smile that crossed her face.

It stretched from ear to ear, hammock style, swinging in the breeze. "Hard rule."

"Got it." Skye paused. "Final question, though. Have you always been a rule follower?"

Gemma shook her head. Then her laughter filled the room, made it brighter. "Never once in my life."

Skye raised a single eyebrow. "Then I don't foresee any issues whatsoever."

Chapter Twelve

It was only a week since Skye started at the vineyard, but Gemma had already noticed the difference. Skye was a sunny presence to have around: she'd hit the ground running and was willing to learn. Plus, she made Gemma laugh. That was rare. The only other people to do that were her sister and her nephews, and that was sometimes unintentional. Gemma had been worried that sharing a workspace with someone new was going to be tricky. However, Skye had slotted in well, leaving Gemma free to run the day-to-day operations. She made coffee, didn't leave dirty cups on her desk, plus she was a self-starter, getting out and about already to meet local businesses. Would Gemma have hired her had she not been desperate? Probably not. It just went to show that sometimes, desperation paid off.

Skye had also volunteered to take a tasting on Saturday, after their lead presenter had come down with food poisoning. It felt like this season's tastings were cursed. Last weekend was the first that had gone to plan with all the presenters turning up, and Gemma and Martha not having to host one. She'd actually had a lie-in and fitted in a little painting in the vines. It had been bliss.

This weekend, she thought she'd have to take both tastings until Skye stepped in. Gemma appreciated it no end. They'd agreed that she'd sit in on Gemma's class and take notes on Saturday. But Gemma had also invited her over tonight so she could go through her spiel, and give Skye a personal tasting class.

Just that. No ulterior motive whatsoever. Although Gemma was pretty sure she never got so dressed up for dinner at hers when her sister or any other of her friends were coming around. She sat in front of her large walnut dressing table with the winged mirror – the one inherited from her gran, the original Martha – and stared at her reflection.

"What are you doing, Gemma?" she muttered. "You've kept it together so far since Skye started. So why are you applying more mascara?"

She knew the answer, but didn't want to acknowledge it. Instead, she checked her watch. Skye should be here in ten minutes. Gemma applied foundation, followed it up with a little powder, and then applied lipstick. She was going for the whole makeup-that-looks-like-you're-wearing-no-makeup look. It was a dark art. She puckered her lips at herself in the mirror. The same ones that had kissed Skye's lips a mere five weeks ago. They'd kept a good lid on things ever since, but there was always something simmering under the surface. Gemma knew that. Did Skye too?

The doorbell rang, interrupting her thoughts. She gave herself a stern nod in the mirror, then took the stairs carefully. Falling arse over tit down them would not be a good look. She heaved a deep breath, then answered the door to Skye.

But holy fucking chardonnay, Skye wasn't going to make this easy, was she? She wore light-blue jeans, artfully ripped at the knee, along with a bright white T-shirt and black bomber jacket. Simple. Stylish. Not at all what she normally wore to work, which was simple and stylish too, but in a more professional, starched way. Tonight's look had far more queer energy, and Gemma, while here for it, needed a moment to fully process. She hoped her legs held firm, because her heart revved and stalled in her chest like the worst learner driver.

Plus, she really should stop objectifying her employees. Martha would absolutely kill her. Her sister wasn't aware Skye was here tonight. It was on a need-to-know basis.

Gemma shook herself. She was staring.

"Come in, come in." She stood aside to make that possible.

Skye gave her a tight smile, then did just that. Her blonde hair gleamed under Gemma's hallway light. Gemma balled her fists at her side lest she reach out and touch it.

Off limits.

"You found it okay?" It was a lame question. Of course Skye knew where she lived. Gemma wanted to slap herself in the face. She suddenly felt very self-conscious in her non-ripped jeans and black sweatshirt with the word 'Happy!' emblazoned across it. Why did she feel the need to signpost her mood? Skye didn't. Gemma crossed her arms over her chest and tried to appear relaxed.

"My navigation skills didn't let me down." Skye took off her jacket.

Gemma hung it on one of the hallway hooks. She'd never done that before. It seemed significant.

She glanced up. Skye's gaze travelled from Gemma's midriff to her face.

When it arrived, Gemma sucked in a large breath.

Tonight felt different. It was the first time it was just the two of them in a non-work space since *that night*.

Skye followed Gemma through to her sparkling kitchen-diner. She'd spent the previous two hours buffing herself and her house to a shine, but wanted it to appear effortless.

"Wow, I love your kitchen." Skye took it in: the antique dresser on the far wall, the paintings, the shiny quartz kitchen counters. "Very industrial meets boho chic."

Gemma was inordinately pleased that Skye liked it. "Thanks. It's been a labour of love." She walked to her kitchen island, and nodded at a bottle of fizz. "I have them ready and waiting. Have you eaten?" She'd scarfed some leftover lasagne her sister had given her – "take it before the boys devour it" – but she had a cheese plate ready, too. Just as they did at the cheese and wine tastings. They were going to do this properly.

Skye nodded, and sat on one of Gemma's high-topped silver bar stools. "Lauren made me this really lovely soup. One that feels like a full meal, so I have enough to soak up whatever you're going to throw at me."

"How's living with her going?" Gemma took hold of the bottle of blanc de blancs, carefully peeled back the foil top and unscrewed the wire, trying to ignore how much her hand shook. Then she grabbed a tea towel to gain traction and popped the cork. Many of her friends were scared of opening sparkling wine, concerned the cork might ricochet off the lamp shade and kill them. There were worse ways to die.

"It's okay, but after living alone, it's an adjustment to share your space." Skye shrugged.

Her bone structure looked gorgeous under Gemma's low kitchen lights. Plus, Skye's lashes were still the longest Gemma had ever seen. She kept both thoughts inside, then congratulated herself.

"What does Lauren do?"

"She's a teacher at the local primary school."

"Martha might know her. Being the dutiful auntie only goes so far. I'm not on first-name terms with the local teachers."

She poured two glasses of the fizz, then handed one to Skye.

Their fingertips touched, and Gemma tried to ignore how hers fizzed more than the wine itself. She sat on the stool next to Skye and clinked her glass.

"Here's to the best blanc de blancs in the business."

"I'll drink to that." Skye took a sip, then nodded. "I told Lauren the same thing the other night when I cooked sea bass and we drank a bottle. She was just over the moon someone cooked her dinner and bought her nice wine. She hasn't had a date in a while."

Gemma laughed. "Does she date men or women, or both?"

"Men," Skye replied. "Always moaning about them, too. Or the lack of available ones."

"She should go out with Martha, they sound the same. I know meeting queer women in the country is hard, but so is meeting eligible men." Gemma paused. "Especially men who like sparkling wine. Somehow, it doesn't fit with being a macho man."

Skye shook her head. "Justin loves a bit of fizz. Remember him from the bar where we met?" As soon as the words were out, Skye winced. "Sorry, I know we're not meant to mention that night. It's in the fine print."

"We're off the clock now." Gemma's words were more daring than she felt.

Skye shot her a pointed stare. "And we're back on bar stools. Let's try not to fall off them again."

Gemma gulped, her bravado wilting under the intense heat of Skye's gaze. She jumped up. "Maybe sitting at the table would be better. A slab of wood between us. What do you say?"

Skye's smile was bemused. "We're grown adults, I'm sure we can behave."

"That's not what happened last time."

"Whatever you want."

Gemma grabbed the glasses, while Skye picked up the ice bucket. She nodded towards the end of the island. "I see Beyonce the Basil Plant is still alive. Good going. How did your aubergine dish turn out? I never did ask."

"Terrible," Gemma replied. "You'll have to show me how to make it. Better yet, cook it for me."

The invitation flickered in the air between them.

Gemma hadn't meant it like *that*.

They settled themselves at the oak table, Gemma avoiding Skye's stare.

"You remember the basic premise of the wine tasting? A little chat about how the vineyard was born. Then how many acres and vines we've got. Always bring up the cow horns and frost alarms. People love that. It's the stuff of romance, even though what they're actually dealing with is shit and the freezing cold in the dead of night."

Skye smirked. "You've got such a way with words, did anybody ever tell you that?"

"I know; I should have been a poet." Gemma paused. "My grandma wrote some poetry about living here. I love having it around, even if it's just scrawled on scraps of paper. I keep meaning to get them done properly and framed, but time is my enemy."

"Tell me you've got them recorded on something other than the scraps of paper she wrote them on?"

"My nephew Leo typed them up for us, so they're stored on his laptop, and somewhere on my email." Gemma could still picture her grandmother, harvesting the grapes every year with gusto. She'd loved the vines like they were her own children. Martha had followed in her footsteps completely. Gemma had been dragged, not quite kicking, but a little screaming.

"You should have them hanging all around the vineyard. People would swoon over that story." Skye paused. "Talking of the cow horns and frost alarms, can you fill me in again? I was too stunned seeing you again when I walked into the tasting the other week. I didn't take much in."

"Consider this your detention, then." A frisson shot up her as she said those words. Gemma had told herself not to flirt, but put her in a room alone with Skye and it was impossible not to.

"Are you the stern teacher?" Skye raised an eyebrow.

Was it Gemma's imagination, or did the heat just go up a little?

"Cow horns." She wasn't going to be thrown off course. "It's all part of the biodynamic way of farming, of being at one with the earth. Cows are seen as symbolic of fertility. We take the manure from a cow who's just given birth, stuff it into cow horns and bury them in winter. The theory is the manure becomes more concentrated underground. Then we dig it up in spring, mix it with water and spray it. It's a kick-starter to supercharge the soil's fertility. It's about faith and holistic energy, but I like it. We've had a few scientists in our tastings and they can be doubtful, but most people like the positive energy and giving back to the earth."

"I never really considered it before now, but it's the way the world's turning."

"It is. Our gran was a bit of a health nut before it was cool in the 1970s. When we decided to turn the farm completely organic and biodynamic, it was an ode to her."

Skye gave Gemma an appreciative nod. "I'm sure your grandparents would be super proud of everything you've done."

Warmth rippled through Gemma like sunshine. Praise was always welcome, especially from someone she wanted to hear it from.

"It might make up for the lack of pride our parents show." Gemma winced at her own words. Often, she thought she was over her parents and their lack of interest in their children or the business, but she still had the odd pang.

"I'm sure they're proud, too. You kept this place alive when they couldn't. They can't fail to appreciate that."

"You'd be surprised." Gemma pictured her parents lounging by their pool. Did they ever give a thought to her and Martha, up to their elbows in cow shit?

"Anyway, back to the frost alarms." She rubbed her hands together. "The vines have to be protected from frost at all costs after bud burst, which just happened. Spring frost is our enemy. People don't understand that even though it might be warm during the day, the nights can be freezing. The next six to eight weeks are crucial. When the temperature drops very low, a weather centre sends a message to mine and Martha's phone, and also to Patrick, our vineyard trainee. When the frost alarm goes off, it means we have to get up and light the bougies, which is French for candle."

"Everything sounds fancier in French."

"It does. We place the bougies in rows by the buds every 12 metres. Lighting them raises the air temperature and creates movement, which stops the frost settling. The shots of all these candles in the dark looks very romantic, but remember, someone has to get up in the middle of the night to light them. Usually me."

Skye shook her head. "I'm sorry, but frost alarms are romantic. There's no getting around it." She glanced around the room. Her eyes settled on Gemma's sketches and vineyard paintings. "A little like these. Are they yours?"

"They are." Blood rushed to Gemma's cheeks. It always happened when it came to her art. She loved doing it, but she wasn't sure she was ready for it to be on public view. "But I just do it for myself. Martha has a few of them up in her house, too."

Skye got up and walked over to one of the larger paintings. She put her hands in the pockets of jeans and leaned in.

Gemma tried to ignore Skye's strong back, her toned arms, the way she rocked back and forth on her feet as she studied the canvas. Gemma's breath grew faster as Skye stared at one of her favourite pieces, a painting of the first vines her grandparents planted on the most southern slopes. She hoped she liked it.

Skye turned, her expression unreadable. "This painting is incredible." She held Gemma's stare, then turned back and spoke to her painting. "The way you've captured the light on the vines, the intricacy of the whole thing." She turned back and put a hand to her chest. "I feel like my words aren't doing it justice, but I love it."

Gemma's insides glowed hot. "Thank you."

"You should make time to paint more. I'm sure you do a great job at the vineyard, but this is a talent you should invest in."

"So everyone tells me. But you know how it is. Especially when my presenters keep phoning in sick."

Skye licked her lips and held Gemma's stare once more. "You've got me now. Use me."

Her words rumbled through Gemma like a freight train. Gemma would love to use Skye. In all sorts of ways.

She bit down on the inside of her cheek, then steadied her hands. They were shaking.

"I will, thank you." She smiled as Skye sat back opposite her.

Skye took in the whole room. "This really used to be one house, and you carved it into two?"

Gemma nodded. "This was the conservatory, pantry and utility room. Martha got the original kitchen when we split the house so we could both stay and have our own space. But I think I won because of the view over the vineyard." She nodded towards the windows. "You can't really see it now, but in summer, I really do thank my lucky stars I live here. Even if there are no eligible women for miles. I've got great views and an endless supply of wine. It could be worse."

Skye laughed. "Talking of which." She tapped her glass. "Shall we taste the other two?"

Gemma poured the Classic Cuvee, and they both sipped. "This is made from chardonnay & the two pinot grapes: noir and meunier. It's made in the same way as champagne, but champagne can only get that label if it comes from the Champagne region in France. It's dry, crisp, and fresh, with summer fruits from the pinots. It's also most people's favourite of the three fizzes on offer in the tasting."

"I love hearing you talk about your wines. Your passion comes through."

"That's good to hear. Sometimes when you do it all day, you worry you become a little jaded."

Skye shook her head. "The opposite. I thought it when I saw you doing the tasting that Saturday, too."

"When you got over being stunned."

"Which took a while. I didn't expect the woman who gave me one of the best kisses of my life to appear again so soon, or ever." She paused. "But I'm glad you did."

Gemma took a deep breath as she considered her response. "I'm glad you did, too." Their stares caught in mid-air, and for a moment, it was as if all the oxygen was sucked out of the room.

But despite whatever was going on behind Skye's radiant blue eyes, and the bedlam in the recesses of Gemma's mind, she knew they couldn't go there. For one, she still had to get Skye up to speed for this tasting. Gemma remembered how scared she'd been before doing her first. In contrast, Skye didn't seem worried at all. Gemma studied her lips as she took a sip of the fizz. Then she tugged her attention away, and poured the Hunter Sparkling Rosé.

She could do this.

"It's the three sparkling wines we're focusing on. The rosé is dry with summer fruits too, but obviously more of the pinot grapes. Hen parties are always a little perplexed by it if they're used to drinking the really pink and sweet stuff you get in the supermarkets."

"I could see they might be surprised. In a good way."

The tension in the room hadn't gone away. Gemma's fingers clung onto her wine glass as she brought her eyes to Skye's again.

She wasn't going to look at Skye's breasts, pert in her T-shirt. Nor her cheekbones, etched on her face like a classic portrait. Nope, she was going to focus on getting her prepared for whatever came her way on Saturday.

But Skye's gaze was focused on her. Gemma almost struggled to breathe under the weight of it.

"Just in case you were wondering, I'm not sorry about our kiss, or being here." Skye paused. "You offered me a new start, and I appreciate that. But I respect your boundaries. I'm not going to press anything you don't want to be pressed."

Gemma's heart screamed in her chest, but she kept her expression neutral.

She didn't want anything pressed.

Nothing at all.

Least of all by Skye.

"I'm still dealing with the fallout from my marriage breakup, so it's probably a good thing you're not dragged into that. It's just nice to be away from Cornwall, away from her, and with space to breathe." Skye held Gemma with her honest gaze. "You know what else? It's nice to be in a place where conversations don't stop when I walk into the room. I hated that."

"I know all about that one. My last break-up, even though the relationship wasn't as serious as yours, left those scars."

"Should I be wary of anyone?"

Gemma shook her head. Things had just settled down. She didn't want to bring that all up again with Skye. "Let's just say, I went out with someone locally, it didn't work out and she's bad-mouthing me somewhat. I've decided the best way to deal with it is to keep my head down and ignore it. But it doesn't stop the pitying looks sometimes. Especially because somehow, wine and vineyards are romantic, aren't they? People don't come to vineyards and get sad. They're pretty, happy places. My sister and I are happy people, but neither of us have a significant other. Every time a possible mate gets away, I feel like there's a collective sigh. Martha says I'm being paranoid, but I don't think so."

Skye stared at her for a few moments. Somehow Gemma felt seen. She had no idea why. Skye hadn't said anything to infer that. But somehow, from what she already knew about her, she knew Skye understood. They had a common enemy in being wronged by women. There was a feeling they were in this together, that they had each other's back. Gemma was only grateful.

"Let's make sure everyone knows that the vineyard is a happy place, run by happy people. Starting this weekend with some storming tasting sessions." Skye lifted a glass. "Here's to us and here's to happiness."

Gemma clinked her glass. "To happiness," she replied.

Chapter Thirteen

The following day, it was time to see if Skye had paid attention to everything Gemma had told her. Outside, the flip-flop weather continued, searing sunshine one minute, hailstones the size of golf balls the next. Skye gripped the bottle of Classic Cuvee and nodded at the man at the front of the tasting room.

"What's the difference between the method of production of champagne, as opposed to this wine?"

Skye remembered this question being asked at her taster session. "The only difference is the place where it's made. You can only call something champagne if it's made in the region of Champagne in France. Our wine is English sparkling wine, but it has all the same characteristics, and as you can tell, the taste is similar."

"I prefer this one."

"That's great," Skye replied. "Feel free to buy more bottles in the shop afterwards. Any more questions before I get the cheese boards? You'll taste four local cheeses, served with our signature home-made chutney. I will be topping up your wine to drink with the cheese, and we will also be serving you a glass of our vermouth. So don't worry, you won't be dry."

A laugh from the crowd. Skye's shoulders relaxed. She nodded at Leo and his friend Jack, and they began setting the cheese boards down in front of the participants. When Skye glanced up, Gemma stood at the door of the kitchen. She gave her a hesitant thumbs up.

Skye nodded back with a smile.

Gemma walked to the door of the tasting room and beckoned Skye over. "Looks like you charmed them."

"So far, so good. Just the cheese questions and wrap-up to do now."

"Brilliant. I'll leave you to finish up, and Leo can help if you need cheese notes. He's done this a million times. Right, Leo? I can't wait until he's 18 and can do the tastings, too."

Gemma's nephew nodded as he passed. "At least then I can put my knowledge to good use. Sometimes I wake in the middle of the night, telling the people in my dreams about pinot noir and English cheddar."

"That's because, one day all this will be yours." Gemma kissed his cheek, before glancing up at Skye. "Come and see me in the office when you're done."

* * *

Skye walked into the main vineyard office behind the tasting room kitchen. It housed four desks and walls adorned with gorgeous framed photos of the sun-drenched vines. The coffee table housed a bouquet of spring flowers her brother Seb would be able to name in five seconds flat. There were pink roses among them. That was about as far as Skye's floral knowledge stretched. On the plush orange velvet sofa, Gemma sat with her head tipped back, eyes closed. Fast asleep.

Skye held her breath, then moved closer. She wasn't sure what the protocol was here. Should she wake her up? Leave her to sleep? Gemma had said she should come and see her. She bit her lip, then glanced around for guidance. None was forthcoming.

She should go. Only, her legs didn't move.

Gemma let out a small moan. If she was having a sex dream, this was *really* inopportune timing.

Skye paused, waiting for whatever came next.

Gemma flinched.

Skye made a snap decision, then sat next to her and put a hand on her leg. "Gemma," she whispered, pretty sure she was breaking some kind of HR code. However, seeing as she was probably staring at the HR manager, Skye was confident she wasn't about to be had up for harassment. Up close once again, she couldn't help noticing Gemma's smooth skin, along with the slight curve of her mouth, as if someone had just told her a funny joke.

In moments, Gemma opened her eyes. When she saw Skye so close, her eyes widened, but her gaze dropped to Skye's lips.

Heat rippled through Skye.

Then Gemma jolted and sat up. "What's going on?" She rearranged herself and stared at Skye's hand on her leg.

Skye did the same. Then she snapped her hand away, but didn't know what to do with it. It hung in the air, both of them transfixed. Skye buried it in her lap and tried to style the moment out as best she could. "I was going to leave you in peace as you looked out for the count, but then you moved and I wondered if you were awake." She angled her head towards the door. "Do you want me to go?"

Gemma blinked again, then shook her head. "Sorry, I was up all night after a frost alarm, and only managed a few hours of sleep." She glanced at her phone, still clutched in her hand. "I just sat down to look at the news, and must have nodded off." She opened her eyes wide, then focused on Skye. "Anyway, first session done, and it looked like it went like clockwork." Gemma crossed her legs, then cleared her throat.

"I stumbled a few times, but nobody really noticed." It was true. "Luckily there were no scientists to rebuke my notions of biodynamic farming, and nobody asking difficult questions about soil. It went well."

"Great." Gemma held her gaze, and Skye was struck again by what she'd seen the first time. Confidence. Directness. A feeling she wanted to embrace.

"You said to come and see you. Did you want anything in particular?"

Gemma nodded. "To check it went well, which I knew it would. Then also, you said the other night you had ideas for the vineyard, and I wondered if you wanted to share? During the week, you were running around and our paths never crossed. I wanted to get a flavour of them before you left today."

"Of course." She rubbed her hands together before she continued. "First idea is music events. I'm not talking festivals, but you've got fabulous outside space, why not make the most of it with sit-down events for a hundred or so ticketed guests? You could set up a marquee too, so if it rains, you've got it covered. I'm talking things like jazz bands, folk singers, mellow evenings with wine, cheese and charcuterie."

Gemma gave her an encouraging nod. "I like it. We've thought of doing it before, but I never know where to start with locating performers."

"Leave it with me. Another thing is, you've got a fully

equipped kitchen and you should be using it more for supper clubs. That way, you don't have to cook, the supper clubs bring the customers to you, and you can sell your wines. These are people who love food and drink and are prepared to pay for it. It's a win-win. Maybe team up with a minibus company to ferry guests to and from the local train station so they don't have to drive, too."

"I love the sound of that."

"Great," Skye said. "I can also get in touch with private members clubs and high-end London hotels and restaurants who don't currently stock us. Give them a discount if they include us as a by-the-glass option, put our wines front and centre. Plus, I have ideas for nature-focused things like trails, weekend nature hunts to bring in affluent parents and their kids, along with self-guided tours of the vineyard. It's about getting footfall here at all times. You already do a great job, but these things can up the ante. Especially focusing on kids to get the grown-ups here buying booze."

Gemma flipped her head back and exhaled. When she came back to face Skye, her smile lit up the room.

"Thank you."

Skye shrugged. "I'm just doing my job."

"I know, but you're doing it well. You've already set up the Easter wine boxes with local vineyards, got us into a few pubs we haven't tried yet, and now all of this. I'm grateful that someone else is taking some of the marketing strain from me. It feels like I've been driving solo for so long." She exhaled again. "Thank you for coming in and just taking it on. Being what we needed here." Gemma stabbed her chest with her index finger. "What I needed."

"You're welcome." Skye went to put her hand on Gemma's knee again, then froze. What the hell was she thinking? Why did she keep going to touch Gemma?

Instead, she limited herself to a tight smile. "I have to tell you, it's not hard to do my job, either. Everyone here has been so welcoming. I wondered after our... weird start... if things would work out. But so far, so good."

Gemma stared, cast her gaze downwards, then back to Skye. "So far, so good."

"One thing I was wondering, though."

"What's that?" Gemma tilted her head.

"I went into The Haunted Hare the other day when I was doing my wine research. Just to see who's stocking us. Of all the pubs in a five-mile radius, that was the only one that wasn't. They only had French champagne. We're on the menu, but there's a *Sold Out*, sticker. Do you know why?"

Gemma looked away again. Something crossed her face, but Skye couldn't quite place it. Resentment? Resignation?

"There are actually three nearby pubs that don't stock us. The Haunted Hare is the closest, the Dog & Dragon in Nuttall, and the Cream Of The Crop in Goosetown. Leave them out of the equation for now. There are issues we're still working out. I'd say focus on pubs further away, and also supermarkets. I know all of this won't happen overnight, but it would be good to have a few things bubbling in the background while you tick off the ones that are easiest to bring to fruition first."

Skye decided not to poke the pub situation more. She was curious, but the longer she stuck around, the more she'd find out.

"Absolutely. I have a contact in one of the big supermarkets, so I'll delve into it."

"Really? That would be brilliant." Gemma yawned, then smiled. "You really are a breath of fresh air." She stared a beat too long.

Something bubbled up inside Skye. She looked away.

"And now I've embarrassed you. I just mean, with your job, what you're doing. Nothing else."

"Right." Skye nodded.

Just a boss and her worker, having a chat on the sofa.

"One other thing I wondered about, seeing as you think frost alarms are so romantic." Gemma tilted her head. "The weather looks terrible for tonight and tomorrow." Gemma nodded out the patio doors. "Even though I can see my sister and two nephews in the car park doing a sun dance."

Sure enough, when Skye followed Gemma's gaze, Leo, Travis, and Martha were flinging their limbs at all angles.

"Has a sun dance ever worked?" Skye smiled as she turned back to Gemma.

Right at that moment, hailstones began banging down on the office's skylight.

In the car park, the dancers sped up, then ran for cover.

Gemma grinned. "It makes them happy, and that's the main thing. But back to my original train of thought. Can I add you to frost alarm duty, so Martha can have a night off? She's done the last two and she's exhausted. You'll get compensation, of course."

Skye nodded. "Add away."

"Fab. In that case, go home, get an early night and expect a call from me in the middle of the night."

Not a booty call, more's the pity.

Skye held her breath.

Had she managed to keep that thought inside?

She had! Success!

Maybe she was getting better at pretending she wasn't attracted to Gemma in the slightest.

Chapter Fourteen

Gemma propped her elbows on the kitchen counter and sipped her nuclear-strength coffee, determined to keep her eyes open. A knock on the front door stirred her. She opened it, still half-asleep. The rush of cold air on the other side made her shiver.

Skye stood on the doorstep, red bobble hat firmly on her head, cute smile and dimple still in place. It was one thing Gemma had noticed since Skye began working here. She hadn't stopped smiling. It was a far cry from the Skye she'd encountered on the bar stool in Cornwall. Had she ridden her bike here, as she had ever since she arrived? Gemma glanced down at Skye's jeans. Yep, there was a bike clip still attached. It was one of Skye's blind spots, but it didn't really matter at 2.30am. Besides, Gemma found it kind of endearing.

Leo arrived behind Skye's right shoulder, wrapped in a green hat, orange scarf and blue jacket. He was not afraid of colour. Her nephew was going to be taller than her soon, and wouldn't that be a hard pill to swallow? His dad had been tall, and her sister was too, so it made sense. He was also starting to bear more than a passing resemblance to her granddad.

"Both of you here, very punctual."

Skye moved aside and glanced at Leo. "I'm being paid,

but I'm in awe of you. If you'd tried to prise me from my bed when I was 15, I don't think you'd have had much luck."

Leo's laugh was deep, just like his voice. "I don't mind doing this when mum needs a break. It's kinda cool. I've only been allowed to do it for the past year or so, since I turned 14. Mum says it's fine, so long as I don't turn into a pyromaniac."

"How's that going so far?" Skye asked.

"Nothing's burned down yet."

"Leo is the perfect firestarter: contained and controlled." Gemma rubbed her hands together. "Okay, let's get this show on the road." She finished her coffee, put the mug on the hallway table, then grabbed her biggest coat, scarf and hat, and banged her door shut. "The bougies are already in place. We just have to light them." She nodded towards the vineyard jeep. "Shall we get in and drive to the first field?"

It was a bumpy ride down the potholed track, and Skye held onto the underside of the front seat. They dropped Leo at field one, with strict instructions to be slow and methodical.

"I know," he said, then rolled his eyes.

"I know you know, but if I don't tell you, your mum will kill me. The same if you burn yourself, so try not to. I'll be back in a bit to check you're okay." Gemma gave him a wink, then drove to the start of the next field. She jumped out, then waited for Skye to follow. "Same goes for you. Slow and methodical. We don't want any fires. We just want to warm the air, okay? Respect nature, and it'll respect you."

All around, the still, dark night enveloped them, the air sharp and crisp. When she turned, Gemma saw the whites of Skye's eyes.

"How are you doing? First time out here in the dead of night and it's quite the thing, isn't it? Yes, this is sleep deprivation and a strange form of modern torture, but there's also something magical being here with nobody else around. Just us, the sky and the vines."

Skye's teeth glinted white against the liquorice night. "There is. When I couldn't sleep after everything happened with Amanda, I used to get up and do some work. I always got so much done in those hours in the middle of the night, because there's nobody to disturb you. It always felt a bit daring, too. But this takes it to a whole new level." She paused. "I don't know what happened between you and your ex, but if she ever helped you do this, surely it must have inspired romance."

Gemma snorted. "Frost alarms only happen in the spring. We were together in the summer and harvest time. But I guarantee you, she'd have hated it. It's lucky I never had to ask her to help." In the whole time they'd been together, Juliette had shown zero interest in the vineyard, telling Gemma it was just a muddy field with some grapes. She'd laughed when Gemma had explained their biodynamic ethos. Juliette thought burying cow horns proved that Gemma and Martha were, in her words, "losing it".

In contrast, Skye hadn't even blinked when Gemma told her. She was open-minded as well as beautiful. That thought stuck in Gemma's throat like a thorn. She swallowed to dislodge it. She glanced at Skye, as her torch illuminated her features. Even at this hour, with ruddy cheeks and wearing that ridiculous bobble hat, she had the kind of face that begged to be sketched. The question sat on the tip of Gemma's tongue, but she swallowed it down.

Ouch. Thorny.

"Her loss," Skye replied, then banged her gloves together. "Because yes, it's fucking freezing, but it's gorgeous. Tranquil. When I couldn't sleep and didn't want to work, I also used to head down to the beach. Being there on your own was beautiful, too."

Her gaze caught Gemma's, and they both paused.

A beat passed. Then two. Then three.

"It sounds like you had a lot of sleepless nights."

Skye smiled, then kicked her foot. "Yes, but they were productive. I decided early on not to mope too much. It's not an attractive quality."

"Sometimes it's necessary, though."

Skye shrugged. "My mourning days are officially over." Skye sniffed the air, and craned her neck. "I smell smoke. Is that Leo already at work?"

Gemma sniffed the air, too. She loved the smell of freshly lit bougies. "It's Leo, but also two other volunteers in the fields behind us."

"Who volunteers for this?"

"People who love wine and romance."

They carried on walking down the row of vines until they reached the first bougie. Gemma pointed upwards. "I've provided a blanket of stars, too. No actual blanket, but close enough."

Skye grinned. "You remembered."

Gemma's body burned from within. "Of course."

She caught Skye's warm gaze, then dropped it abruptly.

There was no time for that.

Gemma squatted down. "Here are the famed bougies. They're the size of a two-litre paint tin, and our job is to light

118

the candles, then keep an eye on them." Gemma reached into her bag and pulled out a safety lighter. Then she got her keys from her pocket, and levered the lid some way off. "Stand back," she said, then kicked the lid free. "Fuck!" She pressed her teeth together. "The first one is always a shock to your feet. You get used to it." She pocketed her keys, held the lighter over the bougie, clicked twice, and the flame ignited.

Skye raised her gaze and grinned. "This is way more fun than answering emails in the middle of the night."

"Good to hear, because we've got 500 to light." Gemma stood and gave Skye her own lighter. "You think you can do the rest of this row on your own while I do the next?" She could already see Leo had made good progress.

Skye nodded. "I think I can do that."

"See you at the other end, then. Loser makes the coffee."

"I thought you said slow and steady?"

"I was lying," Gemma grinned.

* * *

A couple of hours later, the bougies were lit, and Gemma had dropped off Leo and the other volunteers. She'd offered to drive Skye home, too, but Skye had refused. Gemma glanced at her watch. 4am. They probably had a little under two hours until the sun began to rise, and they could go home. Until then, it was a case of watching and waiting. She reached into the back seat of the Jeep and grabbed the flask of coffee she'd made, along with the pack of Twixes. She handed a chocolate bar to Skye, then poured two cups from her big red flask. Skye accepted both with grateful thanks.

"I feel like an undercover police officer on a stake-out.

Like we should have doughnuts. But I think that only applies in New York City."

"Not on the mean hills of rural Surrey?"

"Just coffee and a Twix here." Skye took off her hat, ruffled her blonde hair, dunked one finger of Twix, then sucked it into her mouth.

Gemma tried not to stare.

She focused on the bougies, twinkling in rows in the distance.

"In the summer, I love to sit on the tasting room balcony and look over the vines. It's a bit cold tonight, though."

Skye sipped her coffee, and picked up her phone. She'd just uploaded some photos of the vineyard alight with candles to their official account, and they were already getting some love. "I can't believe how many people are up at this hour. My dad just liked the photo. What's he doing awake?"

"Sleep is over-rated apparently."

Gemma picked up her phone, scrolled to the vineyard's profile and hit the like button. It already had over 200 likes in 20 minutes. One of them was Juliette. Gemma tutted out loud. What the actual fuck? She should block her. Or get Skye to do it.

"Everything okay?"

Gemma rolled the tip of her tongue over the front of her top teeth, then made a decision. She hadn't been honest with Skye about Juliette because she didn't want to seem like a loser. In contrast, Skye had been very transparent with her, albeit because she'd been drunk when they met. Plus, as Martha kept telling Gemma, she wasn't responsible for Juliette's behaviour.

Sometimes, she believed her.

"Yes, it's just my ex. She's already liked the photo. She's

probably up drinking French Champagne, for which she always told me there was no substitute. *She told me that.* That was a red flag, right?"

Skye nodded. "Not the best thing to say to a vineyard owner who produces a brilliant equivalent."

Gemma took a deep breath. "You were asking earlier about why we're not on the menu at The Haunted Hare. It's because Juliette is the sister of the owner and is very persuasive. We went out for six months, and she wanted me to be the life and soul of the party with her. She's also part-owner of the pub, in the loosest possible sense. Her brother Harvey runs The Hare and two others. He's lovely. We were on the menu for years, but then Juliette decided to take an interest in the family business. We started seeing each other, but it all went sour when I wouldn't go to London with her and live the party lifestyle. Then she dumped me, and dumped our wines, too. Harvey keeps telling me he'll get them back on soon, but I'd rather pursue other avenues. Life's too short, you know? But she still has the gall to like our photos at 4am, even though she didn't like much about the vineyard when she was around it."

"She sounds like a charmer."

"That's the trouble. She was, at first." Gemma cringed. "And now I feel really exposed."

Skye let out a laugh at that. "At least you found out before you married or bought a house. Lucky escape, I'd say. We're a right pair, aren't we?"

Gemma smiled. "Apparently we are."

Skye held up her mug of coffee. "But somehow, we're still smiling, still laughing about our heartache."

Gemma touched her mug to Skye's. "Doing romantic things like lighting bougies."

There was a pause as the word romantic bounced around the car.

Skye turned to Gemma. "And we get to watch the sunrise together, too."

Her intense stare made Gemma wobble.

Keep it together.

"Which according to my phone will take place in 90 minutes. You've got 90 minutes to tell me another secret about you. Something fresh. Remember, what happens on bougie duty, stays on bougie duty."

"I thought I just told you my secret? I fell for a loser who didn't understand or respect me or my job, and I overlooked it like it was nothing."

Skye shook her head. "Everyone does that when they fall for someone. Whether they love them or not. Lust does strange things to people. You're not a special case." She finished her coffee, then put the mug on the centre console. "I told you nobody had ever found my G-Spot. Now *that's* sharing."

"You're lucky I finished my coffee already, or I'd have spat it out." Gemma grinned at Skye. "Something to rival your G-Spot woes."

"It's got to be big."

"I'm not sure this conversation is safe for work, and I certainly haven't drunk enough alcohol for it. Which is a shame as we're sitting in a vineyard."

"Dig deep. I have faith in you."

Gemma ate the second finger of her Twix, then scanned her brain. Something she'd never told anyone before. "Maybe that I lied when I said I'd been in love before when we first met?" She'd never actually admitted that before. She'd taken the commiseration about Juliette, but she'd said she loved her. She hadn't.

Skye let out a low whistle. "That's big news."

"It is." Gemma nodded. "I have trouble saying the words, too. Martha would give you a long speech about why. She thinks I need therapy." Another beat went by. "Also, I've never had an orgasm so strong, I've shouted out that person's name in the heat of the moment." Then she immediately slapped her hand over her mouth.

What the actual fuck?

"And I really don't know why I keep telling you things."

"You're trying to make me feel better for blurting out my life at the start of our relationship." Skye paused. "Not that this is a relationship. It's a friendship. A working relationship."

"You done?" She was pleased Skye was just as flustered as her.

"Maybe we should both shut our mouths to stop all these things falling from them?"

"Where's the fun in that?" Gemma paused. "I really can't believe what I just said."

"What happens on bougie duty, stays on bougie duty."

"Okay," Gemma replied. "I think I'm scared to fall in love because of my parents' terrible blueprint. I always think, if you're not serious, what's the point?"

"You're still sharing."

"I'm aware." She covered her face with her palms. "Maybe I should eat another Twix. At least if my mouth is full, I can't talk."

"On the opposite side, though, you told me your grandparents had a fab relationship. I assume your gran loved your granddad as well as the vineyard?"

Gemma nodded. "Very much. He's included in the poetry, too." She took a breath, picturing her grandma's words on the page. "I drink in the wine, and I drink in you. That's one of her lines."

"You know love can happen, then. That it has happened in your family. You're not somehow genetically immune."

"I still have hope."

But it was the hope that killed you.

"That's good to hear. I'm the opposite of you, by the way. I fall in love far too easily. I need you to teach me some tricks to fight it."

"Keep meeting the wrong women, ones who over-promise and under-deliver, and it's easy." Juliette fitted that bill to a tee.

"What about if you meet the right woman, someone who makes you want to shout out her name?"

Something wobbled inside Gemma. She snagged Skye's gaze, and her attention fluttered to Skye's lips. She'd like to taste them again. To fall into Skye's orbit. Could Skye be the right woman? She pushed that thought out of her brain.

"Then maybe I'll shout it."

Skye nodded. "Drop me a text and let me know if it happens. We can come watch the sunrise together and toast your success." She held Gemma's eyes.

Gemma's heart punched her chest. "I promise, you'll be the first to know."

Chapter Fifteen

Skye had dealt with a couple more frost alarms since the first, two weeks ago, but none had been as momentous as that one. She still maintained they were romantic, but they were a different type of romantic when she did them alongside Patrick, Martha, or one of the local volunteers who worked for love and wine. Gemma was still her favourite alarm pal, but their shifts hadn't coincided since the first. Perhaps Gemma was trying to put some distance between them. It made sense. Whenever they came within touching distance, Skye's heart did all manner of gymnastics. Maybe it was the same for Gemma. Hence, no sitting in the vineyard Jeep drinking coffee and looking at the stars. If she wanted to keep her job, that was part of the deal. Even if it was a colossal waste of the natural energy that sparked between them.

However, they'd been using that energy in the business, getting tours of the vineyard set up, and drumming up interest in supper clubs with some social media marketing. Which is what they were doing now. Skye pointed her phone at Gemma, the blue velvet sky behind her, the vines a vibrant green. It was already Insta-perfect, as was Gemma in her flat cap, yellow shirt and dungarees. Skye never believed somebody could be both cute and sexy, but Gemma proved her wrong. She wasn't, however, happy about being in front of the camera.

"I've spent all morning doing the monthly accounts, I'm really not in the mood."

"Just be charming. You do it all the time when you meet customers."

"That's different." Gemma pouted.

Cute, sexy, stroppy.

Skye was having none of it. "Just be your natural self."

"People don't want that, trust me."

Skye lowered her phone and put a hand on her hip. "You said you were up for this. We agreed we need faces on your social feeds. In particular, your face. Moving and saying clever things."

"Come buy wine, it's grapey! How's that?"

Skye sighed. It was sunny now, but rain was forecast later on. They needed to get this done before that happened.

Gemma held up a hand. "Okay, I'll be serious!" She took a deep breath and nodded Skye's way. "Count me in."

Skye trained her phone back on Gemma. "In three, two, one…" When Skye nodded, Gemma launched into her vineyard promo, introducing the vines, explaining the different pinot grapes and how they're used to create not only their sparkling wines, but also the vineyard's signature Hunter rosé.

As the well-rehearsed words fell from Gemma's lips, Skye allowed herself to trail off and enjoy Gemma's performance as a customer might. She was a terrific face to show, her cheeks ruddy, her enthusiasm infectious. Authenticity is what people wanted in businesses these days, along with personality. In Gemma, Martha's Vineyard had that wrapped up. Skye had also filmed Martha earlier in the week, along with Leo, the face of the future. She'd asked Travis, but he'd looked horrified at the prospect, telling her he was more suited behind the camera. She liked an 11-year-old who already knew his strengths.

His aunt certainly did. Skye had told her to make love to the camera, and Gemma had taken her at her word, caressing every syllable with her lips, staring directly at Skye and making her feel like she was talking only to her. It was the closest Skye was going to get to Gemma being this intimate with her. But she wasn't going to think about that. Instead, she tuned back into what Gemma was saying, focusing on her easy manner, her radiant smile, her eyes that Skye already knew she'd see every time she blinked tonight.

The sooner she could shoot this and leave for her dinner with Lauren, the better. She loved this job, but some aspects were less than ideal. Like the fact that every day she spent with Gemma, she liked her more and more. She wanted to reach through her phone, and into another universe, one where she could kiss Gemma amid the vines. Kiss her like she had before. Kiss her so there was no question that she wanted to take this further.

Instead, in this universe, she simply gave Gemma a thumbs-up as she came to the end of her spiel.

"If you want to secure a bottle of our signature rosé – I've already got mine! – log onto our website and reserve yours today for less than £20 a bottle. An absolute steal." Gemma flashed Skye her winning smile, held it for three seconds, then exhaled. "How was that?"

Something hit Skye right in the gut, and she struggled to keep her face straight. Winded by desire. She swallowed down a knot of emotion, then managed a weak nod in Gemma's direction as she hit stop on the recording. "It was just about perfect." She could barely speak. Her attraction had just ratcheted up a notch, hadn't it? She held up her phone with her right hand, as her mouth filled with regret. She had to get out of here. "I'm going to take my laptop home and start my edit there if that's okay?"

Gemma nodded. "Sure. I can't wait to see the final version." She put a hand to her cheek. "You know what, with you behind the camera, that was so much easier than all the times I've tried it before. We make a great team, don't we?"

Skye gave her a tight smile. "We do."

* * *

"So you're not going to move into your brother's place now?" Lauren glanced down the menu as she spoke. She'd put red dye into her chestnut hair this week, and under certain lights like this one, it now looked orange. Lauren wasn't best pleased. They'd agreed not to talk about it.

Skye shook her head. "He's getting some work done to it. Mum and Dad are overseeing that, and taking his cat. I'd rather that finished before I move in. Plus, you're closer to the vineyard. If I moved to Reading, I'd have to drive back and forth all the time, and I'd probably end up staying at yours half the week anyhow. For now, I'm putting the move on hold. So long as you're okay with that?"

Lauren nodded. "Absolutely fine. It's kinda nice to have someone make me a coffee in the morning, and cook my dinner occasionally. You can stay as long as you want."

"Thanks. If this job gets extended, I might even get somewhere closer in the end."

"You know what this means too?"

Skye shook her head.

"That you can come on a park run with me. You've been saying there's no point as you're going to move." She raised an eyebrow. "You're not moving anymore!"

Skye smiled. "I did say that, didn't I?"

"Does your decision have anything to do with a certain vineyard owner? I've seen the way you go gooey-eyed when you talk about her."

"I've no idea what you're talking about. Gemma and I get along. I like the job, that's all. And I like living here." Skye had kept any chat about Gemma to a minimum with Lauren. Apparently, it hadn't worked as well as she'd thought.

"Me thinks the lady doth protest too much!"

Skye rolled her eyes. Lauren didn't even know about the kiss. She'd explode if she did. Then she'd kill her.

She looked around at the inside of The Haunted Hare. It was a fine example of a quintessential country pub with an open fireplace for the winter months, cosy armchairs and sofas, as well as old oak tables to gather around for Sunday roasts. She'd brought Lauren here for dinner to check out the food, which she'd heard was incredible. But also, to understand what happened if she ordered a bottle of Martha's Vineyard Classic Cuvee. This was one of the pubs Gemma's ex was involved with. Gemma was convinced her ex was badmouthing her, but Skye wanted to witness it for herself.

Lauren returned her attention to the menu. "What's good here? Did you say you'd seen reviews?"

"It's got great reviews all round. I'm going to order a bottle of fizz to go with it, so maybe something that goes with that?"

"Is there any food that doesn't go with fizz?" Lauren made a face. "I'll have the monkfish."

Skye got up and went to the bar. A woman with glossy dark hair and a starched white shirt looked up from her phone. She gave Skye a pinched smile that didn't quite stretch across her features. She looked like a school bully who'd steal your lunch money without a care in the world. Was this the famed Juliette who ditched Gemma? Only one way to find out.

"Can I help you?"

Her tone told Skye she really didn't want to. Skye gave their food order, then pointed her finger at the bottle she wanted. "And a bottle of the Martha's Vineyard Classic Cuvee please." There was no 'sold out' sticker on this menu.

Behind the bar, the woman shook her head. "Sorry, we don't stock that anymore."

"Really?" Skye infused her voice with as much innocence as she could muster. "I thought you would, seeing as they're just down the road and the vineyard is award-winning."

The woman's face soured. She leaned forward. "Between you and me, anyone can win awards if they know the right people. Don't get me wrong, the wine's okay, but it's nothing to write home about."

Skye narrowed her eyes but kept her cool. Wow, Gemma hadn't been kidding. Real Cruella De Vil vibes.

"I've tasted a bottle, I disagree. It's pretty good."

"They do the best they can, but it's not a patch on *actual* Champagne. We stock a few bottles of that." She pointed at the menu. Her nail polish was blood red. "I can recommend some particularly good bottles if you'd like to try one of those?"

Skye held her nerve. "You really don't have a bottle? Maybe in a corner of your store room?"

The woman shook her head. "Honestly, save your money. The vineyard's a bit shoddy when it comes to standards, and for me, the sparkling wine is way overpriced." She gave Skye a knowing look. "I'm in the business. I know things, I *hear* things." She tapped the side of her nose in super-sleuth fashion.

Skye wanted to reach over and slap her, but that wouldn't get her very far, would it? Also, she didn't think Gemma would be too happy, either. Instead, she decided to be direct.

"What is it exactly that you know?" She put her elbow on the bar, mirroring Juliette's stance. "I only hear good things about the vineyard."

"PR spin," Juliette replied, then narrowed her gaze. "They say they're organic and biodynamic and all that hippy bollocks, but I suspect they've got industrial chemical sprays making sure their harvests go well. I mean, if you listen to them, they tell you they rely on the spirits of the earth and a bit of shit buried in a cow horn. With the greatest will in the world, only a fool would believe such a tall tale, wouldn't you say?" She rolled her eyes to back up her point.

How on earth had Gemma ever put up with her?

"I assume you're Juliette?"

Juliette flinched, straightened up, and regarded Skye with disdain. "Why do you ask?"

Skye stood more upright, too, then offered her hand. "Because we haven't formally met. My name's Skye, and I'm the new marketing manager at Martha's Vineyard. Someone who believes in biodynamic farming. Someone who believes in our products. Someone who thinks you might have a bit of an axe to grind with the vineyard for one reason or another."

Juliette's perfectly made-up face twitched. Clouds passed over her features. "You tricked me."

"I didn't do anything."

"You did!" Juliette raised her volume. "You came in here pretending to be a normal customer, when you're actually a spy!"

Skye glanced over to Lauren. Was she hearing this? But Lauren was paying no attention, instead petting a brown-and-black terrier at her feet.

"Gravy!"

The dog raised its head slowly to Juliette.

"Get over here!"

Gravy ignored her, then turned back to Lauren.

Lauren shot Juliette a bemused smile.

Skye turned her attention back to the matter at hand. "A spy? Wow, you like to fabricate, don't you? My issue with you is two-fold. One, you're not stocking the wine, which is fabulous. But more crucially, you're spreading lies about the business, which could be very costly and damaging. Whatever your issues with Gemma, don't drag the vineyard's name into it, too."

Juliette crossed her arms over her chest. She had a black bra on underneath her white shirt. Of course she did.

"What's Gemma said about me?"

Skye winced. She shouldn't have made it personal. "That's not important. What is important is you telling the world that Martha's Vineyard isn't what it says it is. That has to stop." Skye's volume increased, too.

"Is there a problem here?" A tall man who looked like he might be asked to audition for the next James Bond appeared from the behind the bar. His jaw was so square, it was ridiculous. "My name's Harvey, I'm the pub owner."

"Co-owner." Juliette gave him a dark stare. "And there's no problem."

"I beg to differ." Skye turned to Harvey. "I just tried to order a bottle of Martha's Vineyard Classic Cuvee, and Juliette told me it's overpriced, the vineyard bought its awards, and doesn't practice the organic farming they claim."

Harvey pinched the bridge of his nose between his thumb and index finger. "For god's sake. Did you really say that?"

Juliette pulled back her shoulders and lifted her chin in defiance. "What if I did? They need bringing down a peg or two, with their lofty ways. Those sisters think they're a cut above everyone around here."

Harvey exhaled. "I'm really sorry about that. Martha's Vineyard is a great friend of ours, we're just out of stock right now because their wine is so good and so popular. But as soon as we're restocked, we'll be selling out again in no time, I'm sure." He glanced at Juliette. "Apologies for my sister, she's not herself right now. Why don't you take a break?"

Juliette scowled at him. "I'm fine."

"Take a break." This time, his tone was firm.

Juliette rolled her eyes, then flounced off without giving Skye a second glance.

Harvey took a moment before he addressed her. "Apologies again for my sister."

"Gemma told me Juliette wasn't best pleased with her, but that was on another level."

He knitted his eyebrows together. "We haven't been introduced. You are?"

"Skye Tuck, marketing manager at Martha's Vineyard."

"Great to finally meet you."

They shook hands.

"Martha's told me all about you, how you're shaking things up."

Skye raised both eyebrows. "She has?"

Harvey blushed. "Yes, when we meet at suppliers and the like. Full of praise." He paused. "I wonder, could we keep what happened between us? I don't want Gemma getting upset again. My sister's caused enough issues already."

Skye stared at him. He seemed genuine. Plus, he was probably right. Skye didn't want Gemma's energy wasted on her past.

"Sure," she replied. "It stays between us, so long as you talk to your sister. I can't do my job very well if she's telling your customers we make bad wine."

"I'll talk to her, don't worry." Harvey gave her a winning smile, and this one did reach his eyes. "Have you ordered yet?"

Skye shook her head. "I tried to, then I got into a fight."

Harvey clicked his tongue. "Then let me take it. Drinks on the house, whatever you'd like. I'll even throw in some free chocolate brownies for dessert. They're our most popular sweet."

"I like you far more than your sister."

Harvey gave her a pained grin. "My parents say the same."

* * *

The following day, determined to come good on her promise of getting the vineyard's wine onto supermarket shelves, Skye tracked down a number for Hugo Stanton. Despite his posh-boy name, Hugo was very much from the mean streets of Derby. Skye had always got on with him at university, and their career paths had crossed in the intervening years, as Hugo had worked in hotels before jumping over to retail. When he'd got the job at John Lewis, they'd had lunch to see if they could do any business. Nothing had clicked back then, but they'd had a posh meal neither of them had to pay for, and left on good terms. That was over four years ago.

Skye checked to see if Hugo was still in the same role – he was – then decided to make her connections count. She might as well use them. As her dad always said, it's not what you know but who you know. Skye hated proving her dad right, but he might have a point. Plus, if anyone deserved to benefit from her contact more than her, it was Gemma.

Hugo answered after four rings.

"Hello?"

"Hey Hugo, it's Skye Tuck here, her of the four-pint jugs from university years." Skye smiled at the memory. She wouldn't dare attempt a four-pint jug now, but back then, it was what you did of a weekend night.

"It's not my abiding memory of you, Skye. That would be the time at Pizza Hut when you loaded your bowl with so much salad, then promptly dropped it on the floor, creating chaos for miles."

Skye's cheeks glowed red. "I'd forgotten that. Great to know you haven't!"

"Every time I go into a Pizza Hut, I still smile. I've told my wife, and all my friends. They'd love to meet the famed Skye Tuck."

"Well, I have a favour to ask. Say yes, and I can make

your wife's wishes a reality. Maybe even recreate the moment in a Pizza Hut for added impact."

"You've got my interest piqued."

Skye grinned. She liked Hugo.

"I've recently started working for a vineyard in Surrey. Martha's Vineyard to be precise, and they produce incredible wines, mainly sparkling, along with a Signature Still Rosé. They've got a great reputation, and they'd love to get into big supermarkets, a little like yours. I'm the marketing manager, and my bosses would think I was a magician if I could get them onto the shelves of Waitrose, and maybe even into the pages of its magazine. Perhaps even run a competition with you to win a tour or a box of wine." She paused, letting her many asks sink in. "What I'm saying is, I'd love to give you a tour of the vineyard, throw in a delicious lunch and show you just how special this place is."

"You always were persuasive. I never wanted to drink a four-pint jug in such a short time. But after you did it, I couldn't say no, could I?"

"I promise I won't make you drink one at lunchtime. Besides, these days, nobody drinks at lunch, right?"

"Frowned upon, apparently," Hugo replied with a laugh. "The short answer is yes. To a tour of the vineyard and lunch with you at least. I can't make any promises about stocking you until I know more. Plus, with the magazine, it's done out of house, but I could definitely put in a word. Can you send me an email with all the information and what you want, then we'll set up a date?"

Skye clenched her fist. She couldn't wait to see the look on Gemma's gorgeous face when she told her.

"Thanks Hugo, I appreciate it. I'll get all the details off to you and look forward to making a date. It'll be great to see you."

"You, too." He paused. "You know, we need a marketing manager here, and you'd be fabulous. Shame you've already been snapped up. If you know of anyone else, do let me know."

"Will do."

Skye hung up, then sat back on Lauren's sofa with a grin. It was nice to be wanted, but she was very happy where she was, making a big splash in a small pond. She'd worked for the corporate machine before, but she much preferred making a difference in a smaller company. Working in Cornwall had taught her that. She cast her mind back to starting at the Seasalter, to big dreams. She'd had them then, but they'd got blown apart. Working at the vineyard was making her dreams come true again. Dreams of making a difference, if not of falling in love. She was doing her utmost to avoid the second.

Even though, every day, Gemma made it exceedingly hard work.

Chapter Sixteen

Gemma buffed up a knife with her tea towel, then stared out over the vineyard. This was the first day they'd been able to throw open the doors and let the spring sunshine in. A group of ten had just passed by on their self-guided tour of the vines which were looking sharp in bloom. Gemma loved telling visitors the story of how the flowers turned into grapes given enough time and space to mature. Their faces were always a picture. Flowers turned into grapes, and then in turn, they turned into wine? It was a potent story, the like of which you'd think was science-fiction or fantasy if it didn't exist in the real world. But it was all true. Gemma often thought that nature was the biggest wonder of all, dispensing magic at every turn.

The self-guided tours were another Skye special, a genius idea. She'd produced a map of the vineyard, including their biodynamic story, along with places of interest to stop around the grounds. It was an activity the whole family could do for free, and afterwards they normally stopped in to buy wine and food, and most had lunch and a glass in the grounds, too. Today, there was also a beekeeping session over in their far field, with their resident beekeeper in charge. The suited-up participants were set to appear in a couple of hours for wine and cheese, and they were sure to buy honey after seeing how it was made.

A gentle breeze wafted across Gemma's cheeks, and the sun's rays heated her forearm. She breathed in the day's sultry flavour.

"Aunty G, is this the table for your meeting?"

Gemma turned to Leo, who held a glass vase brimming with pink roses. "Yep. Are those for the table?"

He nodded. "I just cut them, and Mum ordered me to give them to you."

She took the vase, then gave his arm a squeeze. "What would we do without you?"

"You'd be lost, both of you."

A few minutes later, Gemma stepped back, the table set. The white wooden furniture glowed in the mid-morning sunshine, the cutlery glinted, and the wine glasses shone. Gemma checked her watch. Hugo was due in half an hour for a tour with Skye, and then lunch with them both. This was big stuff. Skye had offered to take the meeting, but Gemma wanted to sit down with the person who might give them their big break, to tell him what it meant to her and the business.

"All ready?"

Gemma looked up, and Martha smiled at her. Just like the vineyard, she glowed.

"The place couldn't look more picture-perfect if it tried, could it? I'd say it's a fabulous omen."

Gemma nodded. "I was just thinking that." She paused. "It's on mornings like this, I feel like I've got the best job in the world. I'd just love it if Gran and Granddad were here to share it, too."

Martha put an arm around her shoulders and squeezed. "They're here in spirit." She stepped back and eyed Gemma. "You're going to ace it today. I have a feeling."

"Hunters always get things done!" they said in unison, and laughed.

"Gran is definitely here in spirit, living in us." Martha waved a hand up and down her sister's frame. "And you look… I can't quite put my finger on it." Martha furrowed her brow, and put a finger to her lips. "Lighter. Brighter. Happier. I can't quite work out the cause, but I like it. It's nice to see you happy in yourself and happy in your work. One thing I know: we'll sell more wine this way."

Gemma looked down. "You'll make me blush." She smoothed down her white jumpsuit and swept back her chestnut hair. Then she pulled back her shoulders and stuck out her chest. "Do I look presentable?"

"Very. Also, like you're standing to attention. You might want to knock off the whole soldier vibe." Her sister grinned. "But your hair looks very shiny indeed. Soldier shiny."

"Fuck off," Gemma replied, laughing. "Seriously." She leaned into Martha, then gave her a full-toothed smile. "No smudged mascara? Lipstick only on my lips, not on my teeth?"

"You are a portrait of beauty," Martha replied. "You're going to knock him dead."

"I'll settle for knocking his socks off. Far less violent."

"Do whatever you need to secure the deal. Love you."

Gemma stared at her, then nodded. "Back at ya."

Martha wagged a finger in her direction. "I'm going to get you to say it properly one of these days. I refuse to let you turn into our parents."

* * *

When Gemma walked around the terrace and to the car park, Skye was already waiting. Her face lit up when she saw her approach. Skye's eyes flicked up and down her, like she was assessing her for a sale. Would she buy? Gemma would love to know.

"Wow, you look incredible."

Maybe she would.

"Thanks, so do you." Skye wore orange trousers and a pink shirt. A daring choice, but one she pulled off like a queen. Mainly because she *was* a queen. But now wasn't the time to tell her that.

Gemma knew exactly what Martha had been referring to earlier and the reasons why. She was glowing because Skye had appeared in her life and shaken it up with *that kiss*. Mixed it up with her professional guile and contacts. But mostly, because Skye was in her life, all day, every day, strutting around looking radiant, pressing herself into Gemma's heart.

Gemma took a steadying breath, then smoothed down her jumpsuit again. She had to remain calm and in control. Both in front of Skye and for the whole of today.

"Ready?"

"A little nervous."

For numerous reasons. One of them being you.

Skye waved a hand. She had dark-red nail polish on her fingers. That was new. Gemma's insides swayed.

"No need. You're fabulous, and Hugo is lovely. Unless there's a good business reason not to work with us, I'd say we're in with a very good chance. Especially after he sees this." She swept her hand across the vineyard.

Gemma hugged herself. "That's the hope." A breeze tickled

her arm and she shivered. It might be sunny, but the air still held teeth.

"Just be yourself, and he'll fall in love." Skye held Gemma with her gaze for a few moments. Then she looked away, twisting the sole of her shoe into the gravel underfoot.

Gemma blinked, her mind playing games. Was the inference that Skye had fallen for Gemma, too? She frowned. She was jumping to conclusions. Ones that made her blood rush and her palms sweat. She took a deep breath and focused on the task at hand.

Skye cleared her throat. "I'll take him on a tour, dazzle him with the vines. Then you sell the wines over lunch, which won't be hard. But remember, this fits with his company's 'Buy British' motto, so fingers crossed for a good result." She leaned in. "If you feel nervous at any point, just remember, Hugo is an old friend, and one I've got intelligence on. If he says no, I'll bring out embarrassing university photos and threaten to put them on his socials."

Just as she said that, a black Audi pulled into the car park. A tall man with fair hair got out, and Skye waved.

"Show time. You ready?" Skye took Gemma's hand and gave it a squeeze.

A frisson shot up Gemma's arm, and she flinched.

She knew Skye felt it, too, but there was no time to reflect on what that meant.

Instead, she gave Skye a quick nod.

"Let's do this."

* * *

The meeting was a huge success, with Hugo making all the

right noises about stocking their wines, as well as showcasing the vineyard in the supermarket's weekly magazine. Gemma was thrilled, and gave him a case of sparkling wine to take away.

Skye saw him off, and then had to dash back to her brother's place after lunch. But not before Gemma had asked if she fancied soaking up the evening sun with some wine, cheese, and charcuterie. Skye had said yes straight away.

Now, Gemma waited at one of the tables in the vines. The sun was still high in the sky, but overnight temperatures were still dropping to frost alarm territory. This time of year was notorious for warm days, but also bizarrely cold nights. Gemma got out her phone and took a couple of shots of the vines with the evening rays in the background. Her gallery was clogged with similar shots already, but she was always in search of the perfect frame. Taking them always brought her joy.

A notification appeared at the top of her screen. Skye was back and asking where she was. She told her she was at table four in the vines. She'd changed into black jeans, a T-shirt and cardigan, because the weather dictated it. A jumpsuit was fine for the middle of a May day, but not for the evening. However, she'd touched up her makeup and resprayed her hair. She wanted to look nice.

For herself.

But possibly also for Skye.

Someone clearing their throat made her look up. Skye strode towards her. Butterflies awoke in Gemma's chest. She took a deep breath. Yes, she'd been nervous about the meeting with Hugo today, but she was possibly more nervous about this. Hugo was business, whereas Skye was far more than that. She moved Gemma. She made her sit up and take notice.

Hugo was head.

Skye was heart.

Gemma stuffed that thought down the back of her evening, then stood. Had she unwittingly set them up on a date? Sort of. But a safe date, because they were on home turf. A friends date. She was pretty sure you had to go further than a mile from your house for a proper date. One with flirting and full-on kissing.

The words *full-on kissing* flashed neon in her head, as if she'd just walked into a retro kissing arcade. She gulped again.

"Wow, this is…" Skye stalled.

"Romantic?"

A flicker of a smile crossed Skye's perfect features. "I didn't want to say that, but yes."

Gemma gave a small shrug like it meant nothing. She was *such* a liar. "Having food and wine at sunset among the vines is pretty romantic. In fact, we had a proposal at this very table last week. It's a popular place to do it."

Skye pulled out a chair, sat, then gave Gemma a quizzical look. "You're not about to propose, are you? Only, I would have put on a better shirt if I'd have known."

Gemma cast her eyes over Skye's marshmallow-pink shirt, which she'd teamed with a red jacket. Orange, pink, and red might be considered an assault on the senses, but it was nothing in comparison to what Skye's presence did to Gemma. She gave her brain fog. Tremors. Heat in all the right places.

"Your shirt looks just fine." Too fine. Especially where it tugged around her breasts. "Lucky for you, I forgot the ring." Gemma's bravado knew no bounds today. "I was going to have wine on the terrace, but then we were bringing these in from earlier picnics, and I thought, why not? Romance is not just for couples in love. It's also for staff who are hopeful of landing a key account, too." There, she'd neutralised the situation. Made it okay.

Or at least, she hoped she had.

Skye's look was intense. "It's perfect," she replied. "Especially for two people with no romantic feelings towards each other. Nothing in their past at all."

If Gemma wasn't held up by her skeleton, she might have melted to the dirt there and then. She might be trying to trick herself with words, but her body wasn't fooled. It knew it was on a date, and her endorphins paced around her body just in case she needed a reminder.

She still held her phone in her hand. She raised it up. A change of subject was needed. "Let me get a couple of shots of you in the vines for social media. You look gorgeous."

That was dialling it back?

For goodness sake, Gemma.

She took a couple of shots of Skye, and ignored how her hand shook. Then she put her phone face down on the table, as if doing so would delete the photos and everything that had come out of her mouth in the past few minutes. Gemma moved her chair back, the need to remove herself from Skye's orbit strong. If she got too close, she might never recover. "Maybe we should invoke the two-metre rule again, just like in the pandemic? That way, no more kissing."

Skye gave her a look she couldn't quite decipher. "You're intent on putting a downer on tonight before we've even started, aren't you?" She smiled. "Shall we pour some wine and focus on Hugo and how impressive you were today? The woman with all the chat?"

Gemma got the rosé out of the ice bucket, then poured a glass for Skye, still with an undeniable tremor. She ignored it and hoped Skye could, too. She worked with this woman every day, and most of the time, she did it without any thought to what had happened between them. Yet every time it was just the two of them, out of hours, away from prying eyes, that kiss and what it had felt like installed itself in her brain and refused to leave. Just like it was doing now.

"You think it's a done deal with Hugo?"

Skye nodded. "I'd be surprised if it wasn't, but I never like to celebrate until the email comes through. But I get a good feeling."

Gemma held up her glass. "Let's cheers to that, then." She held Skye's gaze. "Thank you so much. I couldn't have done this without you." She meant every word. Skye had reinvigorated her work *and* her life. Even if she never kissed her again, she'd always be grateful that Skye had woken her up.

"Here's to my first taste of Martha's Vineyard signature rosé." Skye clinked her glass, sipped, swallowed, then nodded again. "It's delicious. You're right, I can taste the berries. And grapefruit?"

"Yep. We like to think it's the UK equivalent of a Provence rosé. Only it's an original Surrey rosé, of course." Gemma paused. "By the way, I heard from Andi today. She's going to need at least six months off, which means we might need to extend your contract if you're amenable."

"I could be persuaded." Skye held her gaze.

Possibility licked through Gemma. That never happened with Andi. She wasn't sure if that was good or bad. "Great." She had to change the topic. "How are the invites for the rosé launch party going?"

"Really well," Skye replied. "It's a good job you upped the numbers, because it turns out everyone wants to come. We've got local wine club members, local businesses, plus people from bigger hospitality in London, too. I've put on a bus for them from the station, just like we do with the supper club. Plus, I've got press coming. The ones you normally deal with, plus a few new online faces."

"Have I mentioned you're amazing?" Gemma meant it, too. Skye was a step up from Andi.

Skye crossed one leg over the other, her cheeks turning the same colour as the wine. "I'm just doing my job, and you've been a great help, too." Skye tipped back her head to soak up the evening sunshine, breathing it in. "This part of working in a vineyard is the best. Whoever thought of having picnic tables in the vines is a genius."

"Agreed. Especially because that would be me."

Skye brought her head back down. "I would have guessed that. Martha is the more practical one of the pair. You're the creative. The artist. The dreamer."

Gemma squirmed in her seat, but loved it all the same. "Keep talking."

"I'm only saying what's true. You told me I'd made a difference, but you were doing well on your own, whatever you think." Skye paused. "Did I tell you the reason I got in touch with Hugo?"

"You wanted to impress me?"

"Of course, that's true." When Skye smiled, her dimple winked at Gemma. She could stare at it all day. "But also because I went for dinner at The Haunted Hare and ran into Juliette running her mouth off about how Martha's Vineyard bought awards and produced sub-standard wines. I wanted to trounce her trash talk and do it in style. I hope I succeeded."

Familiar Juliette-flavoured annoyance mixed with disappointment rolled through Gemma. She swallowed it down, then poked her tongue into the side of her cheek and shook her head. "I've given up trying to silence her. Harvey thinks she'll be gone soon, that she's already looking into opportunities. She never wanted to be here, so with any luck, that will come true and she'll bugger off."

"Couldn't you have an extra word with Harvey about it? He seems reasonable."

"He is. Martha's more friendly with him, and she has had a word. I just want to distance myself from Juliette. It was an error of judgement on my part. As I think I told you, we don't get many queer women around here."

"You've got one now."

Skye's heated look made Gemma's heart flare.

Then Skye took another sip of her wine, picked up a cracker, added chutney and cheddar. She ate, then made appreciative noises that did nothing to keep Gemma's mind off what Skye might look like with no clothes on. On top of her.

Focus.

"And this lesbian loves your work: your wine, your vineyard, your cheeseboard." Skye sighed. "It's been over two months, you know."

Gemma frowned. "Two months?"

"Since we kissed."

Gemma sucked in a sharp, sweet breath. A butterfly wafted past her head. A vine waved beside her.

She wasn't ready for this conversation.

She thought they'd agreed it was out of bounds.

"Two months of dancing around each other. Two months of avoiding our feelings. Do you think about it as much as I do?" Skye's searing blue stare searched Gemma's face.

It glowed hot.

"Of course I do. But I already told you. I can't work with someone who I'm also dating."

"What about working with someone who you have feelings for? Feelings that aren't going away?" Skye put her glass down, and sat forward on her chair. Then she moved herself and it around the table, closer to Gemma.

Gemma held her breath for what might come next.

"I know you have this crazy rule, and I understand it's concreted in history. It's emotional for you. But don't you think that sometimes, you outgrow the rules? That they're made to be broken? That perhaps kissing isn't even breaking the rules?"

Gemma's heartbeat thudded loudly in her ears.

Skye moved closer still, then put a hand on Gemma's knee.

Gemma's spine stiffened. A fire roared inside. If Skye was the sun, she wanted to lean in like a sunflower.

"You're not your dad, Gemma. You're not repeating the mistakes of the past. You're not married, or having an affair."

She'd heard this before from Martha when she was beginning things with Juliette. Gemma had hesitated over that because Juliette was connected, however slightly, with the business. That hadn't worked out well. She couldn't risk this. Skye was too important to the business, and to Gemma's mental health.

"I know that, but it's a risk. I wouldn't have kissed you in Cornwall if I'd known I'd employ you."

"I like to think of us more as colleagues rather than boss and employee." Skye licked her lips.

That really didn't help.

"We are, of course we are," Gemma replied.

My scorching hot colleague who makes my brain shut down.

"But I had doubts about getting into things with Juliette. My track record with women isn't good. What if this doesn't work?"

"What if it does?"

Skye's words landed right in Gemma's heart. They were the words she'd thought about when she lay in bed at night, wondering if Skye was thinking about her too. Now she had her answer. Skye had been. Skye was. The answer to her question was yes.

Skye held out a hand, then laced her fingers through Gemma's.

Gemma's heartbeat began to sprint. Her thoughts ran. Her rationale laid on the ground, panting.

Skye stood, then tugged Gemma to her feet so their faces were level.

Gold flecks sparked in Skye's peacock-blue eyes. Then Gemma's gaze dropped to Skye's perfect, glossy lips, the ones she'd been trying to steadfastly avoid for the past two months. Now they were in kissing distance.

"I figured," Skye began, then pulled Gemma close, closing her fingers around her hand. "You wouldn't have gone to the trouble of hiding us in the vines if there wasn't the possibility of kissing." She leaned in and placed the gentlest kiss of all on Gemma's neck.

A delicious frisson started in Gemma's scalp, then ran down to her toes.

"If you won't let me kiss your lips, I'll be forced to kiss you everywhere else. Perhaps that's allowed?" Skye kissed the other side of Gemma's neck. Then her ear.

Gemma's breath thickened in her throat. She had to concentrate so it kept coming.

"But when you think about it in reality, kissing shouldn't count. Kissing is not messing things up. Not really. We've already kissed and managed to do our jobs." Skye placed a kiss on Gemma's cheekbone, then on the underside of her chin. All the while, she still had hold of her hand.

Gemma's brain gently fried in her skull, her resolve frayed. Now, she was just a mass of bones and flesh, held together with deafening, silent screams.

Skye kissed her other cheek, then brought their lips level. "I can kiss you all over, but I'd die to kiss your lips. Because I remember how they felt. How they made me feel. How I want them to make me feel all over again." Skye brought Gemma's fingers to her lips and kissed their tips, one by one.

All ten.

At every fingertip, Skye stopped, raised her gaze, pulled back, then barely pressed her lips to Gemma's skin.

Every time, a spark of connection rolled through Gemma.

By the time Skye dropped Gemma's hands, Gemma was a wreck.

Skye stared into her eyes and didn't look away. Her long lashes fluttered invitingly.

Then her steady, intense gaze unzipped Gemma's resolve. Before she knew what she was doing, Gemma leaned forward and pressed her lips to Skye's. In an instant, heat blazed through her. She didn't care if this was wrong, because it felt so right. Skye had been right. It was almost illegal to keep them from kissing each other when they were so good at it.

Gemma's hands, after so long being tied to her sides, roamed over Skye with abandon. Gemma wanted to feel every part of her, if only through her clothes. She wasn't about to get down and dirty in the vines, but she was going to take advantage of the shielded view. The privacy. The small window to do whatever she wanted.

What she wanted most was to slide her tongue into Skye's mouth, feel what it was like again to be inside her, and hear her response stain the air.

Gemma did just that.

Skye reciprocated with a lustful groan.

Gemma cupped Skye's arse with her hand, squeezed, and kissed her until she was dizzy with want. Her hands slid over Skye's back, then returned to her behind. Their breasts pressed into each other. Sparks zig-zagged through the vines, creating a forcefield around them.

Still they kissed. Still they pressed. Still they didn't dare to break apart. Because who knew when this would happen again? When she'd be brave enough to take the leap, to do the very thing she'd always said she wouldn't. Mix business with pleasure.

This was the most pleasure she'd ever felt kissing anyone, ever. This pleasure beat from within, it seeped out of her bones, it took over her very being. This pleasure made her want to root herself alongside the vines, made her want to stay here, with Skye, drinking wine and each other forever.

But all good things came to an end.

Including this kiss.

Skye was the first to pull back.

When it happened, Gemma wanted to wail and stamp her feet like a five year old. She kept her eyes closed, as if that would keep her in her bliss bubble. The one where Skye's lips were on hers, breathing life into Gemma with every press. In her mind, the kiss continued, like a non-stop glitter-soaked showreel. The kiss to end all kisses. The kiss critics would be raving about for decades. She licked her lips, still warm from Skye's touch.

However, she knew real life and rules had to intervene eventually. Gemma opened her eyes and blinked. The surroundings imprinted themselves on the moment. She absolutely hated that. Rude.

Seconds ago, there had only been them: two pairs of lips, two heartbeats. Now, there were flowers, vines, late evening sunshine, wine. She tried to swallow, but her throat was dry. She stared at Skye, whose cheeks were flushed.

Gemma was sure hers were, too.

"I'm pretty sure that broke no rules." Skye's smile was wry.

Gemma took the deepest breath of her life, then exhaled with a grin. "No, no rules at all. Besides, if we kiss in the vines and nobody saw it, did it even happen?"

"Exactly." Skye took a step back, then another, never letting go of Gemma's hand. Then she laid a kiss on her knuckle.

Gemma felt it *everywhere*. Her eyes were glued to Skye as she sat back in her chair.

Gemma did the same, her body still light as air, still

questioning if any of that had even happened. But the thoughts rushing around her head, and the tremor of every muscle she possessed gave her the answer. She stared at Skye, rolled her wine around her glass, let her nerves settle. They were good nerves. Nerves she knew would explode into joy if anything else happened between them. But it couldn't. Could it? Gemma had rules, lines, governance for her life. It hadn't got her that far though, had it?

She shook her head to clear her thoughts.

She wasn't thinking straight.

That was no surprise.

"Only, it did happen, just in case you were wondering." Skye took a steadying sip of wine. "This really is something. Just like its owner."

Gemma gave her a wide smile. "Compliments will get you everywhere."

Skye raised an eyebrow. "Everywhere? Past first base?"

"You know my thoughts on that."

"They don't make sense. We do."

"I've put my line in the sand."

"But you know the thing about sand? Every day, the tide comes in and washes the line away. You can draw it again, or choose not to."

"Do you always know the right thing to say?"

Skye snorted. "Not often, no. But with you, it feels like I need to. To make you see how things could be."

"We work together."

"And we do it well. We kiss well, too." Skye moved closer, then pressed her lips back to Gemma.

It nearly knocked Gemma off her chair. She clutched the

underside of it with both hands. She had to hold onto something, because her common sense and resolve were long gone.

A few golden moments later, Skye pulled away, but remained very much in Gemma's personal space.

"Tell me it's not true. Tell me denying what's plainly there isn't wrong?"

"It's not just me, though. It's Martha, too. We both decided these rules. I had to run Juliette past her. We can't get involved with anyone who has anything to do with our business."

"But being here is living in a bubble. Everyone you meet will have something to do with your business, unless you shag some of your customers. You're both too fixed on it to see how it's hurting you both. Life is all about taking risks. This comes from someone who's newly divorced. If I can say that, can't you?"

"I thought you weren't interested in anyone? That you were still getting over your divorce?"

"I thought so, too, but I was wrong. Being around you has taught me that I *do* want something. My divorce happened nearly 18 months ago. I've moved on, you just caught me on a bad day in Cornwall when I found out about Amanda. That was bound to trip me up. But I'm glad I met you when I did. Because if I'd just turned up here with Lauren on that wine tasting without meeting you first, we'd never have known how perfect our kisses are because you don't snog your customers, as we know."

Gemma sat back. Maybe Skye had a point. If she didn't kiss her customers and she didn't kiss anybody she met via the vineyard, who was she allowing herself to kiss? Nobody. Maybe she'd been living in a box without even knowing.

"Maybe you're right." But she needed more time to process. "Let me think about it."

"I can wait."

Gemma smiled. "Thank you." The sun caught Skye's face, and she shielded her eyes. She was so beautiful. "I'd love to sketch you sometime. I'd love to paint you among the vines. You look beautiful."

Skye shrugged. "You can sketch me or paint me any time you like. But be careful, I might accuse you of flirting."

"I might be flirting." The irony wasn't lost on her.

"Think about what I said. Promise me?"

Gemma sucked in a large breath. "I promise."

Chapter Seventeen

They spent the following week avoiding each other. Gemma had asked for time to think, and Skye knew she needed it before they could take it any further. She'd left once the wine and cheese were finished, and spent a sleepless night wondering when they'd kiss again. Because she couldn't imagine it wouldn't ever happen again. That was unthinkable.

But now, exactly one week since their illicit kiss, they were back in the tasting room on Saturday morning, alone. The one thing they'd both avoided all week. Skye pushed one table of four against another, and set up the left side of the room. Gemma pushed hers on the right, until they came together at the top of the horseshoe of tables they were creating.

When they stood side by side, Skye forced a smile.

"Did the hens deliver all the things they promised?"

Gemma raised a single eyebrow her way. "All that and more. I have a cardboard cut-out of the groom to bring in after the wine and cheese has finished, and we've got games on the terrace once that's done, including some with parts of the male anatomy I'd rather not be privy to."

"We'll leave them to it at that point." Skye glanced around the tasting room. Buttery sunshine dripped through the floor-to-ceiling windows to warm the timber finish. Couple that with the whiteness of the linens and the flowers scattered across the tables, and this was going to be one romantic hen party. She recalled her own, which they'd had together at an Indian restaurant down the road, followed by karaoke in her favourite pub. Amanda had sung to her, and got down on her knees to play an imaginary guitar. She was always the life and soul of the party. Skye hadn't banked on Amanda being in her rear-view mirror already, but she was, and now Skye was only looking forward. She wished Gemma would take a leaf out of her book, too.

Skye took a chance and put a hand on Gemma's forearm.

Gemma stilled at the contact, then looked up.

"I missed you this week. After Saturday, and leaving it up in the air." Skye hadn't meant to say anything, but she couldn't help herself. "Being here in such a romantic setting brings it all back. Last week was romantic. And not in just the 'friends celebrating a new contract' kinda way." She paused. "Was it just me?"

Gemma cast her gaze to the floor, then blew out her cheeks. "Of course not. Last Saturday was… a moment." She paused, as if searching for the next words.

They never arrived.

Instead, Gemma continued with, "Hugo still hasn't sent me through any confirmation."

She really was finding this difficult, wasn't she?

"He was away this week, remember he told us?" Skye replied. "He'll come through, I have faith in him. Just like I have faith in us." She didn't, but the words slipped out, so she must believe it on some level.

"Don't, Skye." Gemma pulled her arm away. "You know

I can't start anything with you because of what's happened before."

"It happened in someone else's life, Gemma, not yours. You don't have to atone for anything. You need to start living. Your grandparents would want that, as would your parents."

"My parents wouldn't give a shit whether I was happy or not, as long as I sent them wine."

"Do it for yourself, then, if for nobody else. And yes, I have a vested interest in what you do, because I want you to start living. And to do that, you need to remember you're not your dad. And you need to get over your ex. To know that not everyone you encounter is out for themselves, and that not all relationships are doomed."

Gemma flipped her head to the ceiling, then back to Skye. "I know you're right, but it's not that easy."

"It seemed like it could be last week. When we were kissing."

Gemma stared, then shook her head.

"What?" Skye wasn't going to let her get away with that. "Why are you shaking your head?"

"You don't want to know."

"I do! Tell me."

"Because you're gorgeous, okay? You're gorgeous, and here, and available, but I'm not. It's the rules, it's Juliette, it's everything. It's frustrating as hell."

Skye clenched her fists by her sides. "You're frustrated? Imagine how I'm feeling. You kiss me, our electricity is palpable, and then we avoid each other for a week. It's fucking crazy is what it is."

"I know," Gemma whispered. "But I can't change it. I can't

get involved with you. Martha lives by the rules and I have to as well."

Skye threw up her hands and went to walk away. "You know what? I'm too old for this shit. Come to that, so are you."

Gemma said nothing. Instead, she busied herself straightening up a couple of wooden chairs. Then she stopped and caught Skye's gaze.

Skye took in a sharp intake of breath. She just wanted to fucking kiss her. Was that such a crime?

According to Gemma, yes.

"You know what you're doing? You're not following your biodynamic principles."

"I'm not?" Gemma gripped the back of a chair and frowned.

Skye shook her head. "You're not. Your love life is like a vine. What do you do to ensure that the vines bloom with the best flowers possible? You get rid of the extra buds on the vines. You make room for the best grapes by removing the less juicy bunches. You make the space for your flowers and your grapes to breathe. It's what you need to do with your life. Clear out the old feelings and relationships. Make room for anything new to bud and breathe. Give it room to grow. Right now, you're stifling that."

Gemma's knuckles whitened around the back of the chair.

Had Skye got through to her? Maybe.

"I want to contribute to this vineyard. But I also don't want to walk away from other opportunities that would make my life better. I'm ready for the next stage of my life. For my next relationship. I'm ready for you. You need to make room for me. But only you can decide if that's something you want to do. Do you want to clear away your excuses and make that room, or are you going to hide behind them?" She stepped towards her and placed a gentle hand on her arm.

Gemma shivered under her touch.

"I'd like to give this a shot. But I'm not going to wait forever. Give it some serious thought. Because right now, you're not making me feel very special. I had enough of that to last a lifetime with Amanda and her affair." Skye paused. "Unless there's something still going on with Juliette?"

Gemma frowned. "We're very much over."

Skye gave an exasperated sigh. "Then think about us. I don't want to sneak around. I can't be your dirty secret. If we can't make this work, maybe I need to find another job. I know you've asked me to stay beyond the month I have left because Andi's time off has been extended, but maybe that's not in my best interest."

Gemma shook her head. "That's not what I want."

"Looks like you have some decisions to make then, doesn't it?"

* * *

When Skye got on her bike to go home, she found herself being pulled in the direction of Juliette's pub. She didn't know why. She could have gone anywhere for a drink, but she headed to The Haunted Hare. What was her plan? She didn't have one. Maybe she wanted to tell Juliette to fuck off. Maybe without the spectre of her hanging around, Gemma would be freer? Skye didn't really know. All she did know was that she'd just left a group of hens deliriously drunk and happy about love, and it was beyond depressing that she could have that too, but Gemma was standing in the way. Gemma had demons and ghosts she needed to slay. If Skye could help in any way, she wanted to.

When she stepped into the bar, Juliette stood at a table by the door, pointing at the menu. As Skye walked by, she heard Juliette tell the customer, "That wine isn't for sale; there are supply issues at the vineyard. To be honest, I think they had a very bad harvest, so we're not promoting their wines right now".

Skye's blood heated, and it wasn't even her vineyard and her sales Juliette was crushing. Then again, ever since she'd taken the job, Skye had a vested interest in the business. She wanted Gemma and Martha to succeed. If for no other reason than they were two women striving to make it in what was still very much a man's world.

She scanned the bar and saw Harvey talking to someone through the doorway that led to his attached home. She'd had enough of being diplomatic. This called for direct action. When he saw her approach, he gave her a beaming smile.

"Skye, how are you?" He glanced behind him, then back to her. He seemed a little fidgety. "Glad to see what happened last time hasn't put you off coming to the pub again. Hopefully our food and hospitality had something to do with that."

"Actually, your food was great, but I just walked in to hear your sister telling someone else that some vineyard was having harvest issues. Probably us. We're not, so she's still spreading lies."

Harvey looked over her shoulder and shook his head. "I'm sorry. I have spoken to her, but are you sure it was about your vineyard?"

Skye put her phone on the bar. Juliette could have been talking about someone else, but she doubted it.

"If you could just have another word with her. I don't want to cause a scene, but maybe that's what's needed?"

Harvey nodded. "I will, I promise. I've told Martha and Gemma I want their wines back on sale, and Martha said she can supply. We're getting them back next week, in fact."

This was news Gemma hadn't relayed. "Really?"

Harvey nodded. "I want to sort this out as much as you do. In the meantime, what can I get you? On the house?"

"I'll have a glass of Newton's chardonnay, please." She jumped off her seat. "I just need the loo."

When Skye came back minutes later, her phone was still on the bar next to her glass of wine. She took a sip, then glanced up to see Harvey nodding at someone in the corridor at the back of the bar. Then he smiled, leaned forward, and kissed someone. Instinctively, Skye leaned back to see who that someone was. When that someone then stepped forward and kissed Harvey some more, Skye's eyes widened.

It was Martha. The sister who apparently didn't live by Gemma's vineyard rules quite as strictly as Gemma did.

Skye's mouth dropped open slightly. Martha was sneaking around behind Gemma's back, but Gemma was fulfilling a promise that didn't make sense? At least Martha sleeping with Harvey had solved the pub's wine problem. She could see how Harvey might well have sped up that solution.

Moments later, Harvey appeared behind the bar, and Skye heard a door slam behind him. How long had Martha and Harvey been an item? Why wasn't Martha coming clean? Why was Gemma clinging so hard to a rule that was out of date and not in anyone's interest?

More to the point, what was Skye going to do now?

Chapter Eighteen

Gemma clenched her fist and pumped the air. Even if her personal life had taken a turn for the better and then a turn for the worse, her professional life had jumped forward in leaps and bounds. Both were down to Skye, but she didn't want to focus on that.

Gemma sat back and re-read Hugo's email telling her he was going to stock her wines, and that she was going to get an interview in an upcoming magazine that would put their wine into thousands of homes. She got up and poured herself another coffee, then walked over to the window. She held up her cup, and gave the vineyard a cheers. Then she walked over to the photo of her grandparents on the office wall.

"This one's for you," she told them. "Our wine is going to be on supermarket shelves all over Britain." Warmth rolled through her. Wherever they were – she liked to imagine her grandparents in a celestial vineyard looking down over everyone – she knew they'd be proud. Pride in her business was something Gemma never had a problem with. Pride in herself and what she allowed herself to do was something else all together. But this was timely. It was the anniversary of the vineyard's opening this weekend, and she and Martha always went out to mark it. Now they'd have something extra-special to toast.

She sat, ignoring the gnawing sensation in her bones, and clicked onto the weather. Even though the sun was out, a frost threatened later. If she had to do an alarm with Skye, that might be awkward after everything. Gemma checked her watch. Skye was normally in by now. She hoped she wasn't avoiding her. She sighed. This was why anything happening between staff was always a bad idea.

Half an hour later, Skye arrived. She gave Gemma a half-smile as she plugged in her laptop at the desk near the door.

"Morning." Her tone was bright, but clipped. A little like the weather outside. "No frost alarm last night?"

"Only a small one. Patrick took care of it. I think we might have to be on standby tonight, though."

Skye nodded, her face far too neutral. Normally they'd laugh about it, or roll their eyes. Not today.

"I can be around if you need me," Skye said.

"Great." Gemma paused. "Also, I have great news. Hugo came through. He's going to stock us, and he's going to feature us in the magazine."

At last, a smile. "That's amazing. Congratulations. Getting your name out there is huge."

Gemma smiled. Skye was saying all the right things, but she couldn't pin down her vibe. Apart from that it was flat. Downbeat. Not the normal Skye. She was pretty sure that was down to her.

"We couldn't have done it without you, so thank you." She held Skye's gaze, and her heart fluttered. "I really mean it."

Skye sucked on her top lip. "I know."

Gemma frowned. "Listen, I know things are a bit awkward between us after what happened and what was said, but I want you to share in the vineyard triumphs, too. I don't want things to be weird." But even saying that, she knew it couldn't be anything but. That's how it went when you mixed business with pleasure.

But Skye shook her head. "This isn't about us and what happened." She paused. "Not primarily, at least." Skye stuck her hands in the pockets of her jeans. Now Gemma assessed her, she saw bags under her eyes. Like she hadn't been sleeping.

"You look tired," Gemma said. "Is that why you're late in?" She winced. Dammit, that had come out wrong. She shook her head, then got up and walked over to Skye's desk. As she got closer, her heart thudded faster. Her body was so predictable. "Sorry, that came out accusatory. I know you're working hard. I just meant, if you're not sleeping, don't rush in. Have an extra hour in bed."

Skye rubbed her eyes before she responded. "I've actually been up early and speaking to local vineyards. Finishing off the finer details of the summer wine box. Remember we spoke about it? I promise I wasn't slacking."

There was a glimmer of a smile as she said the last part.

Gemma grimaced. "I wasn't accusing, even if it sounded like I was." She inclined her head towards the coffee machine. "Can I get you an apology coffee?"

Skye gave her a tired smile this time, but nodded. "You can. And I really am pleased about the Hugo news."

"Me, too."

Gemma got the coffee. When she turned, Skye stood by the patio doors overlooking the vineyard. She walked over and gave her the mug, then stood and stretched her neck beside Skye.

"Thank you." Skye gave her a strange look, then returned her attention to the vines.

When Gemma raised her coffee mug to her lips, her hand shook.

"This is my favourite time at the vineyard, you know. The vines are getting green, the weather brightens, the new rosé is about to release. It's the start of the vineyard year, and people are generally in a good mood." Gemma paused. "Generally." She risked a smile in Skye's direction.

Skye shook her head. "I am in a good mood. Things are going well work-wise. I'd be in a better mood if other things changed."

Gemma flicked her gaze to Skye's lips. She knew things had to. They couldn't keep doing this dance. She put a hand on Skye's arm. "I'm thinking about it, I promise you." She stared into her ocean-coloured eyes. "It's difficult for me, too. Not just you." Standing so close to her and not touching Skye was hard. Gemma wanted to melt into her.

"But you're the one with the power to change it. That's the difference. I have a job I love, with a boss who's way above average. It's kinda strange that's an issue, but it is."

"I know." Gemma squeezed her arm. "I promise I'm working on it. Plus, I need to get you on my good side, because every time we're this close, I want to paint you. To sketch you. You've got extraordinary bone structure, you know that?"

Skye's eyes glinted. "Someone told me recently."

"That someone sounds very clever."

"You know this isn't what normal boss and employees do, right?"

"Do they normally just skip straight to painting the person without them knowing?"

Skye shook her head. "I really shouldn't be talking to you. I should be mad at you. I *am* mad at you."

"But you also can't help being unmad at me, too?" Gemma tilted her head.

"Something like that." Skye sighed. "I've no idea how we've made this work so far."

"Maybe our electricity is our fuel. Maybe if we took it further, our work spark would burn out."

"Which would you prefer? Work spark or personal spark?" Skye's gaze caressed Gemma's face.

"In an ideal world, both."

"We could live in an ideal world, you know." Skye nodded towards the vines. "It's pretty idyllic outside. It's inside we need to change."

Gemma let the words roll around her brain. "Do you want to come for dinner later? Save you going home and coming back for the frost alarm?"

Skye let out a sound Gemma couldn't quite put a name to. "Until you clarify where we are, I'm not sure that's the greatest idea in the world. Remember what happened last time we ate alone?"

Gemma did. She knew she was sending mixed signals. But she couldn't help it.

"Good morning all!"

Martha's voice made Gemma jump a foot to her right, then bustle back to her desk. She was sure her cheeks were burning, even though she'd done nothing wrong. Luckily, her sister seemed oblivious to the crackle of tension in the room.

"We warded off the frost again last night." Martha gave her a wide grin. "Your turn tonight. Any news on your supermarket man?"

Gemma nodded. "Just heard. He's stocking us."

Martha clapped her hands. "That's brilliant news! Well done both." She wheeled around and grinned at Skye, who gave her a muted smile in return. "I'm driving over to the post office to pick up a parcel. You want anything while I'm out?"

"Just the post office? Nowhere else en route?" Skye narrowed her eyes.

Gemma couldn't quite work out the vibe.

Martha frowned. "No, should I be going elsewhere?"

Skye scowled, then shook her head. "No."

"Okay." Martha backed out. "See you later."

Skye slammed her laptop shut, unplugged the leads and stuffed it back into its case. She zipped it up and caught her finger. She shook her hand and swore through clenched teeth.

Gemma walked over. "Are you okay?"

"Fine," Skye bristled. "I have to go. I need to check out some packaging options for the wine box." She put her laptop in her bag, and marched off.

Gemma was left wondering what just happened.

* * *

After the sunshine all day, the frost overnight was a brutal reminder they weren't quite in full-blown summer yet. Gemma arrived at her final row of bougies to light. She kicked the lid off the first candle, then lit it. The satisfying whoosh told her it had been successful. She nodded at the flame, then walked to the next. The lid on the second bougie was harder to budge, and it took three strong kicks to dislodge it. Her big toe smarted after kick three, and she already knew it was going to be bruised tomorrow. Frost alarms were physical work, with all the kicking and marching up and down fields at speed. She'd often thought she could sell it as a new keep-fit regime, but the unsocial hours meant it was unlikely to catch on.

Gemma breathed in the smoke from all the candles, and marvelled at how pretty they looked. She finished lighting the final candle, then caught sight of Skye's head torch. They were almost neck and neck. When she reached the end of the row, Skye was at the end of hers, too. Gemma checked her watch. A couple of hours to sunrise. That was a whole lot of time for them to kill in their new normal.

Skye had clearly thought about it, too.

"I can't really stick around all night, but I'd be happy to come back to help put out the bougies at sunrise. I don't think us spending time together now is the most ideal thing in the world, is it?"

Gemma's heart stalled. This was her fault. She had no right to feel sad. Yet she did.

Nothing in her head made sense.

"I promise, no kissing."

Skye gave her a sad smile. "That's not an encouraging promise, just in case you were wondering."

Gemma winced. She wished they could work things out. That she could run a finger down Skye's porcelain cheekbones. That she could smooth the wrinkles in Skye's mind.

"I'll make you coffee, and tell you another secret about me. Something you didn't know already." She sounded desperate.

"What if I already know more than I want?"

"Please?" Gemma gave Skye what she hoped was a pleading stare.

Skye sighed, then flicked her gaze to Gemma. "I really should say no. You're the one who wants boundaries, right?"

Gemma shrugged on her most confident smile. "You're right. And I'm overstepping them. But it's 3.30 in the morning, and I'm not thinking straight."

"Thinking straight is over-rated."

"Come back to the tasting rooms. Keep me company."

Skye stared, weighing up her options. Moonlight flickered across her features. Then, eventually, she said, "Okay."

Gemma breathed a huge sigh of relief.

They set off towards the tasting rooms and bar, the soil damp under foot. Gemma breathed in the smoke and soil. Being out in the vines had a way of making you feel grounded and connected to the earth. She wanted that feeling with Skye, too. As they arrived, Gemma's step-counter buzzed on her wrist. She'd done her 10,000 steps and it wasn't even 4am.

* * *

"I feel like we should drink." Skye shut one of the big doors out to the vineyard, and sat at one of the rugged wooden tasting tables.

"I feel like that could be calamitous. Even though we are in a vineyard." Gemma ignored the part of her brain that shouted, "drink, drink, drink!"

Skye checked her watch. "How are we going to fill the time until sunrise, then? Sing campfire songs?"

Gemma had a sudden brainwave. "How about we chat,

and I sketch you? That way, we keep a distance from each other, and we have something else to focus on."

Skye thought about it for a moment, her brow creased. "I've never had anybody sketch me before. Is it painful?" She eyeballed Gemma as she spoke.

An arrow of lust caught Gemma right in her centre. She tried to ignore it, but it wasn't easy.

The sexual tension in the air was palpable.

"Only if you make it so."

"Touché."

Gemma put up a hand. "Stay there, make a cuppa, and I'll go grab my sketchpad from the house. I won't be long."

Ten minutes later, Gemma was back, tea was made, and she stood behind her easel, staring at Skye. Perhaps this amount of focus on someone she couldn't have wasn't the most advisable thing in the world, but she pushed that thought from her mind.

"What I need you to do is just relax, and chat to me. I'll take the sketch from there."

"I don't have to keep still?"

Gemma shook her head. "It's best if you stay as still as possible, but I'm not demanding you don't move for the next two hours. Just stay in the same vicinity, with the same light."

"I can do that." Skye took a deep breath, then sipped her tea, and glanced at Gemma. "Sorry, can I move my head?"

Fuck, she was adorable. "Yes, I'm not expecting you to be a waxwork statue, okay? Just relax."

Skye nodded. "Relax. Got it."

Gemma started to sketch, heat coursing through her. In her dreams, she'd done this with Skye lying naked in her bed. Right after they'd had sex. This was a poor substitute.

"How many other women have you sketched in your life?"

"Only one," Gemma replied. "My sister. You're the first," she continued, then stopped. What was she going to say? Love interest? She couldn't say that, as they were currently in limbo. "The first outside my family."

Skye held her gaze. "I wondered what you were going to say."

She wasn't the only one. Gemma tried to gloss over it and started to sketch Skye's silky blonde hair.

"How about we go back to telling each other secrets. That focuses the mind."

"Maybe there are more secrets kicking about right under your nose. Maybe you don't need mine."

"What do you mean?" Gemma's pencil hovered over her paper. She fixed Skye with her stare.

Skye shook her head. "Nothing. Forget I said anything." She sipped her tea, still shaking her head. "Okay, I'll play. A secret about me." She put her fingers to her chin. "I abseiled down Big Ben once for charity. It was singularly the most terrifying experience I've ever gone through, but I'm just glad the bell didn't chime while I was there."

"You really did that?" That was not what Gemma had expected her to say.

"Yep. It still brings a chill even eight years later."

"You're full of surprises, Skye Tuck." Gemma licked her lips. "Are you feeling a little more unstuck being here, by the way?"

Skye exhaled, then gave her a rueful grin. "I think you know the answer. Yes and no."

Gemma gulped. She did know.

A few more moments trickled by as Gemma shaded Skye's

ears. "You've got a perfect heart-shaped face, in case you were wondering. Fantastic cheekbones, too."

Skye didn't respond. Instead, she stared out the window. "The stars look beautiful tonight."

You look beautiful tonight. Gemma's pulse was frantic and her head buzzed, all staticky. Had she said that out loud or in her head? She held her breath. When Skye's expression didn't change, she sighed, relieved.

Eventually, Skye flicked her gaze to Gemma. "What about you? Tell me something people don't know about you."

This was dangerous. Gemma's stomach flipped, and her palms flared hot. There were too many thoughts buzzing around her brain, and she was scared what might slip out if she opened her mouth. The truth was not an option.

"I play darts. Although I'm not a patch on Martha who practises all the time."

Skye smiled. Her face lit up when she did.

"I love your smile."

Oh fuck.

You see, that's what Gemma had been afraid of. She definitely said that out loud. She knew, because Skye's cheeks flared red.

Skye gazed at her, rich with intent. "I love yours, too."

That was news. Gemma's heart stuttered, and she stared right back.

Skye didn't look away.

The moment swayed between them.

Maybe this had been a bad idea. But being here with Skye also felt delicious. Like they were stealing hours they weren't meant to have together.

"I'll tell you something else nobody knows about me," Skye added. "Earlier, when I was stood next to you in the office? I had to stop and walk away because you leaned your head to one side and exposed your neck. The only thing I wanted to do was press my lips against your skin."

Gemma's breath left her body. She pressed down too hard on her sketch, and the pencil lead broke. She wasn't surprised. This had happened since day one. Put them in a room together alone, and sparks flew. Gemma had set the boundaries, and then ignored them. It wasn't anybody's fault. It was just who they were. She clutched her pencil, then her heart.

"But we're not going there, right?" Skye sucked on her top lip. "We're just friends, work colleagues."

Gemma nodded. "That's a friendly thing to say."

"I guarantee you, none of my friends have ever said anything like that to me."

Chapter Nineteen

Skye shook some more unhealthy cereal into her bowl.

"Oh dear, two helpings of Frosties. Is all not okay on Skye Mountain?" Lauren plonked herself down at the table beside Skye. She grabbed a bowl, shook some Frosties into it, then looked around. "Did you put the milk back in the fridge? Since when are you so efficient?"

"I'm on auto-pilot. It just happened."

Lauren rolled her eyes, got up, snagged the milk, then retook her seat. She leaned left and kissed Skye's cheek. "By the way, you look like shit."

Skye snorted. You could always count on your friends. "That's what happens when you're up all night lighting candles in fields and freezing your arse off."

"I knew the magic of frost alarms would wear off eventually." Lauren grinned. "Who were you on duty with last night? Was it the forever out-of-bounds Gemma?"

Skye nodded. "It was. And she sketched me."

Lauren's eyes widened. "She sketched you? And you still haven't had sex?"

Skye shook her head. "Nope."

"I'm sorry, but sketching someone is foreplay, is it not?"

"Maybe back in the Middle Ages."

"You're up in the dead of the night lighting candles to ward off frost. If that's not the Middle Ages, I'm not sure what is."

Skye laughed. Lauren had a point.

"We haven't had sex because of *reasons*."

"Tell me again the reasons? You've mumbled them before, but they didn't make any sense then either."

"She and her sister have this rule about not getting involved with anybody work-related. We work together and she doesn't want to muddy the waters. Although they got muddied a while ago." Skye paused. Was she going to go there? "Right around the time we kissed."

It appeared she was.

Lauren's mouth fell open. She put down the bottle of milk she held over her cereal.

"I knew it! There's this energy, this surge in the air when you even talk about her. Also, you go sort of cross-eyed. But re-the-fucking-wind. When did you kiss?"

Skye winced. Her friend wasn't going to like this answer. "Before we first met at the wine tasting." She leaned back in her seat and waited for the bomb to explode.

It duly did.

"Say whaaaaat?" Lauren couldn't stop blinking. "How did you kiss her before the wine tasting?" She punched Skye's arm. "And why have you been holding out on me all this bloody time? I can't fucking believe you!"

Skye rubbed her arm, pressing her fingers where Lauren had hit her. If it was the other way around, she'd be annoyed too.

"I don't know. Maybe because she kept quiet, so I did too? I can't really explain it." That was the truth.

Lauren made a rolling motion with her hand to indicate she needed more. "Details, please."

"We met in a bar the week of the wine tasting. She was in Cornwall for the day. We met, we talked, then we had this incredible kiss. But it was a one-off. I only knew her first name. I never thought I'd see her again. Until I walked into the wine tasting."

Lauren's eyes were still wide. "This is like the plot of a rom-com, isn't it?" She banged the table with her fist. "And you took a job with her. What the hell?"

Skye gave an embarrassed shrug. "It just all fell into place. Plus, you pushed for it."

Lauren raised both her palms. "I didn't know the backstory!"

"We talked about everything that happened before I accepted. We agreed to keep it professional. And we have."

Sort of.

Lauren gave Skye an incredulous stare, then added milk to her cereal.

The crackle filled the air, and reminded Skye of last night's bougies. The way the air swayed in the heat. The way Gemma smiled at her in the moonlight. Skye shook her head to dislodge the image.

"So let me get this straight. You kissed her, you work with her every day, you have chemistry, but you haven't had sex?"

When she put it like that, it really did sound like a lie.

"I know it sounds ridiculous, but no, we haven't."

"But you want to?"

Heat flooded through Skye. "Of course I bloody do."

Lauren ate a mouthful of cereal, then rested her chin in the palm of her hand.

"Hmmm."

Skye raised an eyebrow. "Hmmm? What does that mean?"

"Could it be that she's having her cake, but bizarrely, nobody's eating it?"

"I don't follow."

"I think Gemma means well, but whether she knows it or not, she's stringing you along. She's kissed you, right?"

Skye nodded. Yes, she'd kissed her. And kissed her again. But Lauren didn't know that.

"Yet nothing's happened since. Again, we're back to the Middle Ages. Maybe it's something to do with the vineyard. At least in the Middle Ages, they had an excuse for not shagging as much as they had so many layers of clothing."

"Frost alarms do need many layers."

"Yes, but there's also central heating now. My point is, Gemma seems to want to keep you hanging on, but she doesn't want to make any changes or do anything to move things forward. You're doing her a favour by doing a great job. What's she doing for you? You're in a holding pattern. You need to get out."

Lauren raised a hand. "And before you tell me that's not what she's doing, she has served a purpose, I'll give her that. She's made you realise that you and Amanda are in the past and you've decided you might like to dip your toe back in the dating waters, am I right?"

Skye nodded. "She has done that, yes. I want to sleep with her. She's the first person that's happened with since Amanda."

"That's good. Excellent! Thumbs up for Gemma. However," Lauren continued. "I don't think that Gemma is the only other person in the world you might want to sleep with. What if it's you who's changed? Yes, Gemma was the catalyst, but if she's not willing, I don't want to see this long face in my house all the time. I want fun, happy, starting-a-new-life Skye living with me. Not sad, brooding-over-a-woman-who-might-not-happen Skye." Lauren chewed some more Frosties before she carried on. "Also, for what it's worth, Gemma does have a point. Sleeping with your boss, even in a small company, has its problems. What happens if you do it, and then things spiral downhill?"

"Now you sound like her."

"I don't agree with her reasons, but maybe now you've realised you're ready, you should have some fun. Go to work, smile at Gemma, do a good job, but then go on a date at the weekend. You can't wait around forever, Skye. You've worked at the vineyard for a couple of months and nothing's happened. If it was going to happen, it would have done so by now."

Skye stuck her tongue in her cheek.

Lauren narrowed her eyes. "Has something happened?"

Skye took a deep breath, then nodded. "We might have kissed again."

"When?"

"Last weekend."

"Oh my god and you didn't tell me that either?" Lauren slammed down her spoon on the white Formica table. "I could get really offended."

She scowled at Skye, but there was a softness behind her eyes. "How was the second kiss compared to the first?"

"Epic," Skye replied. She couldn't say anything else. It was the truth, the whole truth, and nothing but the truth.

"Big words coming from you. Was it a Hollywood kiss?"

It had been all of those things and more. The vines, which

were once just green and pretty, now wolf-whistled at Skye when she walked by.

"It was incredible, just like the first time. Romantic. Hot. Frustrating because she said it couldn't go any further."

"And you were together all last night and nothing more? She just sketched you?"

Something dark settled in Skye's stomach. She nodded. Did Lauren have a point? Was Gemma stringing her along?

"So, one more time. You kissed twice, you have off-the-scale chemistry, but she says she can't sleep with you because she's your boss and because she and her sister have this rule. But you told me you saw her sister snogging a vineyard customer."

"That's about the size of it." Skye exhaled. "Should I tell her about Martha?"

"I wouldn't get involved. That's something they need to resolve themselves." Lauren held up her phone. "You want to know what I think?"

"I have a feeling you're going to tell me."

"You should get online and go out on a date. A date with anyone. Another woman who doesn't scare you. Because until you know if it's Gemma or just someone else you're open to, how do you know you're not wasting your time?"

"I don't think it's that easy. Aren't you the one who's always telling me there are no single men in the area? What makes you think there will be women?"

"How do you know if you haven't tried?"

Lauren grabbed Skye's phone, pulled up the dating app she knew she had on there, and thrust it into her hand. "Do it today. Now is not the time to be waiting around for Gemma. You need to look elsewhere. You could take whoever to The

Cobbler's Rest. Apparently the new chef there is a woman and the food is immense. That way, you score feminism and cuisine points all in one." She gave Skye a look. "You can thank me later."

Lauren left for work, telling Skye to think about it. Skye couldn't think of anything else. One thing she did know was with all this roaming around her brain, she couldn't go in and face Gemma today. She could do everything she needed from home.

That left Skye on her sofa, phone in hand, finger poised over the dating app. Maybe Lauren was right. Maybe she just needed to see what else was out there. Particularly if Gemma wasn't going to change her mind. As Lauren pointed out, she'd had time to think about it. Plenty of time to make decisions. Skye didn't want to give up just yet, but she also couldn't wait forever for Gemma to decide. Why couldn't she fall for someone who was available? However, as Lauren had pointed out, maybe she could. Perhaps it wasn't Gemma she was meant to fall for, and she just hadn't met that other someone yet. There was only one way to find out.

Skye took a deep breath, clicked, then saw a woman named Erica. She was online and available.

Skye thought about it for a few seconds, and then, before she could change her mind, she clicked for more.

* * *

Skye didn't go into the vineyard the next day, either. Instead, she spent the evening working on her CV. What Lauren had said made sense. Gemma said one thing, but did another. Something had to give. Was that her job, or her potential love interest?

Before Skye could decide that, she had to talk to Gemma to give her a chance to change her mind, to make sure she understood where they were. Skye wanted to be with her. If she didn't want to be with Skye, then she'd see if she could pursue someone else. She wasn't sure it was that easy, but like Lauren said, she wouldn't know until she tried.

She pulled up her phone and messaged Gemma before she changed her mind. If she really valued her as a friend and whatever else they might become, she'd make time for her.

'Hey, are you free on Saturday night? I feel like we've got some things we need to talk about and they should be done outside work. Maybe we could go out to a pub to chat?'

Skye's finger hovered over the green button, before she forced herself to press it. Then she waited, a bundle of nerves.

She hoped Gemma was free, and that she understood the significance. She didn't have to wait long.

'I'm not. Saturday night I've got dinner with Martha.'

She stared at the text. Dinner with Martha who Gemma saw every single day? That said something about how important Skye was on her list, didn't it?

'What about another night? I don't want to do another week with things hanging in the balance.' She stared at the message, gathered all of her courage and clicked send.

Then she waited.

Three dots signified Gemma was writing a reply, but it never came. Fifteen minutes later, still nothing, and she was offline.

Thunder rumbled through Skye. Gemma wasn't sitting around thinking about this like she was, was she? That was all on Skye. If Gemma liked Skye in the same way, she'd make the time.

Lauren was right, Gemma was taking her for a ride. Stringing her along. Sketching her, making her feel important, but keeping her at arm's length. Gemma was hiding behind her rules.

Skye wasn't going to let her get away with it anymore.

'Maybe it's a good thing we stopped at that kiss if this isn't important to you. Maybe you were right all along and we shouldn't mix business with pleasure. Let's keep it to business from now on.'

Skye's heart thumped in her ears as she pressed send. Then she made a vow not to look at any reply Gemma sent. She'd wasted enough time. She was glad it was Friday tomorrow, and the weekend very soon.

Instead, she clicked again on the dating app, and scrolled to the woman she'd seen the day before. Erica looked uncomplicated. At this point, anyone was less complicated than Gemma. Skye clicked on Erica's photo, then messaged her to see if she fancied dinner on Saturday night. She got a reply within the hour.

Skye had a date for Saturday night, even if it wasn't her first choice. But Erica had said yes. She'd chosen Skye, unlike Gemma.

It was time to cut the cord and move on.

Chapter Twenty

Gemma pressed down her feelings about Skye, squashing them into a tiny box and tucking them away. It was a skill she'd honed to perfection over the years. Had Skye meant it when she said she wanted to keep it strictly business? Hadn't they gone beyond that already with their kisses? Gemma's emotional compass was wonky. Skye had worked from home yesterday, and ignored Gemma's personal messages, which meant everything was still up in the air.

The ball was in Gemma's court, but she wasn't someone who acted swiftly. She liked to think about things, to deliberate. Skye had a different timeline for life and for love. She'd already told Gemma she fell quickly. Gemma was the opposite. Despite all of that, once Gemma had spoken to Martha tonight and filled her in, she planned to act. It was May, after all. Her favourite month of the year. Gemma was about to take a chance. To turn her life upside down in the best possible way. So long as Skye still wanted her to.

Gemma pushed down the nagging worry in her gut, and focused on the here and now as she pulled her front door closed. It was 48 years since her grandparents had opened Martha's Vineyard, and they were going to raise a glass and eat food to celebrate that. Even if she should have gone to the loo before she left, but the pub was only a 15-minute drive away.

Martha grinned at her phone as Gemma got into her passenger seat. It was a grin Gemma wasn't used to. Her Spidey senses tingled.

"What are you looking so pleased about?"

Martha blinked, then shook her head. "Nothing, just something Leo sent me."

"Is he studying tonight?" Her nephew was in the middle of his GCSE exams.

"Meant to be, but when I left they were both playing Fortnite. Every time I mention it, he tells me it's under control. He told me to have a great time, and promised not to raid the drinks cabinet. It's all I can ask of a 15-year-old, I suppose." Martha gave her sister a shrug.

"Does he see booze differently, like we did?" Growing up in a vineyard meant that alcohol wasn't this great hidden-away thing it had been for most of her friends. She assumed Leo and Travis would be the same. Although it still hadn't stopped her from imbibing her fair share of underage booze on occasion. The more lurid in colour, the better.

"He does. It helps when you know where it comes from, doesn't it?" Martha put her car in drive, and navigated the potholes on their drive like a pro. "Although I suspect Travis is going to be the one to give me more headaches. It's always child two, isn't it?"

Gemma rolled her eyes. "Or maybe it's because child one is such a perfect angel, child two wants to spice things up. Life would get very boring otherwise, wouldn't it?"

Martha laughed as she pulled out onto the country road.

"I haven't seen Skye in a couple of days. Has she had time off?" Her sister said it without a hint of an agenda.

Gemma's muscles tensed under the scrutiny of a simple question, and she knew she had to have this chat with Martha.

"She's been working from home."

Martha nodded. "Makes sense."

The pub they'd chosen was one in a nearby village: The Cobbler's Rest. There was a new chef, and they'd heard good things about the food from a couple of locals, so they'd decided to try it. They were seated in the large dining room at the back, overlooking the lush fields beyond. The vines from a local vineyard bloomed green to their left, as the sun set over the fields.

They ordered a bottle of local pinot, their main courses of fish pie, and pork schnitzel with mash and loganberries, and then settled back. When the wine arrived, Martha poured, and they toasted their grandparents and the vineyard. It was a well-worn evening they performed every year. Gemma always treasured it.

Maybe she should have invited Skye, but it wasn't right just yet. Gemma still had to iron out the kinks in their relationship, whatever that was or could be. Perhaps she'd be here next year. That thought warmed her.

"What do you think our grandparents did for the first few years of their anniversary? Do you think they had anywhere to go for dinner in the mid-70s?" Martha asked.

Gemma sniffed the wine, rolled it around her glass, then took a sip. It was delicious, great depth and body. "I'm sure they did, but they might have been eating bland, beige food. The 70s weren't renowned for gastronomy." She glanced around the wood-panelled dining room, with its sturdy furniture and patterned carpet. "All things considered, I'd rather be where we are today." She paused. "Apart from one thing."

Martha raised an eyebrow. "What's that?"

"I want to talk to you about the rules." Gemma's stomach rolled as she spoke. They'd never brought this up since they'd decided on them a couple of years into running the business. She took a drink of water, then immediately needed the loo. She'd forgotten to go when they arrived. She could hold it a while longer.

"Rules?"

"The rules about seeing anyone related to the vineyard. I think as we're getting older and the pool of people we meet gets smaller, they might need a rethink."

Martha cast her eyes to the ground, then back up to meet Gemma's gaze. "I agree."

That was easier than she expected. "You do?"

Her sister nodded. "Yep. I've been meaning to say something about it, too. Like you say, it's not like we meet a load of people who aren't vineyard-connected." She tilted her head. "Hang on, does this mean you've got your eye on someone?" She tapped the side of her wine glass with her index finger. "Who is my little sister planning on shagging? Don't tell me." She paused. "Is it Dennis at Leathermans?"

Gemma rolled her eyes. "Yes, I've got a crush on the 70-year-old from our winemakers. A great guess especially because I'm a lesbian."

"People are far more fluid these days, you need to get with the times. Stop putting yourself in a box."

"I happen to like boxes, that's the point."

Martha made a face. "Okay. Second guess. Davina from the cheese shop." She sat back, clearly pleased with herself.

"You really think I have a thing for older people, don't you?"

"Davina's only late 50s, so it's coming down."

"It's not Davina."

She sat forward. "So it is *someone*. The plot thickens." Martha's gaze hovered over Gemma's shoulder, before returning to her sister's face. She leaned in. "I hope it's not Skye, because she's just walked in with another woman, so that might be awkward. Could be her cousin I suppose, but she did just pull her chair out for her."

Gemma froze. Skye was here with another woman?

What the actual fuck?

Yes, they'd exchanged a few heated texts and this week hadn't been plain sailing, but she was already moving on? Plus, who the hell had she moved on with in such a small dating pool? Gemma desperately wanted to swivel around and find out, but she couldn't. Panic flooded her, along with a side order of frustration.

"Did she say anything to you about going on a date?" Martha asked.

Gemma shook her head.

No, she very much had not.

Martha beamed. "I bet she hoped she might be able to keep this to herself, but she'll soon learn there's no such thing as that around here." She paused. "You think we should go and say hi? Is it weird if we do? But also probably weird if we don't? Whatever, her date looks nice."

Gemma wanted to slip off her chair and slide out of the pub completely. She wasn't sure if she was pleased Skye had appeared when she was just about to reveal all to Martha. At least she'd saved herself that embarrassment. But it wasn't embarrassment she was feeling right now. That honour went to mortification, along with deep, slicing hurt.

They'd shared moments. Hopes. Secrets. Scorching kisses. Yet Skye was prepared to throw that all away so quickly? Maybe she didn't mean as much to her as she'd imagined. Maybe she'd dodged a bullet. Maybe Skye had done her a favour. The swell of emotions barrelling around her almost made Gemma short-circuit. She took a large gulp of her wine.

"Gemma? Are you okay? You look like you've seen a ghost." Martha swivelled in her chair, then turned back to her sister. "I'm not missing anything, am I? Juliette hasn't just come in?"

Gemma shook her head. "No."

Martha frowned. "It's definitely not Skye you've got a thing for?"

"No!" A little snappy.

That earned a raised eyebrow from her sister. "Only, you do spend a lot of time with her. Far more than you ever did with Andi."

"Andi had a husband."

Shit. That was totally the wrong thing to say.

"My point exactly."

Gemma sat up straight, then shook her head. She had to throw her sister off the scent. "It's just," she started, but then realised she couldn't say anything to her sister. She'd been about to, but that honesty had just been thrown out the window. But Martha was looking at her with concern, and she had to say something.

"I suppose it's just that Skye and me, we've chatted, and I thought we were friends. I thought perhaps she might have said something about going on a date." She cringed as she said it, but it was true. Because all the while they'd been sharing looks and kisses, maybe Skye had been dating the whole time. They weren't anything, after all. Gemma had told Skye that numerous times.

Perhaps though, with the spectre of Skye with someone else on the horizon, Gemma's feelings were sharpening. From being out of focus, they were now crystal clear. She liked Skye. She wanted something to happen with her. She wanted to tell Martha that. But that wasn't going to happen if Skye was on a date with someone else.

With terrible timing, Gemma's bladder pressed down once more, and this time, she couldn't ignore it. Which meant getting up and turning around. She really didn't want to see Skye with anybody else. But she couldn't hold on forever.

"Maybe she wanted to keep it a secret," her sister replied.

Maybe she did. That hadn't worked, had it? "I need the loo." Gemma kept her face steady as she stood.

"Go say hi, it's always good to embarrass your friends." It was a good job Martha had no idea. When and if she found out, she was going to be mortified. But that was not something for today. Hopefully she'd never find out, and Gemma could slot this night into the folder marked 'Best Forgotten'. She had quite the list of nights stored there already. Gemma pulled back her shoulders, gave her sister a tight smile and turned. The table where Skye and her date sat was on the path to the loo. There was no avoiding it. Gemma decided to face it head-on.

She pulled up at Skye's table just as the other woman laid a hand on Skye's arm.

She might as well have kicked Gemma in the gut. She swayed on her feet, then painted on her best fake smile. Whatever happened, she was going to style this out like a pro. She had a lot of practice.

"Hey, Skye." She tried to keep her tone as light as she could.

When Skye glanced up, her face ashened. She pulled her arm off the table, dislodging the woman's hand. Then she picked up her napkin and dabbed the sides of her mouth. She had nothing there, but Gemma assumed she wanted to do something with her hands. Gemma understood. She was fighting the urge to place both of hers flat on the table and shout into Skye's face, "What the fuck is going on here?"

"Hi," Skye replied. Then she got up. "What are you doing here?" Something flashed across her face, and Gemma realised Skye was wondering if she was here with a date, too. She wished she was, but she hadn't been looking. She'd thought someday, she and Skye might go on a date. More fool her.

Gemma indicated towards Martha with her head. "I'm here with Martha. It's the vineyard's anniversary dinner. It's a standing date in our calendar." She held Skye's gaze.

Skye peered around her and waved to Martha, who waved back.

"This is what you had on tonight?"

"Uh-huh."

Skye sucked on her cheek, then nodded.

There was a pause as they both assessed their next move.

Skye broke first. "This is Erica. Erica, this is my boss, Gemma."

There was that boss word again. Gemma took a deep breath, and shook Erica's hand. "Lovely to meet you." Her eyes fell on the wine they were drinking. It was a bottle of their own Classic Cuvee. Gemma had to give Skye points for brand loyalty, if nothing else. "Anyway, I better go to the loo."

She wanted to smack herself in the face. Too much information. "Have a lovely dinner, see you Monday." With that, she gave Skye a steely smile, and left her to it. Clearly, whatever they had and whatever they might have had were more in Gemma's mind than in reality. Skye had done her a favour.

* * *

"That was a delicious dinner, but I'm not sure I should have had the sticky toffee pudding on top of the fish pie. I've eaten enough carbs to last a lifetime."

"Carbs are not the enemy." Gemma flicked on her phone, going to WhatsApp and hoping to see a message from Skye.

She didn't know why.

Unsurprisingly, there wasn't one.

"Skye left pretty swiftly with her date. No dessert for her. Maybe that's how she keeps her trim figure."

Gemma could think of other ways.

"By the way, we never did get back to the subject of dating someone who's connected with the vineyard."

That was because Gemma had studiously kept the conversation away from it for the rest of the evening.

"I'm all for it. Those rules were good when they were made, but they're a bit archaic now, aren't they?" Martha continued.

Gemma nodded. "Yes, they are." Even if it wasn't Skye, it was good to talk about it for anything that might happen in the future. But right now, she didn't want to talk about anything else. All Gemma wanted to do was get home, make a cup of tea and ponder how she managed to royally fuck up another possible future with her epic stubbornness.

"You're not going to tell me who you have your eye on?"

Gemma ground her teeth together. She was normally an open book with her sister. Not tonight. "It's nobody in particular." She was in damage limitation mode.

Martha paused as she pulled into the lane that led to their house. "You sure? Definitely not Skye? I sensed some kind of tension earlier when she arrived."

Every muscle Gemma owned tightened. She kept a straight face.

"No." Her voice cracked as she spoke. She hated lying to Martha. It made her feel seedy. Like her dad. However, this was a needs-must situation. If Martha figured it out, her humiliation would be complete. "I already told you no." She had to close the lid on this now.

The car bucked as they drove over a pothole.

"That's good, otherwise tonight might have been really awkward."

Never a truer word spoken.

Gemma glanced right.

Her sister sucked on the inside of her cheek. Did she believe her? Gemma had no idea.

Martha parked the car, then cut the engine. "Actually, there's something I want to talk to you about, too. You want to come in for a night cap?"

Gemma's brain filled with white noise. Normally, a night cap with her sister would be very welcome. But tonight, it was the last thing on her agenda.

"Do you mind if I take a rain check? It's been a long week, and I feel like I need an early night. Plus, that cheeseboard I had is weighing heavy on my stomach, too."

Martha flicked on the central light in the car. "Are you sure you're okay? Nothing you want to tell me?"

Her gaze drilled into Gemma. How she wanted to spill everything, and have Martha make it better like always. But Gemma had to adopt her best poker face. This was something she had to deal with alone. She'd broken the rules. Now she had to deal with the consequences.

She took a deep breath, then shook her head. "Nothing pressing, no. I'm just really exhausted after a trying week."

Her sister studied her face. "I'm not sure I believe you. But for now, I'll let it go."

* * *

Gemma sat at her kitchen table, as memories of Skye flooded her brain. She got out her phone and called up her photos. She scrolled to the shots she'd taken of Skye in the vineyard. Just before their scorching kiss. The way she looked defiantly into the camera, daring Gemma to look more closely made her heart ache. She wanted to look more closely, but she hadn't been brave enough. Maybe that had cost her. Their kisses had been great, but that's where Skye wanted to leave them. She'd got tired of waiting, and who could blame her? Their timing was all fucked up. Now, they didn't want the same thing. Skye wanted to date. Tonight had made that clear.

The sooner Gemma faced up to that, the better. But it didn't stop the thoughts that scrolled through her mind.

Was that it? The end of the road? After seeing Skye with someone else, her feelings had come into sharp focus. Now, Gemma knew what she wanted for sure. Was she too late? She had to hope the answer was no, because she wasn't ready to let Skye go.

She scrolled to Skye's last message about keeping it professional. She clutched her phone tight. The words swayed in her eyeline. She composed a whole new message, telling Skye she had things to tell her. Gemma's finger hovered over the green send button. She gulped, stared hard, then deleted. Now was not the time. Not when Skye was probably having her date for dessert.

Gemma put her head in her hands and let out a low groan. She wanted Skye's hands back on her and nowhere else.

She had to work out a way to salvage this.

Because Skye wasn't like anybody else she'd dated.

Gemma had finally figured out she was worth fighting for.

Chapter Twenty-One

Even though she wanted to, she couldn't avoid Gemma forever. Especially when she had suppliers coming in with new biodegradable box packaging. Plus, Lauren was at home this week for half-term, so going into the vineyard was unavoidable. Skye much preferred working from there, but the way things had been left up in the air with Gemma made it more than a little awkward. With any luck, Gemma might work from home this morning or this afternoon, so they wouldn't have to eyeball each other all day long. Skye could only hope.

However, when she got off her bike and approached the main office, she spied the back of Gemma's head through the main window. She hadn't prepared thoroughly for this, and now she kicked herself. The car park was already half-full, even before 10am. When she glanced up into the vineyards, she saw families already doing the half-term nature trail. They'd set up picnic baskets for sale to eat in the vines once they were done, too, and had hired an ice-cream trolley, which Leo and his best friend Blake had volunteered to staff. Their pay? £20 each, and as much ice cream as they wanted without being sick.

But before ice cream, Skye took a deep breath and slapped on a smile as she walked in the door.

How should she act?

Like Saturday night had never happened.

Cool, calm, like it hadn't meant a thing. Like she hadn't been worrying about this precise moment for the past 36 hours.

Not one single bit.

"Morning." Gemma's voice sounded normal, but Skye couldn't see her face behind her monitor.

"Happy Monday." Skye had no idea if that was true or not. She set up her laptop, then walked to the coffee pot. Why did she get the feeling Gemma was watching her every step? "Do you want one?"

"Yes please."

Skye poured two cups from the machine, and put one on Gemma's desk. When she glanced up, she looked tired. Skye softened, but she still wasn't sure where they stood. Should she bring up the date?

"Do anything nice yesterday?" Skye settled at her desk, then stretched out her legs.

"I did some painting, and chatted to some customers doing the self-guided tours. They're going down a storm."

Skye smiled. "I'm pleased." They were all the words she could manage. She held Gemma's gaze, and her stomach flared warm. The spring colours were reflected in her eyes, but she had no idea if things would ever warm up between them again.

Saturday night's date hadn't gone well. Mainly because the date wasn't Gemma. Erica had been chatty and pleasant enough, but Skye's heart hadn't been in it. Certainly after Gemma appeared, both her head and heart had been elsewhere. She'd wanted to leave, but she'd stayed seated. She had manners. You didn't arrange a first date, then bail within half an hour unless that person turned out to be the president of the Piers Morgan fan club. And yes, if the person you'd been sharing incredible kisses with was on a table nearby, that was problematic, but something you had to deal with.

She'd stuck it out until dessert, and then pulled the frost alarm card. A lie, but a necessary one. All evening, Skye already had one foot out the door, despite Erica telling amusing anecdotes and the two of them trading dating wounds. She didn't think there was a huge chance with Gemma. Perhaps 10 per cent. Fifteen tops. But while that chance still existed, she couldn't give her all to anything else. Those were just the facts.

"How about you?" Gemma pulled her face completely clear of her monitor. "How was the rest of your night on Saturday? Did she stick around for Sunday?"

Skye shook her head. "Nothing like that. She was lovely, but I'm not sure she's exactly my type." Skye sucked on the inside of her cheek. Should she say more? She weighed it up in her head, then her mouth took over. "I only arranged the date because you wouldn't meet me on Saturday and didn't reply to my next message. It seemed quite final." Anxiety itched in the back of her throat. "A statement."

Gemma frowned. "I thought I did." She reached for her phone, then stopped. "I didn't mean not to reply. Plus, it was the vineyard anniversary dinner with Martha on Saturday. I told you."

"You never said the reason. The special significance of the date. I would have understood that. I thought you were simply avoiding me."

"I wasn't avoiding you." Gemma flicked her gaze away, took a breath, then brought her focus back to Skye. "What is your type?"

Skye gulped. They both knew the answer. She opened her mouth to speak, but no sound emerged. They ended up staring at each other for far longer than she ever wanted to happen.

"I'm not sure I have a type," Skye said eventually. "Just someone who gets me? Who makes me laugh? Someone I have a connection with."

Gemma's gaze settled on her like sunshine.

Skye's heart burned in her chest.

Suddenly, all the air seemed to be sucked from the room.

Outside, the sun froze, and the daytime scene set like jelly.

Skye had no idea how long they both sat there like living statues, both holding their breath. But eventually, she had to breathe in, break the spell. But then, she had no idea what else to say.

Still Gemma stared. Then eventually, she shook her head. "You never know, it might happen with her. You did only go out with her for one night." She paused. "Although, maybe she's not the one for you. Maybe the one for you is staring you right in the face."

* * *

After she signed off for the day, Skye put off getting on her bike and instead went for a walk in the vines. She loved doing that, especially on a warm hug of an evening like this one. The day had been more productive than she'd anticipated, mainly because Gemma had disappeared sharpish after their initial chat. Had she been spooked by her own words? Maybe. She'd gone very pale afterwards. Whatever, it was probably better that way, even though there was so much more to say. But Skye wasn't sure how to broach any of it. Besides, if Gemma wasn't willing to bend on her rules, did she really want Skye enough in the first place? After Amanda, having someone who put her first was a high priority.

Skye walked to the top of the vineyard, with the views out across the Surrey Hills, and breathed in the summer air. She loved it up here; it had quickly grown to be her happy place. The smell of flowers, the low hum of nature all around. If she had a problem, it was impossible to stay sad in this environment. The vineyard, as Skye knew, was bigger than them all. She could see the tasting room and bar from here, along with some people on the upper balcony, soaking up the sun. She also spied the clump of houses at the start of the next village, along with the sweep of the trees that led to a neighbouring vineyard.

The first day of the nature trail had been a huge success, and they'd sold out of ice cream. Tonight, the vineyard was hosting their second night of jazz, presided over by Gemma and their regular tasting staff. Skye had set it up and done the first evening, but she was hands-off for evening two. Maybe she'd stay here and soak up the beats. The twang of guitars and the shuffle of drums echoing across the vines.

She spread her arms as if she was about to take off, and tipped her head to the sun. In the stillness and solace, she could almost forget her troubles. Although as Lauren had pointed out that morning, two women fighting over her was hardly trouble. It wasn't how it felt to Skye. Plus, they were hardly fighting. One was keeping her at arm's length, oblivious to her sister's affair. The other was probably wondering who the hell she'd gone out with on Saturday. Somebody not fully present, completely distracted by Gemma turning up and looking so defiant about Skye being on a date.

Skye had wanted Gemma to slam her water glass down, stomp over, kiss her and demand she push Erica to the kerb. Shamefully, she would have done it in a heartbeat. Skye was sorry Erica had got caught up in this. That she was collateral damage. But Skye's heart wanted what it did. It was just a shame Gemma's didn't want the same. At least, not quite enough.

Why was Skye's love life always so messed up? She had other friends who sailed merrily through life. Even if they got divorced, they met the next person who was single and available. Gemma was single, she just made herself unavailable. Trust Skye to meet the most principled vineyard owner in the country. The one with so many trust issues, she was prepared to cut off her nose to spite her face. Skye shook her head, then crumpled to the ground and took some calming breaths.

A ladybird settled on her forearm. "Do you have the same women troubles in ladybird land?" she asked.

Wouldn't it be wild if that was the case?

A message pinged on her phone. When she checked, it was from Justin.

'It's not the same here without you and your moping face. I have a couple of days off. How about you come and visit this weekend? My spare room is free, you could watch me surf and we could drink beer like old times. Tempted?'

Skye sat up. Maybe that was what she needed? To get away from here, as far as possible. The rosé launch wasn't until next week, she could take a couple of days off and go for a long weekend. A glimpse of the sea, some old friends, maybe that was just the change of perspective she needed.

She messaged Justin back telling him she'd come this weekend, either Thursday or Friday, depending on what days she could get off. Then she messaged Gemma, asking if it was okay to take a day or two off at the end of the week. They had everything covered this weekend, and Skye had been working flat out. Doing it all to make a success of her job and to impress Gemma.

An hour later, Skye made her way back to the main building, where the band were underway, and 80 guests were soaking up the vibes. The band had set up on the patch of grass in front of the tasting rooms, with enough space for guests to dance. The bar was doing a roaring trade, and the cheese boards were selling well. Skye slipped through the main bar and went to leave through the front door when she heard her name being called. When she turned, there was Gemma, radiant in her bumble bee outfit. The same one she wore to that first tasting, where Skye had been gobsmacked.

"I thought you'd left long ago. I got your message about time off. I thought you sent it from home."

She stuck her hands in her pockets. Why did she feel like she'd been caught in the act? She was allowed to relax in the grounds, do what she liked. But everything was far too tied up together, wasn't it?

Skye shook her head. "I was at the top of the field. Just doing some thinking." She met Gemma's gaze. "There's a lot to think about, isn't there?"

She willed Gemma to say something, but she simply nodded.

"Are you going anywhere nice?" Her tone was starched, stretched. Like she didn't want to know the answer.

"Back to Cornwall." Over Gemma's shoulder, the band broke into a jaunty number and a couple of the guests got up to dance.

Gemma followed Skye's gaze, and smiled. "This lot are good, I think they brought most of the guests."

"That's half the battle, isn't it?"

"Sure you don't want to stay for a glass of wine?"

It was tempting. Maybe they'd even dance.

Then Gemma licked her lips, and Skye flinched. She couldn't play along with the will-they-won't-they anymore. Someone had to be strong. It looked like it was going to be her.

She shook her head. "No thanks, I better get back. Lauren's making me dinner."

A lie.

Gemma paused. "One question: you are coming back from Cornwall? It's just a weekend visit?"

"That's the plan. Unless I get a better offer."

Gemma gave a nervous laugh. "You'll be here for the rosé launch next week?"

"It's just a weekend, Gemma. I'm coming back."

Chapter Twenty-Two

The biggest night of the vineyard year was finally upon them: the launch of this year's Signature Still Rosé. Tonight was their glitziest launch night yet, with 150 guests, delicious canapés, a live folk-pop band with an incredible singer, and of course, their rosé as the star.

Gemma had spent all day hanging lights, arranging chairs, answering a million questions and generally making sure that every problem had been foreseen. She hoped it was the case now that 7pm had rolled around. Martha and Skye had been doing precisely the same thing, but now it was time to switch into hostess mode and press the flesh. It was the Hunter sisters' time to shine.

Gemma walked into the kitchen where Barb, host of a super-successful Italian supper club, was putting the finishing touches to her canapés alongside her team. They all looked suitably Mediterranean and delicious. When she breathed in, the air tasted of olive oil, garlic, and basil. She already knew it would go perfectly with the rosé.

"All under control, Barb?"

"Everything is perfect." Barb swivelled and gave Gemma a thumbs-up. "All you need to worry about is looking beautiful for your guests, and you're already doing that, so well done."

She winked, wiped her hands on a tea towel, and went back to putting basil leaves on a tray of bruschetta.

Satisfied, Gemma walked into the main space, the glass wall retracted to make it big. The room shouted 'occasion!', all set up with tables and chairs, plus a few stands on the left with gifts to buy, and an enormous display of wine glasses ready to be filled once the guests arrived. Outside, the band were doing their sound-check. Skye squatted at the side of the stage, adjusting some wires.

Gemma's heart skipped a beat.

Skye could set up a nature trail, find new suppliers, take a wine tasting, and fix a mic.

She could also kiss like nobody Gemma had ever encountered before.

Skye was so fucking capable. Also, off-the-scale hot.

And still not hers.

After she had spoken with her sister, Gemma assumed she'd go out with Skye, tell her they could be together, and they'd give it a go. Instead, Skye had gone out with someone else, Gemma hadn't come clean to Martha, and then Skye had buggered off to Cornwall for four days "to clear her head". Gemma still had no idea what that meant. Clear her head of Gemma? Of her date? Of living here? She'd half-expected Skye to stay where she was, but she hadn't. She'd come back to work yesterday, and flung herself into preparations for the launch. Once it was out of the way, maybe Gemma would ask Skye on a date.

Scrap that, she definitely would. No more doubts. She had to make her intentions clear.

If she got shot down, so be it.

Skye stood, nodded at the lead singer, then threw her head back with a smile. She was a people person. They were lucky to have her. She finished chatting, then made her way back to the main space. When she saw Gemma, she paused for a split second – just as Gemma did – then walked towards her. She stopped when she was within touching distance.

"Ready for your big night?" She smiled, showing off her dimple.

Gemma gulped. "Ready as I'll ever be."

"The place looks great, the wine is knock-out, and the band sounds amazing, so I predict a hit." Skye paused. "Plus, you look incredible, too. Like if you put me in wine detention. I'd go willingly."

She didn't have a mirror, but she knew her cheeks had turned red. "I think most people would like to be put into wine detention, wouldn't they?" Gemma licked her lips and flicked her gaze up and down Skye. She was dressed in green, white, and red, the colours of the Italian flag. If Barb served Skye as a canapé, Gemma would demand her all for herself. She already knew she tasted delicious.

"You don't look so bad yourself." Gemma winced internally. That wasn't the compliment that was in her heart. But she'd said it now.

Skye looked over her shoulder. "Guests are arriving, so I better go greet people."

"Me, too."

They stared at each other for a beat too long.

Again.

"You're going to be great." Skye squeezed her hand.

Gemma froze to the spot.

Skye eyed her, gave a resigned shake of her head, then walked off to greet some guests she recognised.

* * *

Two hours later, the volume was cranked up, the chatter was constant, and the party was truly in full swing. The band had cracked out some crowd-pleasing covers of the likes of Fleetwood Mac, Taylor Swift, and Shania Twain, and the dance floor had been full for the past half hour. Skye ran a hand through her hair, and clutched her glass. The golden rule as the party host was never to actually drink, just be seen to be drinking. She'd been holding the same glass on and off all night. She still hadn't had a sip. She couldn't say the same for Lauren.

"I really like you having this job." Lauren's volume had gone up as the night wore on. "Much better than being stuck in Cornwall. Much better than being stuck in an office." She waved a hand. "Gorgeous place and free wine on tap. Lovely job!"

Skye grabbed an arancini ball from a nearby platter. She gave it to Lauren, whose hair was now almost orange-free. "Eat more food, please."

"On the contrary," Lauren said, wobbling to her left. "You need to drink more booze."

It was probably a mix of both.

"Eat."

Lauren did as she was told. "These are good!" she said, sounding surprised.

Skye leaned in. "Everything's good here," she whispered.

"Including the bosses who you're not allowed to sleep with

for spurious reasons. Only kissing allowed," Lauren replied, using a whispery voice that wasn't anything of the sort.

Skye glanced around, but nobody was within earshot.

"I spoke to her earlier, you know. *Gemma*." Lauren exaggerated her final word by opening her mouth really wide.

"I saw." She'd been concerned about what Lauren was saying, but Gemma hadn't seemed upset after the chat. "What did you say?"

Lauren rolled her eyes way back in her head. "Nothing bad, don't worry." She tapped the side of her nose. "Your secret is safe with me."

Martha walked by and squeezed Skye's arm. "How's everything here, all good?" She looked endlessly elegant in a spring-green sun dress, so different to her normal jeans, wellies and sweatshirt. Behind her, Harvey hovered, trying to look like he wasn't. Skye decided to pretend he wasn't there. It was easier that way.

"Everything's gone like a charm."

"It has, hasn't it?" Martha gave her a final squeeze, then walked towards the dance floor, where the band had just broken into a folk version of a Taylor Swift classic.

Lauren grabbed Skye's elbow. "I love this one, can we dance?"

Did she want to dance? She'd probably earned it. She was chatted out. Maybe something physical would be just the tonic.

She let Lauren drag her to the dance floor, where she was greeted by Martha and Harvey, who were trying to dance with each other like nothing was going on between them, and failing miserably. Or was that just because Skye knew? She couldn't quite work it out.

"Good to see you again." Harvey gave her an unsure grin. "Makes a change for you to be giving me free wine and not vice versa."

Skye smiled. "You're not wrong."

Lauren elbowed her, and she reluctantly introduced them. Skye wanted to look away as the realisation of who Harvey was dawned on Lauren. She held her breath, praying her friend wasn't about to out them to the whole party. But she didn't. Lauren simply smiled sweetly, and told Harvey it was lovely to meet him. Then the bassline kicked in, and everyone whooped and spun. When Skye did just that, Gemma walked towards her.

Shit. Martha looking stunning she could cope with.

Gemma looking as picturesque as her surroundings might be her undoing. But she had to stay strong. Even though Lauren was giving her maximum side-eye.

"Looks like the party's just getting started!" Gemma nudged Martha, waved to Harvey then settled in the weirdest dance circle of all time. Two almost-couples, and a drunk flatmate who knew all of Skye's secrets. Gemma's gaze settled on Skye, and she seemed about to say something to her, then thought better of it. Instead, she closed her eyes and gave in to the moment.

It didn't help Skye, whose internal heating system overloaded as Gemma swayed beside her, head back, silky neck exposed. Skye wanted to place her lips on Gemma's smooth skin and trail her tongue all the way to her full lips. This was pure torture, all of it. She gazed longingly at her, just as Gemma brought her head back and opened her eyes.

When she registered Skye's gaze fully on her, she blushed crimson, and turned her attention to her sister.

Skye blew out a long breath. She had to get off this dance floor. She needed a drink. It was high time she had one.

* * *

It was three in the morning when the alarm went off, and Gemma wasn't ready. Not after a night of dancing, drinking, and studiously not touching or staring at Skye. It had taken it out of her. She stumbled out of bed, dragged on her jeans, bundled up in her sweatshirt, puffa jacket, hat and gloves, then pulled on her sturdy trainers and gave herself a nod in her art-deco hallway mirror.

Skye had left before her, after Lauren had nearly fallen over a table. But Skye would be getting ready for the frost alarm right now, too. Gemma, Skye, and Leo. The intrepid trio. Gemma exhaled a very long breath. She could do this. She'd *have* to do this. She didn't have a choice. When it came to Skye, Gemma had fucked it up. Now it was her job to either work with it, or unfuck it.

Skye arrived on her bike just as Gemma pulled her front door shut. She recalled the first time they'd done a frost shift together. The wonder in Skye's eyes when she'd seen the bougies alight and the vineyard lit up. It was breath-taking, a little like tonight when Skye walked across the gravel and their gazes met.

Skye's jaw trembled as she approached. She licked her lips. "Hi."

Gemma blinked. Skye still had her bicycle clips on. Still adorable. "Hi."

Wow, they were avid conversationalists tonight.

They were still staring – they were doing that an awful lot

lately – when Leo opened the front door and stumbled out. "Steve! Come back!"

The terrier spun in a circle, gave a couple of half-hearted barks, then slunk back to Leo. He scooped the dog up, put him inside and slammed the door. Then he stamped over to them, banging his hands together.

"This whole deal of being woken up in the middle of the night seemed so fucking exciting when it first happened."

Gemma jolted at his words. "Leo!" She might not be his mum, but she still had to react to his swearing as an aunt.

"What?" He rolled his eyes. "Tell me I'm not telling the truth."

"He's telling the truth." Skye smiled. "Shall we get this done so I can get back to the warm bed I was so cruelly dragged away from?"

That thought made Gemma's eyes ping open wider. Skye in bed. Naked. Warm.

She mustn't fixate. It wasn't her place. She led the way to the tasting rooms, and they picked up the gas lighters in silence.

When they stepped out onto the vineyard, the dark night swallowed them up, tip-toeing over Gemma's skin. It was always like this. At first, the fields were desolate. But as soon as the bougies were lit, the magic happened. They each took a row and got to work. There was no time to moon over what might have been. There was work to do and vines to preserve. That had to be the focus for at least the next hour.

* * *

Once the bougies were ablaze and the air warm and smoky, Gemma sent a very grateful Leo back to his bed. He didn't need a second invitation, giving them both a hug as he left.

"Don't do anything I wouldn't do!" he trilled as he walked off, giving Gemma a sly grin.

Turned out, her nephew was cleverer than she gave him credit for. If he was her friend, she'd tell him to fuck off, but she couldn't do that when she'd told him off for swearing earlier. Instead, she followed his retreating form, before taking a deep breath and turning back to Skye.

"You can go, too, if you like." Gemma clenched her toes, her calves, her heart. If Skye did go, she might walk into the tasting rooms and down a bottle of their best fizz. To toast her bad decisions and the smouldering wreck of her love life. Not that it had been that smouldering in the first place.

But Skye shook her head. "And leave you to put out all the flames alone? I wouldn't do that. I wouldn't leave you in the lurch." She inclined her head. "Shall we go back to the barn and make a cuppa?"

"Or we could have some wine?" It wasn't like she hadn't done it before with her sister. There was something about late nights in the vineyard. They were times of reflection however much you tried to avoid them.

Skye gave her a semi-grin. "I thought that wasn't allowed? 'Calamitous' I believe you told me."

"Maybe I'm in the mood for some calamity."

"Let's have both." Skye scanned Gemma's face as she spoke. "I need the tea to warm me up first."

They entered the main building, which had been restored to order, save for the furniture being out of place. She switched on the heater, then went into the kitchen at the back.

Skye followed. "You'd never guess we had a party here tonight. The staff did a great job clearing up."

"They did." Was it Gemma's imagination, or was Skye standing closer than she needed to?

Whatever she was doing, it made Gemma's breathing go shallow, and her concentration waver. What was she doing? Tea bags. Milk. Mugs.

"How was your weekend in Cornwall?" She brought her gaze up to meet Skye's as she poured the hot water into the mugs. "You're not going to tell me Amanda's realised she made a huge mistake and you're running back there, are you?" It was a joke, but it made her breath pause even so.

Skye snorted. "Not quite. It was lovely to go back and see old friends. But it's not where my life is now." She stared at Gemma, her crystal blue gaze open and honest. "This is where I want to be."

A tremor ran through Gemma. That was promising at least.

"In this tasting barn forever?"

"Not quite. But this side of the country. This vineyard, this area, wherever life takes me. I've done west, and that's in my past now."

Gemma handed her a mug of tea and they walked out to the bar, settling at a table overlooking the vineyard.

"That's good to hear. That you're staying. And not buggering off after everything." She gulped as she spoke. "Did you see Amanda?"

A shake of Skye's head. "Amazingly, no. I fully expected it and I was on guard all weekend, but it never happened. I even went to a local supermarket because Justin dragged me, which I thought was exceedingly brave."

"We met over an aubergine." Gemma smiled at the recollection.

"Over an aubergine, in a bar, at a tasting. We have a habit of bumping into each other, don't we?"

"Even when you're on a date."

"I won't be doing that again anytime soon." Skye paused, as if trying to conjure just the right words before she committed to them. She stared at the lit-up vineyard for a few moments before she opened her mouth to speak. "I went to Cornwall to get my head together. To sort out my feelings. Mainly my feelings for you." Skye flicked her gaze to Gemma's face and fixed it there.

Gemma couldn't move even if she wanted to.

She didn't.

A spark of desire landed in her gut. She let it flare, and travel through her body. She hoped the next few sentences out of Skye's mouth were going to be positive, otherwise she might need to uncork that wine quicker than expected.

"They came into sharp focus on my date that you crashed. Which I shouldn't have gone on. It wasn't fair to her, or to me. I already like someone else far too much for any other dates to mean a thing." Skye leaned forward and placed her fingers on Gemma's arm. "That someone's you, by the way."

"Thank fuck for that." Gemma's eyelids fluttered closed for a millisecond. "If you'd said you met someone else at your mate's bar and ended up kissing the life out of them, I really would have had to grab a bottle of wine and down it in one."

"Not the new rosé? That deserves to be savoured."

"It deserves whatever the moment demands," Gemma replied. "Tell me more about these feelings."

215

Skye's lips were just as alluring as ever.

She shook her head. "You know I like you. You know we gel. But I know your rules, so I needed to get away to think about things. To see if I had made a mistake leaving Cornwall. I hadn't. You know what I decided?"

Gemma shook her head, then held her breath. She honestly had no idea. She dared to dream that Skye had decided she wanted her, but she had no right to demand it. But still, her frantic heartbeat showed the outcome she most desired. The result she hoped she wasn't too late to dream of.

"That I didn't need a break. What I needed was things to change here. I'm not exactly sure what that means, but change is needed."

More desire crashed through Gemma. She tried to make it look like it was nothing. It wasn't an easy thing to do.

"I agree," she whispered.

Skye blinked. "You do?"

"Uh-huh. Martha and I talked about our rules on our night out."

"You spoke to Martha about changing the rules? That's a relief. I wondered if she'd speak to you, too."

Weird response, but Gemma crashed on. "Anyway, we did speak about it. And I've got things to tell you. I haven't stopped thinking about you for one moment since we kissed. Not the first time or the second. We keep dancing around, and I can't do it anymore. I'm fed up of fighting my feelings, and really, why should I? I'm not my dad, like you said. I haven't done anything wrong. So yes, I spoke to Martha. We haven't said exactly what will change yet, but it will be something. I hope it's enough to convince you that I want us to happen."

"What about dating someone you work with? You were very adamant."

"I was very stupid. I don't give a fuck about the rules, or work. I'll sack myself if I have to. It means that much, Skye. You mean that much."

Skye stared, her face flushed. She took a sip of tea.

Gemma wished she'd say something. But she didn't. Nervous energy rushed around Gemma's system and she rose. "I'm going to let you ponder your response while I get wine. Lots of wine. All the wine we have if you're about to tell me to fuck off."

Gemma didn't stick around to see what Skye said.

Instead, she hotfooted it to the kitchen, and hoped when she returned, Skye was still there.

Chapter Twenty-Three

Follow her in and kiss her.

The thought pounded in Skye's head as she got up and walked to the tasting room's kitchen. When she got there, Gemma's denim-clad bum greeted her, bent over the fridge door, selecting the wine. She closed the fridge door with a thud, turned, then jumped when she saw Skye standing there. She put a hand to her chest.

"Fuck! You scared the shit out of me." Gemma took a deep breath, then put the bottle on the counter.

Skye moved towards her. She had no idea what she was going to do, but she had to do *something*.

"I'm really bored of talking about the attraction we have for each other." When she got within touching distance of Gemma, she stopped. Her heart thudded in her chest, and her knees almost buckled. She was such a cliché, it was almost comical. She'd finally found a woman who made her knees go weak, but said woman hadn't made herself at all available.

Until this moment.

Until her coded message fell from her lips.

For something to do with her hands apart from slide them all over Gemma, Skye picked up the bottle of fizz, undid the wire, then grabbed a tea towel and popped the cork. The sound echoed around the kitchen, and Skye glanced down to where the air had turned slightly whiter across the top of the bottle as the gas swirled around the opening.

Gemma didn't look at her as she handed over the two champagne flutes.

Skye filled them without a word.

The only sound in the kitchen was their mingled heavy breathing, and the pop of the golden bubbles in the glass.

Skye sucked on her top lip before she dared to speak. "Would you say we're a little like a bottle of fizz? Although, thankfully we haven't had to ferment and stew for two years. Three months has been long enough. Two years might have tipped me over the edge."

"I would have shattered way before two years."

"I really hope so." Something fluttered in Skye's chest. "We put the bottle containing us on the shelf. Are we finally going to pop the cork?" Even saying the words sent a cascade of lust through Skye, which settled, well, everywhere: in her centre, in her mind, in her heart that was about to burst.

"Will you shut up and kiss me?"

Skye's mouth curled into a *fuck-yes* grin, then she closed the gap between them and pressed her lips to Gemma. She tasted exactly as she had the two times she'd kissed her before. She tasted of tomorrow, of the day after that, and the day after that. She tasted like the path that stretched from her head to her heart. She tasted like connection. Like promise. Like home.

Then, everything sped up and out of control.

In the best possible way.

Gemma pushed her up against the kitchen counter, and all Skye's feelings popped, just like the cork, spilling out all over the pair of them. Hot, sticky, insistent dreams. It didn't even matter it was happening in an industrial kitchen. The kitchen staff were spotless, and they'd left it pristine.

Clean surfaces for them to mess up.

Easy surfaces for them to wipe down afterwards.

That thought alone made Skye smile into Gemma's mouth, as the counter pressed into her bum.

Gemma pulled back and surveyed her, eyes half shut. "What are you grinning about in the middle of kissing me?"

"Just that the kitchen surfaces would be easy to wipe down. Just in case this progresses."

Gemma's gaze narrowed. "This is definitely progressing." Then she caressed Skye's breast, pulled her close, and slipped her hot tongue into Skye's mouth. Her kisses were hard, hungry, full of a sureness that surprised Skye. No hesitation. Like she knew where she belonged, and it was right here.

Skye's mind scrambled, and every drop of blood in her body flowed south. From being very anchored where she was, Gemma's kisses suddenly left her all at sea in the best possible way. Then Gemma's hand slid under her top, connecting with her bare skin. Skye sucked in a breath. Gemma bit her bottom lip, then pulled back, eyes wide.

"You drive me crazy, you know that?"

"I do?" This was news to Skye.

"Uh-huh. Every day, I've had to keep my hands off you." Gemma's eyes were dark pools of want. "And every day, I could never touch you. Never kiss you. Never fuck you." She shook her head. "How I've wanted to fuck you."

Ohmyfuckingdays. It took everything Skye had not to strip off there and then, fling herself onto the kitchen island and surrender herself to Gemma's hands, tongue, toy, whatever she wanted to use.

Their eyes locked. Gemma took a very deep breath, then moved her hands to Skye's jeans. She undid the top button, and lowered the zip.

Skye's muscles tensed in the most crazy, delicious way. "I've wanted you to fuck me, too."

Gemma eased Skye's jeans down and off her legs, then slipped two fingers down the front of her briefs.

This was prime knee-buckling territory. Skye reached behind her and held onto the counter with both hands. Then she spread her legs as far as she could, as Gemma pressed her hips into Skye, and brought their lips level once more.

If there was a heat sensor on Skye right now, it would glow red at her core. It took everything she had not to float away.

"How much have you wanted me to fuck you?" Gemma's green eyes swirled dark.

Even in Skye's wildest dreams, this was never how it had gone. Yet here they were. Gemma's warm fingers travelling south, and Skye wondering where her next breath was coming from if Gemma kept on stealing every one. She wanted to answer Gemma's question, but she couldn't find the words.

Instead, Skye moved a shaky hand from the counter, leaned all her weight on the other, then placed her free one on top of Gemma's hand and pressed it into herself.

"This much," she whispered, as Gemma's fingers moved to where she wanted it most.

Skye's knees buckled as the breath flew out of her. But Gemma's other arm was around her, holding her up.

"I've got you," she whispered into Skye's ear as in one

slick move, she slid a finger inside Skye, and her tongue into her mouth.

Skye let out an involuntary gasp, bucked her hips, then allowed a beam to spread across her face. Yes, she'd wanted this, and yes, Gemma was proving there was more to her than meets the eye. Skye was here for it, and she was going to enjoy every second. So, it seemed, was Gemma, as she shed Skye's underwear.

The next few minutes were a blur of action, bliss, and a feeling of inevitability. That this had only ever been a matter of time. Skye moved her hips and spread her legs to give Gemma the best access. Gemma's fingers moved slowly in and out of Skye.

Gemma's lips on Skye's were wild; her fingers were no different. Every slow movement inside her set off a wave of pure starlight, one that filled Skye with a silvery glow. It was like she'd been living in darkness her whole life, and Gemma held the switch all along. To think, they might never have met; that she might never have known such aching, rollicking, sugary bliss. It was unthinkable right now.

"Is this okay?" Gemma asked, her cheeks flushed.

"More than okay," Skye replied, swamped with pleasure.

Gemma simply grinned, slipped out of Skye and found her clit.

Skye threw back her head and squeezed her eyes tight shut. When she'd first kissed Gemma in Cornwall, she'd wanted her to touch her. When she'd watched her fingers caress a wine bottle, she wanted to be that bottle. She'd waited so long to have Gemma just where she wanted her. Tongue in Skye's mouth. Fingers caressing Skye's clit. Her lips whispering sweet nothings in her ear.

"You're so wet." Gemma's strokes were long and sure.

"I know," Skye rasped. "It was all that talk of corks popping."

Gemma threw back her head and let out the sexiest laugh Skye had ever heard. "Let's see if we can truly pop your cork, shall we?"

Gemma slipped another finger inside, pressed it home, and Skye's brain fried. Sunshine yellow leaked into her periphery vision, as red-hot desire streaked through her, landing in her core. Flecks of orange and purple fizzed in her brain, as Gemma flicked and pressed her into the most multi-coloured orgasm she'd ever experienced.

Maybe it was to do with Gemma being an artist. By day, she was a wizard with paint on canvas. By night, her canvas was Skye's body, and Gemma was painting a bona fide masterpiece. When her fingers zoned in and gave Skye just what she needed, her whole body shook and an explosion of want and desire flooded her, leaving her floored.

Nothing in her previous experience had prepared her for this. Not any of her previous lovers, and certainly not Amanda with her selfish attitude. This rush of pure release was fresh and wholly intense. She'd never had an orgasm with someone she wanted this much. With someone who wanted *her* this much. Something slotted into place in her soul, something that made Skye's eyes spring open.

Gemma took that moment to sink to her knees, part Skye's legs as far as they'd go, then suck her to another orgasm, this time one that made Skye clamp her hands to the counter for dear life. She bit down on her bottom lip, drawing blood. It was all worth it. All the hours of staring. All the minutes of hoping. All the weeks of longing. Because now, Gemma was on her knees, her tongue on Skye, and as a final rush of want drenched her, Skye uttered, "Oh Gemma!"

Her whole body shook, then she, too, sank to the ground.

On the floor, Gemma kissed Skye's eyelids, her cheeks, her hair. Then she put an arm around her.

"You're fucking spectacular, you know that?"

For once, Skye did. Gemma had made her feel it in every ounce of her being. In every way that she touched her. Now, when she opened her eyes and gazed into Gemma's own, she saw it in her stare, too. Gemma really thought that. She wanted her in just the way that Skye wanted Gemma, too.

A heat stole through Skye, even though she was semi-naked. It didn't matter. She was in Gemma's arms, and things had definitely moved on to the next level. That was what mattered most. They were no longer kissing buddies. She hoped they were more than fuck buddies. For that to happen, she'd have to return the favour. Was that going to be in this kitchen, too?

"What are you smiling about?" Gemma's voice broke into Skye's thoughts.

Skye laughed. "You don't want to know."

Another kiss to her brow.

She could get very used to this.

"I really do."

Skye took a deep breath. "I was just thinking that of all the places I expected us to get it on, this kitchen did not feature." She glanced to one side, then the other. "I'm currently half-naked with my arse hovering over the kitchen floor. I don't think you're going to be painting this picture any time soon."

Gemma raised an eyebrow. "Au contraire," she replied.

"When you posed for me the other day, all I could think of was that I wanted to paint you naked. I still need to see you fully naked, by the way."

"It can be arranged."

Gemma grinned. "Just so you know, this is a first, too. I've never in my life shagged anyone in this kitchen before."

"I'm glad."

"But while this was spontaneous and hot, we should get back outside where we can see the bougies. We've already left them long enough."

Skye's eyes widened. "If the vineyard's gone up in smoke, please say you forgive me."

"I forgive you. Martha, however, will kill us both." Gemma kissed her cheek and jumped up. Then she washed her hands, giving Skye a sly grin. "I'm going out there, and I'll leave you to get sorted." She picked up the bottle of fizz. "Plus, now there really is something to toast. Rosé launch and the day I finally fucked Skye Tuck."

Skye eyed her, gathering the strength to get up, too. "Sex on the premises. It's very out of character, but I like it. How are you feeling?"

Gemma put a hand to her mouth. "Butch."

"You should be," Skye laughed. "I approve of this side of you, just in case you were wondering."

"I think I do, too." Gemma paused. "Will you bring the glasses?"

"Once I've pulled my knickers up and got my breath back, yes."

* * *

"I don't quite know how, but it looks even more beautiful now." Skye sat at the table next to Gemma on the upstairs balcony, and put the glasses in front of them. Outside, hundreds of paraffin candles danced in the moonlight, and Skye thanked whatever higher power had introduced her to Gemma in the first place, and whatever had brought her back to Surrey so they could meet again.

Somehow, Gemma had turned into her north star, and going back to Cornwall had only heightened that sense. Nothing had felt right there. Yet as soon as she was back in Surrey, she'd felt at peace. Places you belonged were never about the location itself. They were always about the people, the memories you held, and the ones you hoped to make. Gemma and Skye fell very much into the final category. They'd made a good start tonight.

Gemma poured the wine, then held up her glass to Skye. "To us. To whatever started here tonight. People have always told me that getting up for frost alarms was romantic. I always told them to try seven nights in a row, which is what we had to do three years ago."

Skye laughed. "That's brutal. And you never had sex in the kitchen to cheer you up."

"Exactly." Gemma leaned over until their lips were close. "But this right here? This is romantic. Sex, then sharing a glass of fizz with you under the stars. I couldn't have written it better."

"If I'd written it, maybe I would have had a softer surface to fall down on post-orgasm than the kitchen floor."

"I disagree. Writing's all about drama, right? That's drama. Having sex in a bed is boring. I've said it before and I'm sticking to my guns."

"Wow, I'm learning a lot of things about you today. Here I am, a bed enthusiast, and there you are, an exhibitionist. Is this going to be an issue before we've even begun?"

Gemma laughed. "I hope not. I didn't hear any complaints from you earlier."

"Absolutely no complaints here." Skye brought her lips to Gemma's and kissed her. Slowly at first, then deeper, richer. She didn't know how much time had passed when she pulled back and stared at Gemma's perfect cheekbones, her delicate mouth. "You can take me whenever and however you want to."

A smirk crawled onto Gemma's face. "Music to my ears." She sat back and blew out a long breath. "But right now, shall we actually drink this wine we uncorked." Gemma clinked her glass, and they drank. "What are the tasting notes on this again?"

Skye's mind was blank. "You might have to fill me in. My mind's still a blur."

Gemma held up her glass and swirled. The moonlight caught the faint bubbles in the glass. "This wine has been matured for two years in bottles, and it's perfect for drinking in the early morning." She laid a hand on Skye's knee.

The effect washed through Skye like an energy burst.

"Especially after you've just had sex in the kitchen and want to revel in that a little longer," Gemma added, kissing Skye's shoulder.

Now they'd finally touched, it was impossible not to stay connected at all times.

Skye picked up the bottle and ran a finger over the label. "It actually says that on the tasting notes? What are the chances?"

They shared a grin, then a kiss, then sipped their wine.

"Does this mean you won't be having a second date with Erica?"

"I think it might." Skye turned her head and caught Gemma's stare. "I shouldn't have gone out with her. I was just mad at you. But now you're going to sack yourself, everything's fine." She lifted one eyebrow. "For clarity, I'm not expecting you to sack yourself."

Gemma drank some more wine and turned her head back to the scene outside. "I am sorry about it all. Keeping you a secret. I wasn't being fair to you. I shouldn't have kissed you in the vines and then pulled everything back. I have to be in or out, I get that."

"For further clarity, I'm glad you kissed me in the vines, just not the part that came afterwards."

"I know."

"But thanks for saying you're sorry. I don't want to be your dirty little secret. In fact, it's the very last thing I want."

Gemma reached out a hand and ran it through Skye's hair.

Skye closed her eyes. It felt gorgeous to be touched like this. Delicately. Intimately. By someone who mattered.

"When the candles are all out, do you want to come back to mine?"

Skye smiled. She could think of nothing she'd like more.

"I love you."

Holy fuck, that is *not* what she meant to come out of her mouth. If she was on her bike right now, she'd be desperately back-pedalling.

Skye sat forward, heat crawling over her skin. "I mean, I'd *love to*. Not, I love *you*." Skye winced. "Although I do love you."

Stop it! "But that might be my orgasm talking. Or the wine. Or the fact that I do love you." Her mouth was a runaway train, and it was never coming back.

Gemma stared, but said nothing.

An awkward tension hovered on the balcony.

Skye flexed her toes, then faked a yawn. She wanted to break free of this particular moment as quickly as possible and never speak of it again. Why had it spurted out of her mouth in the first place?

Although it did make her wonder.

Did Gemma have feelings for her, too?

She wasn't going to ask now. Not when they'd just had sex for the first time.

She wasn't needy.

Much.

She held up her glass and wished she could rewind the last couple of minutes. But she couldn't.

"To us?"

Gemma wouldn't meet her gaze. "To us."

Chapter Twenty-Four

Gemma woke up later that day with a warm arm across her back. It took her a few minutes to remember what had happened, but when she did, a liquid grin crept across her face. She moved her eyes, then her head ever so slowly. She didn't want to wake Skye, or break the spell. This moment was perfect. She wanted to keep it that way. However, her bladder had other ideas.

Eventually, after a few minutes she had to move. She picked up Skye's arm and moved it gently to her side of the bed.

Skye opened her eyes and gave Gemma a bleary smile. "Morning."

"Actually afternoon, but let's not get hung up on technicalities." Gemma kissed her lips.

"What time is it?"

"Just after midday. We got back at five, and I'd say we've had a good three hours sleep?"

"Generous." Skye gave her a sultry smile. The one that had got them into this trouble in the first place.

"Totally worth it. I messaged Martha to tell her we'd be late. The perks of being a boss."

Gemma jumped out of the bed and ran to the loo. When she walked back in, she kicked the pile of clothes on the floor, discarded quickly once they came home in the early hours.

Skye wrapped her in her arms again. Perfection was back on the menu.

"I missed you." Skye kissed her cheek.

Gemma rolled her eyes. "Did you pine the whole time I was in the bathroom?"

"Sobbed."

"That's what I like to hear." Gemma slung a foot over Skye's leg, and shuffled into her embrace as far as she could. She was happy to note that Skye was a hugger. "Did you sleep okay?"

"The little I got was divine. I slept like a log. A well-fucked log, obviously."

"My favourite kind."

"Mine, too." Skye kissed Gemma's lips, then pulled back. "How do you manage to look so perfect, by the way? Your hair looks like you just styled it. I bet mine's sticking up at all angles."

"I used my brush in the bathroom."

"You cheated."

"I cleaned my teeth, too. Got to reel you in with fake news before I present you with the facts."

"I'm sure I'll like the real news, too." Skye stifled a yawn.

"Your eyelashes are still illegally long this morning, just in case you were wondering." Gemma paused. "Any regrets? You didn't spend the whole time I was in the bathroom working out how you could slip out of my bed and out of my life?"

"Slipping out of your life would be pretty hard." Skye crinkled her forehead. "No regrets here. Unless you do, then I reserve the right to change my mind."

Gemma shook her head. "Nope. This was what I wanted to do last night, this morning, and if I'm honest, ever since we met. I know I've fought against it, I've put up barriers, but we make sense. Times change, don't they?"

"Apparently they do, and I'm glad. Otherwise, I might still be in a hotel in Cornwall trying to avoid my ex every day." Skye shivered. "Meeting you was the catalyst, so thank you."

Gemma shrugged. "You were the one who made the decision and moved here. That was nothing to do with me. So I shouldn't get all the credit. Maybe two per cent."

"I'll give you ten. Especially if we factor in that you're one of the main reasons I stayed here. This job. Your smile. You." Skye went to say something else, but then stopped.

Was she going to say she loved her again? Gemma had skilfully navigated around that last night, but she wasn't sure she'd be able to do it a second time. She wasn't ready to say it. It was too soon. The quicker she could steer Skye off the topic, the better.

"Sweet talker, but I'll take it." Gemma rolled onto her back and exhaled.

"Big sigh."

She crooked her right arm above her head on the pillow, then turned to Skye.

She did love her.

She was pretty sure.

It just took her longer to get there.

"It's not about you, more about me. I was just thinking, you were right about what you said. That I'm not cheating on anyone, that I'm not my dad. I guess I saw the destructive pattern that relationships with staff could wield. But I know they can work, too. You just have to be honest and open about them. I haven't been so far, but things are going to change."

"You're not your dad. If you start shagging one of the Saturday staff, then we have an issue."

"Although Polly is cute."

Skye elbowed Gemma in the ribs. "I agree, but no sleeping with Polly."

"Got it," Gemma replied with a grin. "But I promise, no more secrets. If we're going to make a go of it, it's a must-have. Honesty and openness."

Skye blinked, then rolled into Gemma. "We're making a go of this?"

"I think we are." Gemma's skin tingled with happiness.

Skye slung a leg over her, then stopped. "One other thing. When you were talking about secrets and changing your rules. What did your sister say?"

"That the rules were outdated. That we both needed all the help we could get when it comes to love and relationships." Gemma couldn't quite read Skye's face, but she looked... puzzled. She had no idea why. "Should she not have said that?"

"No, she definitely should have." Skye stroked Gemma's naked torso. "Just, speak to her."

"About us?" Gemma replied. "I plan to, but I thought it best to speak to you about it first. Just to be sure you were in before I told my sister."

Skye smiled. "The correct order. But speak to your sister."

Gemma slid slightly away from Skye, pushing her body up the bed. "What secrets is Martha keeping from me?"

"None that I know of."

But Skye wouldn't meet her gaze.

What did Skye know that she didn't? And *why* did she know something she didn't?

"What's going on?"

"Nothing. It's not a big thing, but speak to her."

Skye pulled Gemma towards her, then rolled on top. She settled her body weight, a knowing smile on her face. As their naked skin pressed together, Skye let out a low, primal groan.

Heat roared in Gemma. She wasn't sure what Skye had been hinting at, but Gemma wasn't going to ask now. If this was her idea of distraction technique, it worked well. Having Skye on top of her was sheer bliss, from the curl of her toes to the whisper of hair falling into Gemma's eyes. She was here for it all.

"Is this your way of changing the subject?"

"Is it working?"

Gemma licked her lips and wiggled her arse. "It seems to be." She'd talk to Martha later. For now, she had far more pressing matters. The big thing about it, too? Quite often Gemma woke up paralysed with fear about having a woman in her bed. Mainly because all the previous ones hadn't worked out very well. But with Skye, there was none of that. Gemma was properly at ease. It didn't feel weird to have Skye naked in bed with her. It just felt right. Like this was the way it should have been all along. Gemma could kick herself for not acting sooner. But at least she'd got the ball rolling.

"Back to what you were saying earlier." Skye moved her body to the left, then slipped a hand between Gemma's legs. "We're making a go of this, are we?"

Gemma's thighs tingled. Her heart began to thump fast. "I'd like to if you would."

She moved her legs apart, then threw an arm around Skye's neck. She knew exactly what was coming, yet, she knew nothing. Skye was the great unknown. A surprise Gemma was still processing. She'd wiped the slate clean, and Gemma was ready to start again. To give it her all. "You're making me believe in fairy tales."

Skye responded by sliding a finger into her. "Let me make you believe a little more."

Gemma stared up into Skye's bright blue eyes. They told her to relax. To let Skye take it from here. Skye's finger trailed up and through her slick core.

Gemma sucked in a huge breath.

Then Skye was back inside her, all around her, stealing breath after breath with her skilled lips, but breathing life back into Gemma with every sweep of her tongue, every touch of her hand. It was crazy, it wasn't what Gemma was used to, but that made it all the more glorious.

This morning felt different, too. Last night, the first time had been frenzied. Something inside Gemma had snapped. She simply had to have Skye in the kitchen. They'd laughed about it later, but it had been primal. Rough. Hot.

Today, they knew each other that tiny bit more. Knew a little about what the other liked. Not everything. That would come. But enough. They were no longer a blank page to each other. It would take some time to fill in the whole picture, but that was part of the process. Gemma couldn't wait for the next part. Neither, it seemed, could Skye, as she moved down Gemma's body, never taking her fingers away. When her mouth was at the same level, she stopped.

Gemma glanced down.

This would never get old.

"Have I told you how sexy you look between my legs?"

Apparently, overnight she'd turned into a lothario.

"Wait until I've got my tongue on your clit." Skye raised an eyebrow.

Desire flooded every ounce of Gemma. "Don't tease, then," she growled.

Skye gave her a final look, then lowered her gaze, before she slowly placed her tongue at the base of Gemma's clit and swept it upwards.

Gemma melted into the bed. Right at this moment, she had no idea where she ended and Skye began. What's more, she didn't care.

Was this the best morning she'd had in a long time?

Hands down.

Could she get used to starting every single day like this?

Hell, yes.

She'd spent far too long on her own. Far too long worrying about the business. They were doing well, now. They had a good reputation. It was time to work on her reputation as red-hot lover. Starting right now.

Chapter Twenty-Five

They made it into the office by 2pm, after a shower, a grilled cheese sandwich and a very strong coffee. When Skye checked her phone, there were a bunch of messages from Lauren.

'Please let me know you've fallen into Gemma's bed and not down a well. Your mum would want to know about one, not about the other.'

Skye smirked, then messaged back.

'Not in a well ;0)'

Lauren sent back a row of dancing ladies, along with one word: 'Halle-fucking-lujah!'.

Once they were ready, they walked the short distance from Gemma's house, down the lane to the main building. As they approached the door to the offices, Skye squeezed Gemma's bum.

That brought a stern look.

Skye immediately removed her hand.

"No touching," Gemma hissed. "Not until I've said something to Martha." She glanced left, then right. "There are eyes everywhere in this place, and I'm sure Leo suspected something last night."

They stepped into the offices, but there was nobody there.

Martha was probably in the vineyard, her favourite place to be.

"Leo didn't suspect a thing. He's 15. He's too wrapped up in himself to think about his aunt."

Gemma frowned. "You might be right. But still."

Skye held up both palms either side of her face. "I promise these hands will come nowhere near you. Even though that will be hard after the past 12 hours we've shared."

Gemma grinned. "You're not kidding there."

"But I know your relationship with Martha is more important. So go open your emails, and I'll make us both a coffee." She paused. "But you definitely shouldn't come in the kitchen with me. You've no idea what might happen."

When Skye returned, Gemma was staring at her screen. She looked up, and her face softened. Even more so when Skye handed her a coffee.

"Thank you. I think I might need this to stay awake today."

"You and me both."

Gemma snagged her gaze. "But it was worth it. All of it. I'd do it all again. Especially the bit where you fucked me in the hallway." Then she got up, took Skye's mug from her hand and pulled her close.

"I thought this was exactly what you told me not to do? I'm getting very mixed signals…" Skye's words were swallowed by Gemma's lips as she brought them together. They kissed like that for a few moments, until a gust of wind flew in and ruffled Skye's hair. She broke apart from Gemma, but it was too late.

Martha stood at the office door, staring.

Skye winced, then took a step back.

"What's going on?" Martha waved a hand. "I mean, I can see what's going on, but what the hell, Gem?"

Gemma sprang around the desk, and shook her head. "This is just what I didn't want to happen." She looked at Martha. "This isn't what it looks like."

"It's not?" Confusion and suspicion stained Martha's voice.

"Isn't it?" echoed Skye. Of all the things she'd expected to come from Gemma's mouth, that wasn't it.

Gemma didn't look her way. "I mean, this is new. It only just happened. It's not something I've been hiding from you."

Skye frowned, but said nothing. Gemma was trying to play this like they were new? The unexpected blow winded her. Yes, they'd only just slept together, but this had started way back in Cornwall. With that stunning kiss at the bar. But nothing had been plain sailing ever since. She had no reason to believe it would start being so now. All she had was Gemma's word. However, at the first sign of trouble, Gemma had rowed back.

Skye took a deep breath and crossed her arms over her chest. This was between the two sisters. She'd keep her mouth shut. For now. But something needed to be said later on.

"I can't believe you wouldn't tell me this. After everything from our past." Martha put a hand to her chest, as if to steady her emotions.

Guilt draped itself over Skye. Despite what she knew about Martha. When Skye glanced at Gemma, her face had drained of colour. If Skye felt bad, she could only imagine how Gemma was feeling. But then again, she'd brought it on herself. Now was the time to change it. Just as she'd promised she would.

"Plus, isn't Skye dating someone else?" Martha shook her head slowly. "After everything we've gone through, are you really going down the route of our dad and having an affair? I knew something was going on, but you repeatedly denied it."

She had some nerve, Skye had to hand it to her. Although when she said the final part, a flash of guilt crossed her face. She quickly wiped it away.

"I guess this explains why you wanted to talk about the rules and how they weren't helping you." Martha cupped her right hand behind the back of her neck and exhaled. "And now you going all quiet on anniversary night at the pub makes sense, too." She pointed at Skye. "You taking time off last week, was that connected?"

Gemma shook her head vehemently. "It's not like that, and I'm not like Dad. Please don't say that, it's the worst thing you could possibly say. This is something that really has only just started. Last night, in fact. I wanted to talk to you about it first because if it's going to cause a problem, we need to discuss it."

Now Skye couldn't stay silent.

"Excuse me?" She stared at Gemma. "We haven't just started, Gemma. This has been rumbling for months. And are you saying I'm a problem? That this might not work? Because that's not what you said in bed this morning." It was like Gemma was Jekyll and Hyde.

Gemma blushed furiously, then screwed up her face. "Of course not."

"Then why aren't you telling the truth? After everything we said, you're still lying. I don't know your dad, but maybe Martha's right. Maybe you did pick up some tricks from him."

As soon as it was out of her mouth, Skye knew it was the wrong thing to say. The words tasted grim, and when Gemma's face twisted in anguish, she wanted to grab them back and bury them. But they were out, and they'd slapped Gemma in the face. Hard. If Skye had wanted to make a point, she'd done it with aplomb.

She had to try to rectify what she'd said.

"Gemma," Skye began.

"Just don't. I'm trying to talk about things with my sister, and you bring my dad up? How dare you? You don't know me that well, and you don't know him. Don't go treading where you don't belong."

Ouch. Gemma was giving as good as she got. Yes, Skye had overstepped, but so had Gemma.

Skye couldn't quite comprehend how quickly this had unravelled.

A few hours ago, they'd been in bed. Now, she looked at Gemma and realised she didn't know her at all. Maybe there was a reason she'd been holding her and them at arm's length. Because she truly wasn't ready.

"You know what, you're right. Maybe I don't belong here. I've tried to belong for the past three months, but you've constantly pushed me away. If you can't tell your sister we're an item and that this has been on the cards since we met in Cornwall, that's all I need to know." Skye turned to Martha. "But before I leave, if you're coming in here and pointing fingers, maybe you need to be honest, too."

Martha raised her gaze to Skye, then dropped it abruptly. "What do you mean?" Her tone was unsure, but Skye swore she saw a flickering of understanding behind her eyes.

Skye inclined her head. "Really Martha? You're not going to fess up about you and Harvey? Don't even try to deny it, I saw you with my own eyes kissing him. Before you come in here talking about being honest and open, it's a two-way street." She exhaled. "I'm not even sure why I'm sticking up for Gemma when she clearly thinks I'm disposable, but maybe that says more about her than me."

"What the hell is she talking about, you and Harvey?" Gemma did a double-take.

Martha made an anguished face, then bowed her head.

"You and Harvey? Juliette's brother? Seriously, Martha?"

Behind Martha, two cars full of hens arrived, the women tripping out onto the gravel in jeans, branded T-shirts and tiaras.

Martha shut the door properly. "Can we keep the noise down? We're still open, still working."

"Who's doing this tasting?" Gemma asked. Like they were in the middle of a normal morning.

"Annabel, with Katy, Polly and Leo on clear-up," Martha replied.

"I guess if we're not together, you can go ahead and shag Polly, now." Skye hadn't meant to spit the words, but that's how they came out.

Martha frowned, her stare drilling Gemma. "You're shagging Polly too? What the hell?"

Right at that moment, Leo strolled through the car park. When he saw his mum, aunt and Skye, he walked up to the office door with a smile.

Martha opened it a touch, and told him to go straight into the tasting room. He looked puzzled, but took the hint and left.

She shut the door and turned back to her sister. "What's this about shagging Polly?"

Gemma blew out a long breath. "Nobody is shagging Polly. I'm barely shagging Skye. Unlike you and Harvey, so stop trying to change the subject. How long have you been seeing him behind my back?" She creased her forehead, then put a palm to her cheek. "I really can't believe this. After everything you just said to me, you were doing the same thing?"

"I wanted to tell you, but the timing was never right. I tried to tell you after the anniversary dinner, but your head was elsewhere. Now I know why."

"You should have tried harder!" Gemma's voice shook the rafters of the office.

Martha flinched at the volume, as did Skye. However, neither said a word.

Gemma put her gaze to the ceiling, then back to her sister. "Every time I see him, he asks after you." She shook her head. "You were dancing together last night." Another pause. "Now I know why you agreed so readily to us changing the rules, too. I'm such an idiot."

Martha clasped her hands tight. She looked like she'd rather be anywhere else in the world but here. "You're not an idiot."

Skye had heard enough. "As charming as this family chat is, I'm going to leave you to work out what you both want because honestly, you need to be a bit more open with each other. If you had been in the first place, maybe things would have worked out better." She turned to Gemma. "Gemma, Martha is seeing Harvey." She wasn't sure where this bravado was coming from, but she was through being used.

She turned back to Martha. "Your sister kissed me months ago, but refused to do anything about it because of your rules. Because of something your dad did years ago." She looked from one to the other. "But here's the thing you both need to understand. You need to carve out your own lives. This is your vineyard, and you run it how you want. You don't run it as your parents or your grandparents did. So why would you run your personal lives according to some weird stuff that happened ages ago? You need to stop living in the shadow of other people. My ex-wife cheated on me, which is a major reason I left Cornwall. In the end, it was drama I didn't need." She pointed at Gemma. "You're cheating on me with your family drama. You've been ignoring what we could be. And you're still not ready to face it. You need to clear the air, and sort yourselves out."

Skye gathered all her emotions together, as if she were a football coach.

"I'm going to leave you to it," she said to Gemma and Martha. "Good luck, I think you're going to need it."

Chapter Twenty-Six

Gemma arrived at Martha's front door and rang the bell. She had a sore throat, but that was to be expected. No sleep plus stress. Not even fantastic sex could save her. Especially when it looked like it would never happen again. Skye had ignored her texts all afternoon since she left – no great surprise – but she had to sort this out with her sister.

If Skye chose to leave, Gemma would survive. Just. It would take time to heal. Time she never wanted to contemplate. Damn it, she really, truly, madly hoped it wouldn't come to that. That Skye would find a way to forgive her. That what they'd had in the past could be replicated in their future, and made ten times better. However, if Skye walked away, she'd be broken, but she'd limp on.

On the contrary, she couldn't survive without Martha. It was a physical and mental impossibility.

She rang the bell, and Steve barked behind the door.

Travis answered in his football kit. Gemma didn't think he wore anything else. Steve jumped up, and she bent and ruffled his wiry fur, instantly feeling calmer. It was true what they said about pets. They were a great leveller. However, Gemma could barely take care of herself, never mind anybody else. She had no idea how Martha did everything alone.

Although, now, of course, she wasn't alone. There was also Harvey. Did the boys know?

"Is your mum in?" It was seven on Thursday night. She wouldn't be anywhere else.

Travis nodded, then disappeared to the garden, Steve following in his wake. Moments later, the rhythmic thud of a football being kicked against a wall began, along with Steve barking.

Gemma walked through to the kitchen, following her nose and the smell of onions, garlic, and cream. When she arrived, Martha turned. She stared, then a flash of relief crossed her face. She took a glug of wine from her glass. The bottle sat on the counter, already half empty.

"You cooking for yourself, or for you and Harvey?"

So much for 'we come in peace'. Gemma shook her head and held up a conciliatory hand. "I didn't mean that the way it came out, I promise." She winced. "I was just asking the question. I want to know more about what's been going on. Also, when did you have time to fit in an affair with Harvey?"

Martha's face twitched before she answered. "It hasn't been going on that long. Not as long as you and Skye, from what she said. Plus, I was going to tell you, too, when the time was right. There just never seemed to be the right time. The perfect time."

"No such thing."

"I know that now." She held her gaze. "I'm glad you're here."

Relief flooded through Gemma. It was going to be okay.

"I know you're already cooking, but I wondered if you fancied a bottle of wine at the top of the hill. Some chat in the open to help clear the air? Skye said a few things I didn't agree with today, but she got that right. We do need to talk."

Martha tilted her head to one side. "You want to eat this dinner first? There's enough. It'll be half an hour in the oven. Although I've been up the hill all day tending to the vines, so that part doesn't hold as much allure. Can we take the cover off the hot tub and have some wine in there instead? I know Travis put it on earlier, so it'll be warm."

A hot tub with her sister. A weight lifted from her shoulders. Not that she'd really doubted they'd recover, but Martha was her security blanket. Her rock. Anything that knocked that, knocked her. "I'm in the wrong and you're going to feed me? Does that mean you still love me?"

Martha smiled, then blew out a long breath. "We were both in the wrong, and I'm really sorry I lied to you. But at the end of the day, we have to stick together, don't we? Otherwise, we're both buggered. Set the table. Then you can tell me what's really been going on with Skye, not this broken timeline I have in my head."

Gemma walked over and rubbed her sister's back.

Martha leaned her head into Gemma. "You're lucky I'm so bloody forgiving."

"I know." She paused, staring down at dinner. "And you're lucky I am, too. Are you making my favourite smoked haddock and potato gratin by accident?"

"Pure fluke." Martha gave her a full-beam smile.

"Lucky me twice, then."

* * *

The sky was dark pink with purple hues by the time the sisters got into the water. Martha pressed the button, then poured fizz into two plastic flutes.

Gemma had powered through the day on three hours sleep, but immersing herself in the hot tub gave her body permission to unwind. The tub had been Martha's insistence when they got the place, and it turned out to be a wise investment. The boys loved it, and Gemma often looked out and saw Martha relaxing in it. She should use it more often. Especially on nights like this. She should use it with Skye. But that might never come to pass now.

She wasn't going to focus on that.

Tonight was about her and Martha.

Her sister rested her arms on the ledge of the hot tub.

"I'm still fucking mad at you."

"I know."

"Just how long have you been sleeping with Skye?"

Gemma shook her head. "Last night was the first time. That's the truth. I'm really not lying about that."

"That's not what she implied."

"Remember when I went to Cornwall? To visit that vineyard?"

Martha nodded.

"On the way home, I stopped off at a bar on the seafront. I had a couple of hours to kill before my train, so I thought, why not? I went in and I met Skye."

"Right."

"Yes. We got chatting, one thing led to another, and I ended up kissing her." Gemma waited for her words to sink in.

Martha's eyes narrowed. "You just started kissing a stranger in a bar? That's not something you'd normally do."

"It was complicated. She was getting over her ex getting engaged again, the barman and I were being supportive."

"Did he kiss her too?"

"She's gay," Gemma replied, rolling her eyes.

"And you were the nearest woman available?"

"We chatted for a while. We got on. She said she'd never kissed a stranger in a bar, and I thought, what the hell? I'm never going to see her again. So I did. But after that, I couldn't get that kiss out of my brain. And then coincidentally, she turned up here for a tasting, told me she was moving back, and I offered her a job. It made sense at the time. We sort of knew each other. But I also told her that nothing could happen because of our rule. She accepted it at first."

Martha leaned her head back, then took a swig of wine. "Bloody hell. There was me thinking you just happened to hire a genius marketing person. But what you actually hired was someone you wanted to shag." She let out a hearty laugh at that. "My sister has hidden depths I didn't even consider."

Gemma smiled. "I know it sounds ridiculous, but it was never that premeditated."

"Nothing happened when she arrived?"

"No! I was being true to our rules. I tried to tamp down any attraction there was. She did, too, although as the weeks slipped by, she was less happy. So was I, but I just got on with it. Until I kissed her again a few weeks ago, which might have muddied the waters."

Another snort. "You think?"

Gemma gave her sister a pointed look. "But now, because I didn't stick my neck out, tell you and make things okay, I may well have buggered it all up."

Martha shook her head. "You didn't come across well today, denying it. But I think Skye just needs time to cool off. If you

249

like her, life's too short not to act on it. It's time to throw the rulebook out the window."

"She knew the deal when she arrived. I told her nothing could happen. She needed a job, so she took it. Plus, the rules were there for a reason. I went against them when I went out with Juliette, and the fallout from that hurt our business."

"But Skye and Harvey aren't anything like Juliette. I've no idea how she and Harvey are related. I'm sure there was a mix-up at the hospital. Harvey's a sweetheart. So is Skye. She's done a great job. She was a great hire. But I wish you'd told me what was going on."

"I wish you and me had both talked about what we were doing." Gemma eyed Martha, and took a sip of her drink. The jets fired up and the bubbles mingled with her thoughts.

"I don't know what to tell you. We got chatting not long after you broke up with Juliette. I went there for dinner with Leo – it was his choice, not mine, you know how he loves the chocolate brownies at that pub."

"They are good." When she'd broken up with Juliette, she'd had more than one moment when she'd mourned never eating one again.

"We were there, and Harvey came over to say hi. Then I went in one day to pick up some more brownies for the boys as a treat, and we got chatting. We got on. About a month later, he found me in the vines and gave me some more brownies."

"There are a lot of brownies in this story."

Martha smiled. "He bakes them himself. He's a man of many talents."

Gemma raised an eyebrow. "I bet."

"Anyway, then we had dinner on our own. Nothing

happened for a while because you and Juliette had broken up and things were thorny. We decided to just be friends. But a little like you and Skye, maybe we should have been honest. We've been seeing each other for about six weeks properly. But I use properly in the loosest sense, because he can't come here, and going there is hard when Juliette's around. We've had to keep it quiet from everyone we love."

Gemma shook her head. "What a pair we are."

Martha nodded. "However, Juliette walked out today and flew to LA to start a new life with someone she met on the internet. So neither of us have to worry about her anymore."

Relief and shock barrelled through Gemma. "LA?"

"Apparently. Said she's fallen in love with some rich woman. I thought you'd be pleased with that news, at least."

"I am. For both of us." Gemma paused. "But it still doesn't solve the Skye issue." She wasn't sure what, if anything, was going to solve that. She kept replaying the look on Skye's face as she walked out earlier. Had she packed up and got on a flight somewhere, too? Gemma wouldn't blame her.

"What's to solve? You can date her now. Everything's out in the open."

"But you heard what she said earlier. What I didn't say. I'm not sure if she'll give me a chance."

"That's for you and her to sort out. But if there's something there, you should try to."

"You'd be okay with me dating someone who works here?"

"You're not Dad, Gem. So long as you're not having sex in the office every day, I'm fine with it. Gran and Grandad managed to run the business as a couple without shagging anybody else, or shagging in the office."

Gemma raised an eyebrow. "That you know of."

"Please!" Martha screwed up her face and took a sip of her wine. She tipped her head to the sky, then back to Gemma. "I'm sorry I didn't come clean about Harvey. I'm sorry how you found out. I hope you understand the reasons. But I was honestly planning to say something as soon as Juliette left."

Gemma reached out a hand and squeezed her sister's arm. "We'll cope. But I'm thrilled for you. Harvey is a sweetheart, and you deserve one of those."

Martha grinned. "I really like him. He's the first person since Stu died that I've felt comfortable with. It's only taken ten years. We're not fast movers in the relationship department, are we?"

"Apparently not. But you're taking a chance. That's good."

She nodded. "I am. Plus, now you know, I just need to come clean with the boys." Martha grimaced.

"I wondered if they knew. But they'll be fine. Leo will be pleased, and Travis will love him because he plays football. More to the point, how will Steve take it?"

Martha's shoulders shook as she laughed. "I haven't worked out how I'm going to break it to him." She paused. "But seriously, hopefully everything will work out. For both of us."

Gemma sighed. "What will be will be."

"No." Martha sat up, taking the water with her. "What will be is whatever you do. It's a big ask, but I know you're up to the challenge. Know how I know?"

"Tell me."

"You're a Hunter. Hunters always get things done."

"Dad took that motto a little too far."

Martha howled into the dusky sky. "Again, you're not Dad. You know that, right?"

Gemma nodded. She did. She just felt a huge weight of responsibility being his daughter.

"I'm glad we're fixed. Now I need to fix things with Skye. The woman who I went a bit too far in keeping under wraps. When I think about it, it's not the most flattering tactic, is it?"

"Not really," Martha agreed. "But repairing is totally possible. The world would stop otherwise. You forgive, you move on. If Skye likes you enough, she'll do that too."

"I hope you're right."

Martha gave Gemma her best older-sister smile. "Aren't I always?"

Chapter Twenty-Seven

"Are you totally sure about this?" Lauren turned as she jogged, her face sweat-free and not in the slightest bit pink.

She wasn't even out of breath.

How was that even possible? They were in the second week of June now, and the weather had definitely taken a turn for the better. It was about time. Today, the sun's rays gently tickled Skye's scalp through her hair.

"Because you really like this woman."

Skye sighed. That was true, but she was tired. She needed to do something for herself. Finally coming on this park run with Lauren was one such thing. She'd admired Lauren for doing it every week, rain or shine. However, it was only now she was five minutes in, Skye realised just how unused to running she was. The only bracing movement she'd done recently, apart from cycling to work, was traipsing up and down the vines and kicking off bougie lids. That thought sent her spiralling into a Gemma spin. Skye shook her head to rid the thoughts. Back to the park run, which, while not simpler, was only short-term pain. Gemma was anything but.

"I do like her. You know me. I like her a great deal."

Understatement of the year. She'd fallen for her, but that

didn't matter to anyone but Skye. Gemma hadn't fallen for her, and that was the key point. Skye dodged a stick and tried to regulate her breathing. Easier said than done. Her nose tickled as the smell of freshly mown grass filled her senses. Most people loved that smell, but Skye always found it too over-powering. She blamed all the summer nights she'd spent raking her childhood garden. It was why she'd never had a garden wherever she'd lived.

"But I've just had months and years of drama with Amanda. I don't need more. I think the best thing to do all round is to hand in my notice and chalk it up to experience."

"But you like the job, too, right?"

"Is this just because you won't be getting any more free wine?" Skye stumbled as they hit a slight incline.

"Of course not." Lauren couldn't help the smile that crept onto her face. "I wouldn't base my advice on whether or not you could supply me with free wine. Much."

"You can always count on your friends." And now she had a stitch. Skye held her side and grimaced at the sharp, niggling pain. They weren't even ten minutes in. "You can go ahead if you want."

But Lauren shook her head. "We started together, we'll finish together. We can walk for a bit."

A woman who must be pushing 80 overtook them.

"I thought I was fitter than this."

"I thought you were, too." Lauren slowed to a walk. "Back to your decision. Did you call supermarket man?"

Skye nodded. "Yep. I'm meeting Hugo on Tuesday. Whether he gives me a job or not, I need another one. I can't stay working for Gemma. Too much has happened. Plus, I'm not a masochist."

Lauren widened her eyes. "I had you down as one after you stuck around in that Cornwall hotel to see Amanda get engaged to her sous chef."

Defeat rolled through Skye. "Maybe I learned from that lesson. I didn't leave fast enough there. I'm not going to make the same mistake twice."

After the debacle that was the morning after the night before, she went home, took a long, hot bath and tried not to think about how well she and Gemma had fitted in bed. How she'd never wanted to leave. While she was talking with her body, Gemma was perfect. It was just when she opened her gob things went awry.

Skye started to run again, and Lauren fell into step beside her. Skye's stitch was still there, but she'd run it off. She hadn't got up this early on a Saturday morning to walk around a dusty field. She had to at least jog for most of it, even if it killed her. She made a mental note never to do this again. She loved the theory of jogging. The practice, not so much.

"Has she messaged you today?"

Skye shook her head. "Not yet, but it's early." She pictured Gemma in her king-size bed. Then pictured herself beside her. Then cleared her mind.

Skye was prepared to walk away, but she never said it was going to be easy. However, if she moved into her brother's place, at least she'd be out of the area. No chance of bumping into Gemma, Martha, or Harvey anywhere she went. That, at least, would put her mind at rest. Maybe she'd even date after she moved. Although even the thought made her frown. Maybe she'd move to Reading and just be. Wouldn't that be novel?

"But she's messaged most other days since you slept together two weeks ago?"

"She has." Sometimes about work stuff as they tried to wrap up Skye's involvement. She'd officially handed in her notice via email, which Gemma had accepted. But Gemma had also messaged her privately, telling her how sorry she was, how she'd spoken to Martha, how everything was going to be different if she'd give them another try. Gemma was convinced they could work and be together. Skye wished she shared her conviction, but it was all a little late. She was going to the vineyard on Friday as a final handover, and she wasn't looking forward to it.

"Can we stop talking now so I can concentrate on getting to the finish without dying?"

Lauren grinned. "I warn you, I'm going to sprint to the line. It's what I do."

Skye had tried to sprint to the line with Gemma, but she'd tripped on an invisible hurdle and fell flat on her face. Slow and steady obviously won the race, if not the girl.

* * *

Skye arrived at the vineyard at 5pm on Friday as arranged. She put her bike in the rack. Leo's wasn't there.

Skye steadied herself, then banged her knuckles on Gemma's front door. She shucked her backpack from her right shoulder.

Gemma answered pretty quickly.

"Hi." This was the first time they'd seen each other since the office showdown, so Skye wasn't surprised that Gemma's voice held a wobble.

A waft of coffee hit Skye's airwaves. Gemma made great coffee.

"Did you get your hair cut?"

Gemma touched it instinctively. "I did. Martha arranged it. Said I could use cheering up."

Skye's heart pulsed. "It looks good. The pixie cut suits you."

Gemma caught her bottom lip with her front teeth. "Thanks." She stood back. "Come in, please."

So formal. So different from when she'd ended up in Gemma's bed three weeks ago.

Skye's heart ached.

"I just brewed some coffee. I know it's late, but I figured the more alert we both were for this, the better."

Skye followed her into the kitchen, then sat on one of her stools. Her memory flicked through the few times she'd been in here before. The first, for the wine tasting. The last, after they'd spent the night together.

Gemma put a coffee in front of her, but stayed where she was. Standing, on the other side of the kitchen island. Skye was all for some distance between them. She glanced right and noted the basil plant.

"Beyonce still lives." Skye nodded at it.

Gemma's sad smile broke her heart. "Beyonce survived longer than us, didn't she?"

"That wouldn't be hard." Skye's words were true, but she didn't mean them to hurt Gemma. Despite everything, that was the last thing she wanted to do.

"I emailed you everything you need to know about the clients and all the upcoming events I've arranged. I've put it all in a schedule too, and printed it out." She reached into her backpack, held up a pink folder, then got up and put it on the kitchen table. "Any questions, the answers should be there." Skye sat back on her stool.

"Thank you." Gemma's words were laced with regret. "How have you been this week?"

Skye didn't want to prolong this. She'd taken this week off, but just seeing Gemma again made all Skye's thoughts and decision go hazy, as if they'd been plunged under water. But she wasn't going to be deterred. She'd met women like Gemma before. They were well meaning and probably believed all the words they said. But when it came to actions, they didn't match their words, and people rarely changed.

"I've been job hunting."

She didn't look all that surprised. "I wondered if you might. Did you have any luck?"

Skye nodded. "I have actually. With Hugo, would you believe? He told me when I contacted him if I ever needed a job, he was always looking for good people. He's said he'll create a role for me. I'm moving into my brother's place finally, which my parents will be happy about. They've been looking after his cat, Winston." She paused. "Perhaps it's all worked out as it's meant to in the end."

"There's nothing I can say to change your mind? I'd love you to stay. If you push aside everything to do with us, you've done a great job." Gemma clutched the kitchen counter. "Not that I want to put everything that happened with us aside. That's the very last thing I want, to be clear."

Skye took a steadying breath. This was harder than she'd anticipated. The job stuff paled in comparison. All she wanted to do was crawl over the counter and kiss Gemma. But she couldn't.

"I think it's best all around." She paused, and took a deep breath. They hadn't spoken about them since that day. Skye had asked for space, and Gemma had given it to her. "I also think it's best if we call us off, too." Skye moved her mouth left, then right. She hated being the reason behind Gemma's watery eyes, but she didn't know what else to do. "If there is an us at all. It was short-lived to start with."

"Of course there's an us." Gemma said it like she'd never had the slightest doubt.

That wasn't how she'd acted over the past few months.

"You're very sure now, but you haven't been ever since I arrived. You started off perplexed, freaked, scared. You gave me a job, which was great, I've loved working here. But you created this weird rule, and turned your feelings on and off at will. I've been thinking about it all week, and it's made me realise you're not ready for a relationship. And weirdly, it's not to do with Juliette. A touch, maybe. But it's more to do with your family. Of being scared of any relationship. Of having any woman encroach on your space. Maybe if you get over that, then you'll be ready. But you're not right now."

"I am!" Gemma looked startled at the piercing volume of her reply. She cleared her throat before she continued. "I was saying this to Martha the other day. I know we had these weird rules, but sometimes you just follow something because you always have. It takes someone else to come in and ask why you've been doing that, and why you want to continue. That person was you.

"You asked questions about the business, then you asked

questions about me. They made me confront things I've been hiding behind. Yes, every relationship pushed me back a little, but I've started to see you're right about my family and their influence." Her eyes were still shiny. "I know I fucked up that morning with Martha, but it was a reflex action. What I've always done. Now we both know who we want to be with and so does everyone who matters. There is an us, I promise you."

"I want to believe you. You say the right things, but you don't follow through. Not when we met, and not now."

"But everything's changed now, including me." Gemma dropped her head and put down her coffee. When she looked up, her cheeks were flushed and wet. "Thanks to you, I've also been working out how I can tie my job and my passions together. I've decided to run an art class in the vineyard in the summer. I wouldn't have done that if I hadn't met you."

Skye's stomach lurched. When she walked in, she'd convinced herself there wasn't an 'us' when it came to them as a couple. But she knew now there was definitely an 'us' when it came to them and friendship. She didn't want to lose that, but she couldn't have it all. They weren't going to stay friends if she walked away from *them*. The pull of the 'what if' was there, but it wasn't enough to make Skye change her mind. There was too much evidence stacked against Gemma in the past few months.

"I think it's great you're doing the art classes. Just like the music events, the supper clubs and the tours, people will come to them. People want spaces to congregate in, especially with good food, wine and activities in a gorgeous setting. You tick every box. Plus, when the presenter knows her shit, I'm sure it'll be a great success."

Gemma gave her a weak smile. "Don't compliment me, I'm not sure I can take it. If you're going to break up with me, be nasty, please."

That almost made Skye slump. "I could never be nasty to you."

"I was nasty to you. I didn't mean to push you away."

"I know." And she did. "I'm moving into my brother's house as that's an easier commute to London. But Reading isn't a million miles away. Maybe I'll run into you."

Gemma didn't say anything in reply. She must know that would never happen.

"But we never even shared a hot tub together."

"You've got a hot tub?"

Gemma nodded. "It's in the garden at the side. Martha and I were in it the other night, working our shit out. We did work it all out, and she's going to make a go of things with Harvey, which is great. Juliette's left the country by the way, so that's one less headache in my life. Martha thinks I should make a go of it with you, too. That's two people who think it."

"I have to think it, too."

Gemma reached out and took Skye's hand.

She nearly crumbled then. She'd been fine with the counter between them, no touching. But just the feel of Gemma's fingers brought back all the memories from the other night. They were still fresh enough. If she wanted, she could walk around, take Gemma in her arms and kiss her. But Skye couldn't get over that when push came to shove, Gemma had said they weren't anything. She didn't fully trust her, and that was crucial.

"Please don't do this," Gemma pleaded. "What about

the night we had? It meant so much to me. What about us, everything we've shared over the past few months? I've had a lot of time to think about everything, and I miss you. We only just got started getting to know each other. That can't be it. I can't just walk away."

"But you were prepared to when you told Martha what you did." Skye took her hand back and shook her head. Talking about it brought back all her initial anger. It was still there. Gemma wasn't forgiven. Which was why she had to go. "If you really wanted us to work, you could have made it happen earlier. This isn't easy for me. I want to kiss you. It started with a kiss. A magical, dreamy, drunken kiss."

Gemma let out a whimper.

"But the other issues haven't disappeared. Something needs to give, and that something is me. I fell for you, Gemma. I fell in love with you." Her whole body thrummed with the enormity of it. She was in love with her. She'd known it ever since that first kiss. It's how Skye worked.

It wasn't at all how Gemma worked.

"Can you even say it back to me?"

A single drip fell from the kitchen tap.

Gemma's eyes went wide.

She couldn't.

Even after everything, she couldn't tell Skye she loved her. Either because she couldn't, or because she didn't.

Skye stared at Gemma for the longest time, then she walked closer and kissed her cheek. She lingered a second or two longer than she needed to, just to breathe in her scent and lodge it in her memory. Then she pulled back. "It started with a kiss, let's end it with a kiss. I'm really sorry it turned out this way. I'll do what's needed next week, and then I'll be gone."

Skye gathered up all her resolve, pulled back her shoulders and walked out of the room, down the hallway, out the front door and out of Gemma's life.

When she got on her bike, she heard the front door open behind her. She battled with herself, but she couldn't help it. She turned.

Gemma stood at the door, tears streaming down her face.

Skye nearly broke. Nearly said something. But she didn't.

Because Gemma hadn't.

Instead, Skye took a deep breath, swung her leg over her bike, and rode away.

Chapter Twenty-Eight

Gemma spent the rest of the week in a daze, doing the dance of tastings, private bookings and supper clubs. Skye promised to come and do her bit to help, as long as Gemma promised to make herself scarce. She'd reluctantly agreed. Martha made Gemma sit in the house while Skye was there, and came to tell her when the coast was clear.

"Even if you want to tell her how much you miss her, you can't go bowling in there. You didn't tell her how you felt when she told you. Everything can't always be on your terms." That last comment had stung a little, but she knew it was true. She'd failed at the crucial moment. Now, she had to live with the consequences.

Instead, while Skye was around, Gemma went to her garden and painted. She painted through the blur of pain, ignoring her legs that wanted to run out the door and beg Skye to give her another chance. When that urge overtook her, she mixed. While she painted, she sipped a glass of rosé and remembered drinking it with Skye. In another lifetime. One where everything was still on the table. Before she buggered it all up with her family issues and her stubbornness. Would she say something different now if Skye told her she loved her?

She wasn't sure. Just saying the words was an obstacle for Gemma. She rolled her eyes. She infuriated herself.

She walked over to the wooden garden table and chairs and sat, shielding her eyes. The weather had finally bucked its ideas up, so frost alarms were a thing of the past. That, at least, was something to be thankful for. Although, it was frost alarms that had thrust her and Skye together. Left them alone with nobody else around. Now Skye and the alarms were in the past, it felt like the end of something big. An era that had seen Gemma open her heart more than she ever had before. Now she'd opened it, she didn't want to close it. But she wasn't sure how to turn it around.

"Nice painting, Aunty G." Leo loped across the grass and slumped into the chair opposite her, a can of Coke Zero in his hand. "You really should do those art classes you talked about."

"I intend to." She paused. "Would you come if I need to swell my numbers?"

Leo crinkled his eyes. "Not really my jam. But I'll tell all my mates' mums for you."

Gemma laughed. "That would be great, thank you." Family ties only stretched so far, and she'd just broken Leo's.

"How are your exams going?" Leo tolerated school and exams at best. Luckily, he found them easy.

Her nephew moved his floppy fringe from his forehead and frowned. "Okay. Last one next week, then we're done." He shrugged. "I can't wait to break up, then I can get an undercut. School won't allow it."

"That rule's still in place?" She remembered it from her school days.

Leo nodded. "Mum says I can get one as it'll grow out over summer, so I'm counting down the days." He put his hand up over his eyes. "She's letting me get my ears pierced, too. For my birthday."

Martha had mentioned it.

"What do you want from me? Anything in particular, or just cold, hard cash." Gemma knew the currency teenagers dealt in.

Leo took a glug of his Coke. "Cash would be great. I also want to go axe-throwing. I mentioned it to Skye before she left, and she was into coming too." He studied Gemma before he continued. "I like her a lot."

Gemma licked her lips. "You and me both."

Leo sat forward. "So do you think she'd come?"

"You could ask her, but I don't think so. Not if I'm there."

A few moments passed while Leo absorbed that.

"Something happened between you?"

Gemma's insides wobbled. "Yes, it did. But I fucked it up."

"Aunty Gemma! Language!"

She laughed. She deserved that.

"But you still like her?"

"Yes, very much."

"Does she know?"

"Know what?"

"How much you like her?"

Gemma winced, then shook her head. "Not really. Sort of. I don't know. Whatever, it's all a bit late now."

"But shouldn't you at least tell her?"

He'd been hanging out with Martha far too much. Nearly 16 going on 30.

"It's not that simple."

"Isn't it? I just saw her, and she looked sad. She was just leaving as I walked in. She got her bike from the rack and stared at your front door for quite a while before she saw me."

Gemma sat up. "She did?" The urge to run out the front door and down the lane after her was so strong, Gemma almost had to hang on to the table. But that was all at least ten minutes ago. Skye would be almost home now. The moment had passed.

"I could invite her to the axe-throwing if you wanted? Or you could do it?"

Her nephew was better at relationships than she'd ever been. Should she invite her? Leo did want her to come.

"Let me think about it."

He nodded. "Okay. But I'm not inviting many people. You, Mum, Travis, Harvey, plus Jack and Blake." The latter were his two best friends, also part of the vineyard's weekend staff.

Gemma sipped her wine. "How are you feeling about Harvey?"

He shrugged. "Fine. He cooks well, and Mum seems happy. It's nice to have someone else look out for her."

A wave of love washed over Gemma. Leo had taken on that role ever since his dad died when he was five. He grew up fast. It explained why he was an old head on young shoulders. She'd tried to step in, but it wasn't the same. If Harvey gave Leo the chance to focus on himself and not Martha, that was another tick in Harvey's column. That, and the fact that Martha was walking around beaming from ear to ear every time she saw her. It was amazing what being out in the open and having regular sex could do for a person. Gemma only wished she'd had the chance.

She had, but she'd blown it.

"Do you love her, Aunty G? You've got a very faraway look in your eye."

He wasn't letting this go, was he?

Gemma thought about the question, ignoring her tremors. She did love Skye. She knew that now. But she still hadn't said it. Not to herself, not to Skye, not to anyone. Maybe she should change that now. Leo would be perfect practise.

"I…" she began.

Then stopped.

For fuck's sake, Gemma.

It's just three words.

"I know you have trouble saying it."

She blinked. "You do?"

He gave her a slow nod. "I have eyes. And ears. Plus, Mum always tells us you were never told as kids. It's why she's always saying it to us."

Stuart had made Martha believe in love, as had her children after he died. She was far better acquainted with it than Gemma.

But maybe Skye was Gemma's Stuart.

"I do." She sat up straight, emboldened, then cleared her throat. "Yes, I love her." A rush of endorphins sailed through her.

Oh my god, she'd admitted it.

An enormous weight she hadn't even known was there lifted from Gemma's shoulders.

Now, she wondered what the big deal ever was.

Opposite her, Leo gave her a thumbs up. "Mum's going to be pissed she wasn't here."

"Hello!"

Her sister's voice made them both turn their heads. She walked in, with Harvey close behind, grins on their faces. When she looked at Leo, then Gemma, she frowned.

"What have we interrupted here?" Martha pulled up at the table. "You look like you lost a tenner and found a pound."

Leo stood. "I just got Aunty G to admit she loves Skye."

Harvey made a noise, and Martha nudged him.

"She said it out loud?" She turned to Gemma. "Like, you actually uttered the words in a sentence?"

"I'm still in shock, in case you were wondering," Gemma replied.

Martha frowned. "Say it again please. I won't believe it until I hear it."

Gemma cleared her throat, then stood. "My name is Gemma, and I'm in love with Skye." She eyed Martha. "And I love you, too."

Martha's mouth fell open, then she rushed over and picked Gemma up in an embrace.

"Well this is cause for celebration!" She put Gemma down and held her at arm's length. "Now you just need to tell Skye before she disappears from your life."

That realisation hit Gemma dead centre.

"Is she in again tomorrow?"

Martha nodded. "Final supper club. Then she moves to Reading this weekend. Time's ticking, little sister."

Gemma was well aware.

* * *

It was her last throw of the dice. She'd tested it earlier in the evening, with Martha on the balcony telling her where to move the bougies for maximum impact. They had blankets, wine and a picnic all ready. Now it all depended on Skye turning up. That part, Gemma had no control over. She just had to hope that Skye responded as she always had. She was still on the pay roll. Just.

She messaged Leo to tell him to override the weather system and send out the frost alarm to a party of one. Hopefully the ends would justify the means. In half an hour, she'd find out. Then Leo had promised to light the bougies before they arrived. Gemma had everything crossed.

Sure enough, just over 30 minutes later, Skye arrived on her bike, sans bobble hat. Yes, it was midnight, but there was no longer a chill. She parked her bike and jumped off, then walked over to Gemma, holding out a hand as if testing the air.

"I wasn't sure if this was a mistake, but I didn't want to leave you in the lurch." She rubbed her fingers together. "Although, it doesn't feel that cold. Are the vines sensitive tonight?"

Gemma put on her best poker face. "I think they might be." She tried not to focus on her heart nearly springing out of her chest at the sight of Skye. Gemma's body had always known it loved her. It was just Gemma who'd taken a while to realise. She gulped, then nodded towards the tasting rooms.

"There's something I want to show you before we get going. It won't take a minute. It's up on the terrace. Follow me?"

Skye frowned, but nodded.

Gemma took a shaky step forward, then led the way. Sweat trickled down her back. Was she crazy to do this? She was about to find out.

"Is Leo already out there?" Skye sniffed the air. "I can already smell the bougies."

Gemma nodded, but didn't turn around. "He is." She walked through the tasting room to the stairs on the far side, then took them one step at a time, every move taking her nearer to her fate. When she reached the top floor, her heart thumped so hard in her chest, she was sure it was about to fling itself onto the floor. This was her time to shine. To show and tell Skye how she felt. The very thing she'd never been any good at. Tonight, she had to make sure that changed.

She walked to the start of the balcony, where a bottle of fizz sat open in an ice bucket, two glasses beside it. She glanced out to the vines, but couldn't bring herself to look properly. She was far too nervous. When she turned to Skye, her guest frowned.

"What's going on?"

Gemma took a very deep breath. "Before you say another word, close your eyes and take my hand."

Skye creased her brow, then glanced at Gemma's outstretched hand like it was poisonous.

If she wouldn't do this bit, Gemma was fucked.

"Please?"

Something crossed over Skye's features, then she nodded, and took Gemma's hand.

"Close your eyes."

Skye complied. She still had a bicycle clip on one leg.

Gemma pulled her around the table, and to the edge of the balcony, then placed her hands on the metal railing. Only now did she dare to look at the bougies.

"Open your eyes."

Skye did as she was told, then stared. She took a few moments to take it in, before her bottom jaw dropped open slightly, and she turned to Gemma.

Gemma glanced at the bougies. Placed and lit strategically, they spelled out, *I love you*. The suspicion in Skye's eyes had gone, now replaced with curiosity and something else Gemma couldn't pin down. She hoped it was something positive.

"You did this?"

"With a little help from Martha and Leo. It said *I live you* for a while, until Leo fixed my mistake." She risked a smile now.

"And do you mean it?" Skye's knuckles turned white as she gripped the railing.

Gemma nodded slowly. "I really do. I know I couldn't say it last time we spoke. I should have, but I've never said it to anyone. You know that. And even though I felt it, I couldn't get the words out. So I thought I'd show you instead." She placed a hand over her heart. "I'm really slow on the uptake, I know that. If you decide to give me another try, that fact still remains."

At last, a smile from Skye. That was enough for Gemma to carry on. Her biggest line was yet to come.

She turned to Skye fully, and took her hands in hers. This time, Skye didn't object.

"I know I hurt you, and I'm sorry. It's my stuff, and I'm going to work on it. But what you need to know is that I really do love you." Thank fuck for the Leo practice. This time was way easier than the first. "I'm sorry it took me so long to realise, but I hope you might reconsider leaving? If not the job, then at least us." She stared into Skye's gorgeous, crystal blue eyes. "I want to give us a go. You and me as a couple. These last couple of weeks have been awful. I've missed you so much. I want you in my life. What do you say?"

Skye stared at Gemma for a few seconds, then dropped her gaze to their joined hands.

Fuck. Gemma hadn't thought what her exit strategy might be if Skye rejected her. In all her imaginings, Skye had always said she loved her too, taken her hand, and they'd kissed and drank wine.

But she still hadn't said anything.

Gemma's brain went fuzzy.

"Are you sure?"

"That I love you?"

Skye nodded.

"I don't light bougies for just anyone." She squeezed Skye's hands. "Skye."

She lifted her gaze back to Gemma.

"I love you. I want to see where this goes. Will you be my girlfriend?" Why did she feel 14 saying that?

Skye narrowed her eyes. "Say it again."

"Will you be my girlfriend?"

A shake of the head. "The other bit."

It was like jumping hurdles when she was at school. They'd seemed impossibly high at first. Something other people did. However, once she got in the rhythm, there was no stopping her.

"I love you."

Another eternity passed, before suddenly, Skye moved towards her and pressed her lips to hers. The whole world went fuzzy. Gemma swayed on her feet. When Skye pulled back, she swore she saw stars.

"Is that a yes?" She hated herself for being so needy, but this was important.

Skye gave her a grin. "My head says no, my heart says fuck, yes. I'm choosing my heart. Don't make me regret it."

Gemma shook her head. "You won't, I promise." She leaned forward and kissed her again. Confetti fluttered inside her. "Damn, I missed your lips."

"I missed yours, too."

"Then why have we wasted so much time?" Gemma cringed, then held up a hand. "That was a rhetorical question, I know the answer is 'it's my fault', so let's crash on."

She pulled Skye to the table, then poured two glasses of bubbles. "Candles, wine, and over there," Gemma pointed to the far end of the balcony, "a blanket for us to lie on and look at the stars together. We only lit 40 bougies max, which means far less smoke, and way more stars."

Skye licked her lips. "You've thought of everything."

"It's about time."

Skye flicked her head to the stars. "There's a lot out tonight. They all wanted to be here to hear you tell me you loved me."

"Apparently so." Gemma raised her glass. "To us?"

Skye nodded and raised her own. "To us. Although, I'm still leaving my job. That hasn't changed."

It's what she'd expected. "When do you move to Reading?"

"This weekend." Skye winced. "A little ill-timed now."

But Gemma shook her head. "Do you want some company? I can call in a few favours and take a weekend off. Help you settle in?"

Skye nodded. "I'd like that." She paused. "Does this mean I still get my staff discount when I come back?"

"You might even get the odd free bottle. Perks of sleeping with the owner."

"There was me thinking that was a perk enough."

Gemma pulled her chair around so they were next to each other, then kissed Skye one more time. Heat surged through her, along with pure contentment. Was that what love was? The feeling of being just where you should be, a feeling of home? She was so glad they'd met. So glad Skye had brought that gift to her.

"Lauren's going to be pleased, too. She was a bit grumpy when I told her I'd left and we'd broken up. She likes your wine." Skye paused. "One more question. If we're giving this a go, will I still be on the frost alarm rota? Because I'm not sure I can hold down my other job and do this all the time."

Gemma grinned. "The only 2am calls will be booty calls, promise."

Skye took her hand and kissed it. "Those are the kind of calls I can very much get behind." She kissed Gemma again.

Gemma stood, downed her drink, then held out a hand. "Come on, Skye Tuck. We're going to lie on a blanket, hold hands, and look at the stars. Tonight, I'm giving you the happy ending you always deserved."

They settled into each other on the blanket, then stared upwards. Contentment smudged itself into Gemma's core.

Skye gripped Gemma's hand, and placed it on her stomach. She turned her head. Her eyes sparkled in the moonlight.

"Thanks for my happy ending."

Tears stung the back of Gemma's eyes, but she held them back. She squeezed Skye's hand. "Thanks for my fairy tale."

"You're welcome. Although this feels more like a new beginning than a happy ending."

"Can't it be both?"

Euphoria trampled through Gemma. "Let's make it both."

They were silent for a few moments.

"I'm still yet to dance naked in the rain, by the way."

Gemma snorted, then kissed Skye's cheek. "One day at a time. I promise, I'll make it happen." She caught Skye's gaze. "Do you believe me?"

Skye considered the question for a few moments, then nodded.

"This time, I think I really do."

Epilogue: One Year Later

"**M**um, come and look at this bathroom! It's so tiny and cool!" Leo poked his head out the front door, and Steve appeared at his feet, barking his head off as only tiny dogs did, closely followed by Gravy.

Martha rolled her eyes, but walked over to the brand-new pods they'd installed in the clearing beyond the main building. Guests could now come to a tasting or event, and stay the night in one of their four wooden pods that were small, but had everything you needed. A kitchen, bedroom, bathroom and lounge in a compact, energy-efficient space. The pods had been Harvey's idea, after he took Martha to stay in one in the New Forest. They'd both come back enthused and got the project under way. Now, Leo and Travis were threatening to move in when they were free. Gemma thought Martha was half considering it.

"Have you seen the finished product?" Gemma asked Skye.

Skye nodded. "Leo showed me around earlier. He's like a proud dad."

"He did put up all the loo roll holders, so he's invested."

Gemma took Skye's hand and tugged her to the barbecue area, where Harvey was in charge of a full grill. To his right, Travis kicked a football against a low wall.

"Is it always the man's job to do the barbecue?" Skye asked.

"It was always mine before Harvey showed up, so I'm all for it," Gemma replied, patting her brother-in-law on the back.

His and Martha's relationship had progressed at speed, and they married within a year. As Martha said, "no point hanging around if you know something's right, we might die tomorrow." Luckily, Juliette had not flown back from LA for it, so Gemma had thoroughly enjoyed the day. Skye had never been more thankful.

"How many are we expecting for the official pod opening?" she asked.

"Just us, my parents, and I think Lauren's coming too?" Harvey directed the last part to Skye, who nodded.

"She is, and she's bringing her new boyfriend. We have to be nice and normal so we don't scare him away." They'd been together for three months, and Lauren declared herself "the most hopeful she'd ever been". He was a widowed dad from school and they'd met at a parent-teacher evening.

"Where's the fun in that?" Harvey replied with a grin. "How's the move going, Skye? Nearly in?"

Skye's job was going well, but a year on from moving into her brother's place, he'd returned after his Australian adventure fizzled out. Amazingly, he'd got his old job back, and now it was as if he'd never been away. Skye had considered moving elsewhere, but after chatting with Gemma, they'd decided to give living together a try. It made sense.

Their first year they'd spent as much time together as they could manage, but it had never been enough. Martha had a point. When something's right, run with it. Hugo had agreed she could work from home when she didn't have meetings, so everything had slotted into place. Skye was excited to live on the vineyard. Beyond excited to have a hot tub in her back garden. It was the stuff of dreams.

"Nearly there," she told Harvey. "I travel light. My brother's bringing his van this weekend." She put an arm around Gemma. "And this one has already got me roped into doing a tasting on Saturday."

Marketing manager Andi had come back, but she wasn't working this weekend. Gemma gave Skye a butter-wouldn't-melt grin. "Got to make you work for a living. I'm doing my art class, and we're a presenter down since Liz had her baby." She winked. "I'll make it worth your while."

"TMI!" Travis piped up, sticking his hands in his ears.

"What's going on here?" Martha walked around them and squeezed Harvey's bum.

"The ladies were regaling Travis with their sex life. He took offence," Harvey said.

"Suck it up, Trav," Martha told him, giving Gemma a grin. She walked over to the ice bucket and got the Hunter rosé out, then topped up everyone's glasses, including Leo.

"A toast. To our grandparents, for setting up Martha's Vineyard. To everyone here for helping us make it what it is today, and to our record harvest and bumper year all round. But mostly to our grandma, for making us strong women, going after what we want and getting it." She grinned at Harvey, then Skye. "To the Hunter women. We get things done."

* * *

"Sometimes I can't believe this is where I'll be living full time. It's pretty incredible." They were in their back garden, looking at the stars. It was a favourite and regular pastime these days. "Which one's that again?" Skye pointed upwards, then turned to Gemma.

"A shiny one," Gemma replied. "I bought you that astronomy book so you could teach yourself."

"That would involve reading it, though. I prefer staring in ignorance."

Gemma laughed. "That, we can do all night long."

Skye scrambled to her feet.

"Where are you going?"

She raised a finger. "I brought you a present. I just remembered." She arrived back minutes later with a wrapped gift. "Open it."

Gemma took it, a smile on her gorgeous face. She ripped the paper, then pulled the frame from the wrapping. When she saw what it was, she gasped, and put a hand to her heart.

"I can't believe you did this." She stared, then shook her head. "How did you get hold of it?"

"My pal, Leo, of course." Skye had truly bonded with him over the past year. When she came across Gemma's favourite poem of her grandma's in a drawer recently, she got Leo to mail her the typed-up version, found an artist to draw it, then got it framed. "Do you like it?"

"I absolutely love it. Martha's going to love it, too." Gemma shook her head. "You're going to make me cry."

Skye sat next to her and took her free hand. She kissed it gently. "I didn't do it to make you cry. I did it so you can always see your grandma's words. The ones about love. Because I think she cast a spell over this vineyard, and now look at it.

It's thriving with love. The vines are feeling it, you're feeling it, everyone's happy."

"I'm happy because of you. I'm thrilled you're finally moving in."

"Me, too." After the trial year, this time, she really believed this could be her happy ending.

Gemma ran a fingertip across Skye's knuckle. "I love you, you know that?"

"I do, mainly because you tell me all the time."

"I've got a lot of lost time to make up for." Gemma paused. "One final thing. I was thinking after you move in, we could decorate. New colours to make you feel at home. Maybe we could choose a new couch. Get a new rug, too?"

"So long as it's not goatskin."

Gemma tipped her head back and let out a belly laugh.

"No goatskin. You have my word."

THE END

Want more from me? Sign up to join my VIP Readers'
Group and get a FREE lesbian romance,
It Had To Be You! *Claim your free book here:*
www.clarelydon.co.uk/it-had-to-be-you

Did You Enjoy This Book?

If the answer's yes, I wonder if you'd consider leaving me a review wherever you bought it. Just a line or two is fine, and could really make the difference for someone else when they're wondering whether or not to take a chance on me and my writing. If you enjoyed the book and tell them why, it's possible your words will make them click the buy button, too! Just hop on over to wherever you bought this book — Amazon, Apple Books, Kobo, Bella Books, Barnes & Noble or any of the other digital outlets — and say what's in your heart. I always appreciate honest reviews.

Thank you, you're the best.

Love,
Clare x